The experts speak about *Brimstone and Lily*!

"Call me disgusted."
—*Herman Melville*

"The manuscript that corrupted Hadleyburg!"
—*Mark Twain*

"Please, sir, I want no more chapters."
— *Oliver Twist*

"From hell's heart I stab at thee!
For hate's sake I spit my last review at thee!"
—*Captain Ahab*

"~~It was the best of books,~~ it was the worst of books."
—-*Charles Dickens*

"All right, then, I'll **go** to hell...
as long as I don't have to read that book again."
—*Huckleberry Finn*

Also by Terry Kroenung
www.terrykroenung.com

Novels
Jasper's Foul Tongue
Jasper's Magick Corset
Paragon of the Eccentric
Rapiers & Rogues
The Gaze of Zeus

Drama
The Three Musketeers
Coolness and Courage
Blood and Beauty
Gentle Rain

Nonfiction
HeartSnark

Anthologies (contributor)
Customs, Castles, and Kings, v. 2
Broken Links, Mended Lives
False Faces
Found

Awards
Colorado Gold Literary Award
Paragon of the Eccentric (winner)
Brimstone and Lily (finalist)

Independent Publishers Book Award
Brimstone and Lily (Bronze Medal)

Next Generation Indie Book Award
HeartSnark (finalist)

Colorado Short Story Contest
"The Day the Earth Couldn't Stand Still"
(winner)

The Legacy Stone
Book One: Part One

Brimstone and Lily:
A Blade of Dubious Glory

The adventures of Verity Sauveur
and her most Righteous Blade of Wrath,
the Fell Sword Morphageus,
hereafter known as Jasper

Terry Kroenung

RARE MOON PRESS
Longmont, Colorado

Brimstone and Lily:

A Blade of Dubious Glory

(revised edition)

Printed in the United States of America

Cover image by Solarbearstudio

ISBN: 978-1-7378947-4-2

www.terrykroenungink.com

To Janet
For 27 years of saintly patience

&

Alaena, Freya, Brigid, and Jasper
for lending me your names

Contents

A howdy-do from y'all's intrepid narrator

Ma says I oughta make sure y'all understand about this here book. I hafta admit it sure looked like the south end o' a north-bound horse when I first scribbled it (sorta like this here introduction). I tend to get purty good grades in English Literature but Miz Finch threw up her pudgy hands and declared that the Pennsylvania State Normal School sure never prepared her for my grammar. Thought she'd expire o' the vapors when she first eyed the rough copy. But betwixt her and Ma, they wrassled the words into a rough sort o' shape that swanky, educated folks like yourselves kin read without too much eyestrain. We cleaned up the narration parts some but tried to leave most o' the dialogue stuff alone, so y'all get the flavor o' the thing.

I just don't wanna misrepresent that I'm some sort o' literary stylist, 'cause I sure enough ain't. Took a month o' Sundays t' put lipstick on this here pig, let me tell ya. Miz Finch might be contemplatin' a career change. If I'd known what a trouble it was to write a book I never would o' tackled it.

As far as the talkin' bits go, I guess I oughta apologize in advance fer Jasper. You'll see what I mean.

Thanks,
Verity

Brimstone and Lily:
A Blade of Dubious Glory

...the most magick-hunted person on Earth.

1 / Verity
Friday, June 20, 1862

Right past my eye! Too close. The wasp-sting of the Fell Knight's sword point buzzed so close to my nose that for an instant I saw two of them. A drop of sweat leapt from my face as I jerked back and the bead split itself on my foe's steel. *Move, move, move!* Giving his rapier blade a quick tap upward with my parrying dagger, I cart-wheeled right. As I'd expected, my enemy's own poniard gouged jagged woodchips where my foot had just been. I shrugged my dripping hair out of my eyes and squared off to meet his new attack. *Ain't much more than a warm-up so far.*

"You're too predictable," I told him with a smirk. *The saucy heroine must **always** smirk at the villain. I think it's a rule.*

"Predict this!" he sneered, giving me a feint thrust to the left shoulder. I moved to block it with my rapier but he deceived it. His tip dipped below my guard and licked at my wrist. Ready for him, though, I knocked it aside with a snap of my dagger. *Is that your best move?* In that same second he stepped in hard with his own short steel to dispatch me with a jab to my right flank, his intended target all along. *Clever boy.*

But he hadn't reckoned with the rattlesnake responses of Verity the Valiant. I paralleled both of my blades and spanked the knife out of his cruel fingers. With a yelp he tried to take my head off with his sword. *Good thing I can do a fast split!* His long edge tickled my ginger cowlick as my feet slid apart and I dropped to the floor. I looked up, catching him out of position from his follow-through. Scissoring my legs back together, I rose to his exposed throat with my blades crossed. I placed the iron X at his sweaty neck, feeling his frightened pulse pounding through my edges.

I snarled, "Do you yield, monster?"

The Fell Knight gave me a haughty laugh. "To the likes of you? Never! Do your worst, wench!"

"I take you at your word, then!" My weapons clattered to the stage floor as I began tickling him in his bony ribs.

"Hey!" Tommy shrieked, his defense against my wiggling fingers as vain as his swordplay had been. "You'll make me wet my pants!" High and ringing, his voice echoed in the empty theatre.

That only increased my gleeful assault. I pinned him against the stage left proscenium arch. "Give?" My arm wrapped around his neck and I Dutch-rubbed his scruffy brown noodle. "Give? Say uncle!"

My stage brother squirmed like a trapped rat but that got him nowhere. I'd always been stronger. "Oww!" He threw up his dirty hands. "Okay! Okay! Uncle, then! Don't scalp me like a red Injun!"

I released him with a grin and staggered out the stage door into the alley for some air, making the cats and rats scatter. Tommy followed, gasping. *Lordy, it's hot.* Side-by-side, arms around one another's shoulders, we gazed east toward the half-completed Capitol dome. *They still ain't finished the darned thing, or the Washington Monument, neither. Prob'ly have to wait for the war to end now.* I'd heard, though, that President Lincoln vowed to keep working on the dome, no matter what Jeff Davis tried to do.

We flopped onto a pile of just-delivered scenery canvas. Later we'd make flats out of it, transforming it all into mountains and skylines and forests. Already I could smell the glue. *Ick!* That reek of that stuff always made my head hurt. Near as bad as the smell of the Canal. Seemed the farther into summer we got the worse the raw sewage stunk. Made you wonder why the Confederate army would want the place. Richmond sounded ever so much nicer than Washington. Our capital still needed paved streets and decent plumbing. I'd seen the mud so bad that a fire engine drove onto the wooden sidewalk so it wouldn't sink. Some days I wished Ma had never moved us here from the Maryland farm where I'd been born.

Touching his own aching noggin, Tommy made a face and offered me the jug of water he'd brought out. We panted and sweated in the summer humidity. "I get to win next time. You can be the villain."

"Only if you invent the fight moves. Them's the rules. Besides, I like givin' bad guys their comeuppance."

He nodded through the door toward the hole he'd made in the apron floorboards. You could see it even from that distance. "We have to fix that quick. If Mr. Ford sees it we'll be the ones getting the comeuppance."

"If you hadn't stabbed so hard you wouldn't've put a dent in his new floor. It's just pretend, you know."

"I know, but it has to look proper." Tommy sure loved *proper*. Proper speech, proper clothes, proper manners. Everything had to be correct. That's how you could tell we weren't real kin.

"You're gonna get a proper whuppin' if you don't fill that back in and paint it before their dress rehearsal tonight." I led him back inside and nudged a pot of glue at him with my toe. "Here. Put the big chunks back, sand everything off even, and then slap some black paint down."

Tommy sagged. "I don't know how to do all that. I'll make a hash of it. Can't you?"

I sighed, something I did a lot around him. "You're a piece o' work, Thomas Stubb. How is it you can paint the prettiest pictures but you're useless for paintin' a floor?"

To be honest, Tommy couldn't really have been as useless as I let on. Mr. Ford paid him a nickel apiece to make color sketches of scenery and costumes. No adult could do them as well. Mr. Sherburn, the company carpenter, and Ellen Sauveur, the wardrobe mistress and my ma, used them as references.

Tommy shrugged. "I don't know. It's just different. Not like designing makeup or styling wigs."

I snorted. *Different's the word, all right.* He'd fooled us all once, Ma and me included, by waltzing into the lobby of Ford's Athenaeum dressed as a snooty rich lady. For ten minutes he'd complained about the ticket prices, how uncomfortable the seats felt, and the ruffian next to him spitting tobacco juice on the floor. Then he stuck his snoot in the air and stormed out. We might never have discovered him if he hadn't come to supper with a tiny bit of rouge on one cheek. Mr. Ford announced that soon he'd put Tommy on stage. Even at twelve years old, he acted that well. Most of what I know of disguises and accents I learned from him.

Tommy was a lot prettier than me. I hate that word. *Was.* It still takes some getting used to, that he's gone. Taken by the Bullies. You know what that means. *Dead, or wishin' you was. Magicked into something horrible, not even able to make a human scream.*

Anyhow, Tommy had a prettier face than me, though that ain't saying much. Prettier than his three girlfriends, too. Everybody called me a tomboy. 'A ragamuffin,' Mr. Ford would say when he got cross at me. Too-short red hair, snub of a nose, mouth as wide as a barn door, and as many freckles as stars in the sky. Dresses made me itch and corsets made me cry. All that girlie stuff left me cold. Seemed to me that all that girls and women got to do boiled down to three things: embroider, stay clean, and giggle. I preferred hammers and wrestling and swordfights. *And maybe that's why you only have one friend in the whole world. Who wants their kid to be seen with the freak?* Ma always said I'd grow out of it, a terrible thing to contemplate.

"You're only twelve," she'd told me that very day. "When you're a bit older you'll see."

I stood up and stretched, looking around. Old Mad Molly crouched over down the alley a piece, hunting for who-knew-what in a trash heap. She'd lost her husband in the last war, the one where the Britannic army had burned Washington. Everybody said she'd lost her mind from grief back then, too. Walked about town living on handouts, babbling. Tommy and me gave her a dime now and then, but mostly avoided her. There were lots of poor old widows in town, left with no one to care for them. Now the new war minted fresh ones faster than anybody could count.

We finished up the water jug and shuffled back inside, muscles creaking from over an hour of stage combat. When I planned the fights Verity the Valiant triumphed, a spunky unbeatable righter-of-wrongs with a heart of gold and an arm of iron. The Fell Knight had no chance against her. But whenever Tommy designed the routines poor Verity fell, a rube from the countryside who scarcely knew which end of the sword to grab. A helpless pawn caught in the ruthless designs of her social superior. Today I'd won the coin toss.

"Battle of Agincourt?" blurted Tommy in a snooty Britannic voice. *Aha. Time for Round Two.*

"1415," I answered, returning his serve with a Gaullic tone. "Fall of Constantinople?"

"Which one?" he asked with a grin, batting his huge chocolate-brown eyes. His lashes were long for a boy, and the left eye did a funny little twitch sometimes.

"Both, smarty-pants."

"1204, sacked by Christian knights during the 4th Crusade. Then the Turks took it for good in 1453. Shakespeare's birthday?"

I made a *ppfft* sound with my lips. Too easy. "April 23, 1564. How many angels can dance on the head of a pin?"

He hesitated for just a second. "Straight pin or safety pin?"

We had a good laugh at that. I punched him on the arm a couple of times. He made-believe that it hurt. Like I said, Tommy could act. Sometimes he'd sham weakness. It helped him keep the rowdies away every now and then, since they couldn't look very tough picking on a 'sissy.' Fooled them, too. They'd saunter off to find bigger game and the next thing they knew, a rock would ping them between their shoulders, fired from around a corner or up on a balcony. He never missed. Tommy worked on proper marksmanship, along with everything else he did.

While he rubbed his arm he peered at me like he wanted to draw my face. I twisted up my nose and mouth, and then stuck out my tongue. "Whatcha doin'?" I asked.

"Your eyes look bad. Are you sleeping okay?"

I looked away. "Sure."

"None of them dreams?"

I rubbed the dark circles under my eyes. "Uh-uh."

He pulled me back around and gave me his 'you can't lie to me' face. "Verity."

Sighing, I gave in. "Oh, all right! Just a couple o' times this week is all."

"Maybe you need to see a doctor."

"What for? He'll just say I need to quit eatin' raspberries before bed or some other fool thing. Doctors don't know beans."

"Maybe not, but you need to do something. You tell your ma?"

"Not after the first time. She gave me a look like I'd just confessed to murder. Don't want to see that again."

Tommy frowned. "Same exact dream? Every time?"

I nodded, pulling glue and paint out of the tool cupboard. "Never changes."

"The man with the gold skin? The big black dog?"

"Yep, all of it." *Fallin' down a dark hole. Weird letters that move around like ants. The grandma with sharpened teeth. And blonde kids with long scary hands, reachin' out for you. Like havin' that Edgar Allan Poe feller in your head.* I got spooked just thinking about it and wanted to talk about something else. "I'll be okay. They come in bunches for a couple o' weeks, then they go away. Should about be done." I held up the glue jar. "And we should be about done fixin' the floor, if you'd quit yer jawin'."

I made a deal with Tommy to trade chores for the day. He'd wash costumes for me and I'd beat the lobby rugs for him, plus fix the floor. His funeral, I figured. Washin' is ever so much more work, to my mind. So while he went out with our hired freedman Romulus to fetch water for the tub, I patched the nick in Mr. Ford's apron floor. When I'd finished you'd never have known it'd been there. That's what I've always been good at, hiding mischief.

Just as I put the paint away in the stage right cupboard Mr. Ford strolled in through the upstage entrance, dapper and handsome as always. One of the lead actors came with him. They didn't see me because I snuck behind the cupboard door. They talked about the dress rehearsal that night, picking their way through papier-mâché Scottish rocks. *Macbeth* always pleased the crowds and no mistake. Mr. Ford seemed to think that his witches weren't scary enough.

"They should move in an inhuman way," he said, inspecting his theatre as he spoke. Yanking on a rope to see that it stayed secure, he continued while the other man followed. "Perhaps like spiders at times, or slithering snakes. Their heads might jerk as birds of prey do, eyes never blinking. I want the audience to be disturbed."

"If you truly desire to upset your patrons, double your prices," said his companion, as good-looking and well-dressed as they come, even for a star actor. Dark curling hair and a fierce moustache set off his square jaw and pale skin. His eyes matched his voice. Both struck me as deep and restless, with half-contained fire. After chuckling at his own joke he went on in a different tone, one that made my skin crawl. "Or you can re-cast them with the prettiest blonde children in town, all with black eyes and long fingers."

What did he say? I tilted my head and crouched close to the floor where I could see and hear them without being noticed.

Mr. Ford froze and glanced around. He seemed scared to be overheard, even alone in his own theatre. "Not funny, Booth."

John Wilkes Booth gave him the same smile boys made when stepping on bugs. I'd have bet his Thane of Glamis would give you more chills than any witch he shared the stage with. "Jumpy, aren't we? Next you'll be intoning, 'The very walls have ears!'"

"It's not the walls that I'm worried about. It's the cat by the fire, or the rat that raids the pantry, or my housekeeper's canary." *Are they talkin' in some kinda code?*

"Relax. As long as you don't rock the Merchantry's boat they won't try to sink yours."

Merchantry? What's that? He'd pronounced it like a Gaullic word...mer-SHAN-tree.

Mr. Ford frowned and stared at the precise spot that I'd just patched, even though he stood twenty feet upstage of it. "My boat is not my chief concern. I'd just prefer not to wake up one day as a dung beetle."

"Well, let's just work to put on a good show and the rest will take care of itself." Booth glanced at an expensive-looking watch plucked from his brocade vest. "I'm off to the Willard for a brandy, and perhaps some socializing with a couple of the Army bigwigs. See if I can find out what's going on in the Peninsula. No one seems to have a clue about this Lee, the Rebels' new commander. Coming?"

"Lee doesn't matter. As long as he's fighting McClellan, that bragging little —"

"Full of sound and fury, signifying nothing!" Booth boomed into the empty house. I had to admit, he sounded darn good.

Ford laughed and slapped his star on the back. Booth stiffened for a second, but Mr. Ford didn't notice. "If you deliver all of your lines like that one, it'll signify fat profits for us both!"

"Stay awhile, I will be faithful." Booth shook Ford's hand. "Adieu."

The actor bounded off through the wings, humming. Mr. Ford moved downstage. Now he could see me in the paint cupboard, the picture of innocence. "So," he purred, "was it your sword or Tommy's?"

I blushed. Nothing ever got past him. Of course, the pile of weapons near the prompt box sort of gave it away. "Tommy gets too enthusiastic sometimes."

"Which is why we all love him." He stood right above my floor patch. "Good work. If I hadn't seen it from the upstage side, angled in the light, I never would have noticed. I presume that this is your work and not Tommy's?"

"Yes, sir. He's out back scrubbin' linens for Ma. She's in the green room gettin' things ready for tonight's rehearsal. I'm gonna beat the lobby rugs for you."

"Good girl." He squinted. "Where's your necklace? I thought you never took it off."

I gasped and dug a hand into the back of my overalls. "Forgot! Didn't wanna have a sword point catch it." A smooth red stone glowed in the afternoon light. The gift Pa had put around my neck the day of my birth. I had nothing else of him. No pictures, no letters, nothing but a flat speckled rock on a black silk cord. Shaped like a long blunt-nosed arrowhead with a vertical oblong slit in its center. Ma called it my Legacy Stone, a piece of jasper Pa'd claimed that he'd had since he'd been a boy. I slipped it over my head and tucked it inside my shirt.

"Still doing well in school? I've been bragging to everyone about how sharp you are." As proud of me and Tommy's school work as if he'd been our own daddy, Mr. Ford kept close watch on our learning. Since he paid for us both to go out of his own pocket, he had the right, I guess. Sometimes I wished he had been my real pa. I had no memory of my father at all. Ma said she'd lost him the day of my birth. Never would tell me more. Must've been real hard on her.

"Oh, yes, sir. Perfect marks in History and Literature last term. My grammar and cipherin' still need work, though. You won't want me countin' your receipts, that's for sure. Can't wait fer summer to be over so we can go back." I didn't lie. Believe it or not, I loved school, except for having to wear shoes. You can call it girlie, I don't care. Guess I had a knack for it, especially for Shakespeare and other storytellers. I reckoned I knew just about any book you could name, backwards and forwards. Me and Tommy would have competitions in history, too, trying to stump one another. It amazed our teacher, Miz Finch, that we could be that sharp. Me in particular because I didn't appear the studious type. 'Tweren't natural, she'd say. High praise from someone who looked unnatural herself. *Never saw such a backside on a woman. Broader than a hay wagon.*

Reaching into his coat pocket, Mr. Ford drew out a peppermint stick and handed it to me with manicured fingers. "Here. Make sure you give him half." When I reached for it he withdrew the candy. "After you put the swords back in the property closet."

I smiled and stared at my big, booted feet. Just like at school, I wasn't allowed to be barefoot in the theatre. "Yes, sir." I collected my treat and scampered off with the blunted rapiers, their daggers stowed inside the caged hilts. Mr. Ford in a good mood, sweets in my hand, and Tommy doing my chores...all was right with the world.

As right as that twisted war-torn world could be, on the last happy day of my childhood. Before I became the most magick-hunted person on Earth.

I punched his boy-bits with all of my might.

2 / Romulus

My ma folded shirts in the green room, on account of it being cooler than in the costume shop. Sweat soaked her blue calico dress. Some crazy person had built Washington City in a swamp, so summers always sweltered. Before the war those who could had always left town come June. It felt that miserable. Most years Mr. Ford booked little or nothing into the Athenaeum for June, July, and August, there being no audience to speak of. But the attack on Fort Sumter the year before had filled the city with troops. Now he had a chance to pack the house full of free-spending Army officers and War Department workers. That's why the popular Booth had brought his company, to perform for folk starved for entertainment to help them forget the war.

Giving me that look she always used when I'd disappointed her, Ma said, "You switched chores with Tommy? What did I tell you about—?"

"I didn't take advantage of him," I protested. *Well, maybe a little.* "He asked me to help him out of a fix."

She smoothed her damp dark hair out of her gray eyes. Short

and curvy, she wore spectacles on the end of her sharp nose. They made her look like Ben Franklin's sister. The glasses usually sat atop her head, except for when she sewed or when she wanted to glare at me about something I'd done. I don't look much like her. Guess I got Pa's face. At least that's what she tells me. I don't recall him. *Sure wish I could, though.* "You might have said no."

"And then he'd be onstage right now, in a world of trouble with Mr. Ford. I did him a favor."

"And since you're so considerate for your best friend, you'll do him another. Go help with the wash...now. Then you'll both beat those rugs."

I started to argue, but knew it would be useless. Jamming the peppermint stick in my mouth, I clumped out.

"Don't forget to give him half of that candy," she called after me.

Oh, a big one for honesty and fairness, my ma. She based everything she did or said on those ideas. Whether portions at dinner, kids' games, or national affairs, she considered *right* more important than *convenient*. Even though Tommy didn't really count as my real brother—Mr. Ford had found him on the street and let him live at the theatre—he got treated as such by us. And Ma had hired Romulus to help with odd jobs, paying him the same as a white man. Him being somewhat simple didn't matter to her. As soon as Mr. Lincoln had freed all of Washington City's slaves in April she'd made it a point to give a job to the first colored person who'd asked her. Didn't care who knew it or who objected, neither. Of course, she expected the same from me, too.

Me and Tommy spent a miserable hour wrestling with a mighty mess of shifts, drawers, and shirts. Boiling water, boiling lye, and boiling sun, combined with stirring what seemed like eleven tons of waterlogged fabric, made us woozy and weak. The sultry air could have almost drowned you trying to breathe it. Romulus helped out a bit (well, more than a bit), truth be told, or we'd likely have fainted. The biggest man I'd ever laid eyes on, he had the kind of strength you read about in fairy tales.

Big old loyal Romulus. He'd come to Ford's asking for a job, any job, the day he'd got his freedom papers in April. Ma hadn't needed any help, but she told me that something about him made her feel safe. Faithful and brawny, he looked after us like a kindly uncle. Though sometimes he watched over me so careful that he resembled a sheepdog guarding his flock from wolves.

After some time in the shade back of the theatre—and about a gallon of Ma's lemonade—we beat the lobby rugs till we almost choked to death. The beaters made good pretend-swords, so we performed Macduff vs. Macbeth for Romulus, poor Mad Molly, and a few scruffy alley cats. Tommy got to win that time—his last victory, come to think of it. Shaved head shining in the sun like a big buckeye, Romulus clapped his giant paws as he watched. Sitting in that odd way of his, upright on his toes with his hands between his knees, he looked like a happy old mutt, tongue lolling.

Ma let us loose after chores, so long as we got back at five for supper. Dress rehearsal started at six and we had to help. I'd shift scenery and Tommy would work with Ma and the costumes. That gave us over an hour. We ran west to the Potomac, my horrid boots left at home. *Woo! My tootsies can breathe!* The guards around the President's House returned our wave. They were used to seeing us. Once Mr. Lincoln had even said hello while watching Willie ride his pony on the South Lawn. Willie had been the same age as us. The typhoid got him just four months before. Now the poor President didn't come out much anymore.

President Washington's monument-to-be rose a ways to our left, a whitish mess that didn't look like something dedicated to a great man. Seemed more like a gravestone. In fact, some kids we knew said it was haunted. Weird things happened there, they claimed. People would come out of it wearing clothes from long ago: Napoleon's Gaulle, or the Middle Ages, or the Thirty Years War. We laughed, of course. 'About as believable as the Headless Horseman'. But with the sewage smell of the nearby Washington Canal smacking you in the face, you could believe it a half-built castle from Ivanhoe's time.

Hoping to see the *Monitor*, we peered at the river from a high point near one of the Heavy Artillery batteries that pointed downstream and toward the Virginia side. *Harper's Weekly* had run pictures of the new iron gunboat, wonder of the Navy, and we itched to catch sight of it. No such luck. It probably cruised down by Richmond, making sure that the Confederates' own ironclad couldn't do any mischief against McClellan's army. Seemed like he needed all the help he could get. The papers said his siege had turned into a retreat, thanks to the new Rebel general, that Lee. Big battles brewed that could decide the war.

We gave up looking for the wonder weapon and sprinted along the shore. Funny how the heat's intolerable when there's work to be done, but you can play in the same sun forever and never feel it. Pretending we were the giant guns of the battery, Tommy gave me orders like he'd heard their officers doing. I'd go through the loading drill for a 100-pound Parrot rifle, then cock my arm. When he'd shout, "Fire!" my rock would blast out to sink the enemy. Many a driftwood gunboat suffered our righteous wrath. I wasn't as accurate as Tommy always was. Once I misfired and the shot landed amidst a bunch of bathing soldiers. They seemed to think that Southern sharpshooters had found their range, for they dove under the water like frantic ducks. Laughing at the sight of so many naked fish-belly-white bottoms, we tore off back through town.

Our laughter faded quick when we saw that we'd made a dumb decision. To save time after being held up by a slow-marching regiment, we turned off our normal route. Trying to cut across the grounds of St. Usher's, a posh school for Senators' sons and the like, we hoped we wouldn't be spotted. Our previous dealings with those kids had taught us not to truck with them. *Advanced Orneriness* must've been a required class there. Once they'd stripped Tommy's trousers and sent him home with a whipped backside. What is it about money and power that makes some people so cruel?

We figured we were pretty safe, it being summer and no school, so we didn't take it as careful as we should have. Three-quarters of the way through we started to relax. No one had jumped us or even yelled, 'Boo!' The big sandstone building that the boys lived and studied in sat there like a forgotten mausoleum, all shadowy and dead. Weaving between the spooky old oaks on the lawn, Tommy and me started giggling from released nerves.

The first one dropped out of a tree behind us like a well-dressed monkey. His three friends popped up from behind a woodpile and a trash heap, cutting us off in all directions and closing in. Two carried sticks. Another had a length of chain. Tommy already started to shake beside me. As the noose constricted I recognized their leader, the one who'd been up in the tree. *Time to apply some butter.*

"H'lo, Horace," I said with as big and goofy a grin as I could manage. Our best chance would be to act stupid and harmless, maybe disarm them enough to make them drop their guard and then we could run for it. "How ya'll doin'? Nice suit."

Horace returned my smile with one of his own. Since it looked like a hyena licking its chops, it didn't reassure me much. He looked down at his blue velvet jacket. "This old thing? Just the rags I like to wear on days like this so I don't get the blood of interlopers on my really nice clothes."

Interlopers? Somebody's been payin' attention in Britannic class. "We're just tryin' to get home fer supper. No need to make a fuss."

His greased dark hair looked like a shiny skullcap. He lacked a front tooth, but otherwise looked the rich kid, a banker's boy from New York. "Fuss? No fuss needed to teach you two your place. And because it's so hot, I think Tommy might appreciate being stripped buck naked this time."

The trio lurking between us and home snickered along with him. Wilbur and Hawthorne, the pair with sticks who dressed like Horace, except more sloppy, took a couple steps toward us. Tommy started to whimper. I nudged him with my hip to be quiet and to start sidling toward home. When he began to move I followed right behind him, but backing up to keep my eye on Horace.

"Y'all oughta be home. School's out. Why ya hangin' 'round here?" I said, as cool as I could manage. To be honest, I felt like making Tommy-noises myself.

"My father has a position with the War Department now," Horace announced in a grand tone. *Means he's sellin' rations to the Commissary, emphasis on the **r-a-t**.*

"Yeah? That's swell." The boy with the chain slid sideways. Our move hadn't been as slick as we'd thought. Looked like we wouldn't be able to dash after all. Oh, well. I had a back-up plan, but it depended on some luck. And on Tommy not fainting before we started.

"Swell...that's what your heads are going to do when we break 'em," whispered Wilbur, thumping his stick into his fat palm. With his thin hair and round pink face he looked kind of like a pig. Some folks said Wilbur had been thrown out of public school for setting fires and talking to spiders, so his wealthy family had got him out of Pennsylvania and dumped him at St. Usher's. They never visited, I heard.

Horace played the leader, the cool customer. Hawthorne and the kid with the chain seemed to be followers, trying to be popular. Wilbur looked like the one I could get to make a mistake. Anyhow, he stood closest and I wanted his stick. *Oh, please, let this work. Oh, please...*

I turned toward him. "You're clever. You must be the boss here."

Horace cackled. *Thanks for being predictable.* Wilbur puffed himself up and looked at the three kids beside him. "Well, ya know how it is..."

"No," said Horace in a dark voice. "Suppose you tell us how it is, Little Willie."

Oho! A snotty nickname. Better than I'd hoped. I could feel the heat rise from Wilbur's wounded pride. "Shut yer trap, Horace!" he spat. "I do what I want, when I want."

"That so? And what do you want, Little Willie? Huh?"

"I want to whale on these two fer a bit, then I'll tan your hide!"

"Well, get to it, then. I'm waiting.

Wilbur eyed me, almost with an unspoken apology. He preferred going after Horace, but he'd been boxed in. *Boys!* I could see him wavering. But I needed him to go after me first. Otherwise his two buddies might just charge at us while he attacked Horace. So I helped him make up his tiny mind.

"Afraid ya might lose to a girl?" I smiled. Then I blew him a kiss.

Of course he swung at my face as hard as he could, like a batter playing rounders. I counted on it. Blood thumping in my ears, I dropped into the same split I'd done with Tommy earlier that day. The stick whooshed over my dipping head in such a big circle that it forced Hawthorne to hop back. *So far, so good.* Before Wilbur could recover from his stroke I took him out of the fight as only a ruthless girl can: I punched his boy-bits with all my might.

Just so you know, it hurts a girl to be hit there, too, but it seems to *mean* more to a boy, somehow.

Wilbur's yard of oak plopped onto the grass as his knees buckled. Pushing him as hard as I could, I scrambled forward quick as a bobcat and grabbed the club. Hawthorne almost fell over him as Little Willie staggered backwards clutching his groin, then dropped. Chain-Boy reacted quicker than I'd expected. He ignored me and went for Tommy, who just stood there paralyzed in terror, eyes wide as a frightened bunny's. That hunk of chain zizzed through the sultry air. Try as I might, I couldn't get up fast enough to stop it.

But it didn't hit Tommy's noggin. My stage brother justified Mr. Ford's confidence in his acting skills. His scrawny form dove straight at his attacker, inside the arc of the chain. *You were pretendin', you sneak!* Chain-Boy's swing had been a bit lazy, counting on Tommy's staying frozen. They looked like one of those dances the soldiers sometimes had when there were no girls around. Swirling together, they spun away from the rest of us and crashed into a tree.

I couldn't watch anymore, because Hawthorne and Horace had recovered from their surprise. Now they played it more careful, their overconfidence replaced by cunning. Hawthorne scooted around to cut me off from home. Wilbur struggled to his feet and headed my way. He looked real mad. *OK, Verity, now you're in trouble.* I let Thorny have it with my new weapon, but he blocked it with a neat wrist snap. *Darn! St. Usher's must have a single stick class.* I tried again, feinting this time and jabbing at his breadbasket. That worked, but he hopped back just enough so that the thrust landed weak. *Crud! Time for my secret Verity the Valiant attack, a combination of cleverness and grace that'll stun the world.*

Before I had a chance to think of anything close to that, Wilbur screamed like a banshee and hurled his nasty self at me. My stick smacking his shoulder didn't even make him flinch. I hit the grass hard, his weight knocking my wind out. In a second he straddled me, knees pinning my arms down tight. No amount of squirming helped shake him loose. I relaxed, hoping he'd think I'd given up and lower his guard. No such luck. He may have looked creepy and dumb, but refused to be fooled twice. While he gloated over me, Chain-Boy drug poor Tommy over and dumped him next to us. Each of them had a swollen lip. *Good for you, Tommy.*

"I'm gonna enjoy every minute of this," sneered Wilbur, raising his fist.

Horace grabbed his arm. "Wait." He looked over at Tommy's captor. "Roderick, move Pretty Boy over here next to her."

Tommy's bruised face appeared next to mine. His fear looked real now.

With a nasty chuckle Horace stood over us like an over-dressed Colossus. "Since you two stuck your big noses where they don't belong, I think I'll trim them a little." His delicate rich-boy fingers drew a long blade from his coat. It had a queer-looking pattern of swirls in the steel like nothing I'd ever seen. *A knife? Jiminy, Horace, this is just a kids' fight!*

"Come on, Horace, what are you doin'?" I said, more hoarse than I'd planned.

"I'm slitting your nostrils, that's what I'm doing. We've been ordered to keep all trespassers away from St. Usher's."

"Ordered?" asked Tommy, wriggling. No use. "By who?"

Horace got an odd look in his eye, like someone testifying in church. "We're Merchantry men now."

While I digested what that might mean, he leaned down, knife tip hovering over my sweating face. I craned my neck to get away from the evil blade. It looked sharp enough to cut a hole in the air itself. Fear must've made me see things, because I swear the swirls in the blade began to move like snakes. Just as it almost touched me Tommy pleaded, "Get away from her!"

Horace Hadleyburg flew back a full thirty feet, landing on the lawn in a screaming heap. *Whoa! How'd you do that, Tommy?* Wilbur rose straight up as if levitated by a stage magician. He squeaked out a froggy croak, feet kicking like a hanged man, then crumpled sideways off of me. *What on earth's goin' on?* I wrenched myself up and looked around in a daze. Hawthorne and Roderick scrambled away from us, shakily brandishing their weapons as something huge and dark growled above my head.

Romulus towered there, almost smoking with rage. I'd never seen him like that, or ever imagined such a thing. He snarled in a way that you'd imagine Cerberus would do in the Underworld. His eyes had lost their calm loving look and almost seemed to glow. Our hired man crouched low, almost on all fours. Where had he come from, without making a sound or being seen? The man stood as tall as President Lincoln and weighed close to 300 pounds. Stealth shouldn't have been in his vocabulary.

I had to give Wilbur credit, he didn't back down once he got over the first shock. With a howl and a curse he brought his oak cudgel down. I flinched as it caught Romulus square on the head...and snapped clean in two like a straw. Blinking, I felt my jaw drop. *That should've laid him out cold.* Romulus just shook his head and howled at Wilbur. The boy's pants darkened as he wet himself and sprinted off toward the school building, Hawthorne at his heels. Roderick half-dragged Horace in the same direction.

"Cave! Amicis meis epularer custodiuntur!" Romulus roared with the voice of a lion.

Tommy and I got to our feet, shaky but not hurt too much. We stared at each other, then at Romulus. *Did he just yell in Romish?* Now that our attackers had fled, he seemed to be shrinking somehow. His breathing got back to near normal and that ungodly light left his eyes. There stood our old Romulus again, harmless as a new puppy.

"This a bad place," he told us in a soft voice. Well, as soft as he could ever manage. It still sounded like a locomotive ready to pull a load uphill. "Don't you two come here no mo'." He got no argument from us. "C'mon. Yo mama's waitin' supper."

All the way home I kept sneaking sideways looks at our rescuer. Something didn't smell good and no mistake. I remembered that weird knife against my nose, and how Horace had been so ready to cut me up just because we walked on his stupid school's lawn. 'We're Merchantry men now.' *What **is** this Merchantry?* Tommy grabbed my hand tight. It looked like he thought the same thing. *What's goin' on at St. Usher's?*

"Be extra careful this evening.
I have a terrible feeling that they've found her.
And tonight...things... will be abroad."

3 / A Weird Chamber

"What did I tell you two about that place?" Ma said, holding a beefsteak on Tommy's black eye. We sat in the kitchen of our tiny house, a half-block north of the theatre. I could smell the chicken boiling for supper. My mouth watered despite how much I hurt all over.

"We didn't think anybody'd be there this time of year," Tommy told her, wincing.

"They was awful nasty," I said, rubbing all the parts of me that ached. "Acted like they guarded it or somethin'."

Ma shook her head and muttered, "Merchantry men, they said?"

"That's what I heard Horace say, whatever that means. His pa's company, maybe? I'd like to find out."

"No!" We jumped a little at the violence of that word. Ma'd gone white as a sheet and started shaking. "Don't even think that!" She grabbed me hard under the chin. "You stay away from

St. Usher's. And anyone starts talking about anything you don't understand, particularly about the so-called Honourable Merchantry, you skedaddle away as fast as your legs'll take you. Hear?"

"Yes, ma'am. But I don't understand why—"

"Were any of the boys blonde? White-blonde, with coal-black eyes?"

Tommy and I looked at each other as we replayed the fight in our minds, then we shook our heads.

"Well, they wouldn't be out in the sun anyhow, I guess. That's good." She still looked as scared as I'd ever seen her, fidgeting with the dinner plates and her apron.

Romulus clomped up the back stairs into the kitchen. I saw no sign of the horrible blow Wilbur's club had struck his bald brown head. Not so much as a bruise. *How can that be?* He leaned against the door jamb, facing sideways so he could look out at the street and still talk to us.

"Looks okay, Miz Sauveur. Everything seems normal, like." He pronounced our name like we said it, not the proper Gaullic way: sew-FAIR. She heard plenty of jokes at Ford's about that being the perfect costume designer name.

"Thank you," Ma said, looking as grateful as could be. She stirred the stew pot and added some onions. "Can you check around the theatre after sundown? And keep a lookout during the rehearsal?"

"My pleasure, ma'am."

"Do you have your mirror?"

He patted the pocket of his gray cotton shirt. "Never go anywheres without it."

I felt confused. Tommy looked just as puzzled. "Lookout for what?" he asked. "They're just kids."

Ma eased herself down at the dinner table. She looked tired and worn, like a soldier after a battle. "It's not Horace's gang I'm worried about."

"Who, then?" I asked, sitting on her lap. "And why does Romulus need a mirror?"

She hugged me tight, then gathered Tommy into her arms with us. "Oof! You're getting to be big, missy. What happened to that little huckleberry I could carry around all day? It's about time to tell you, I suppose. Only right and fair that you know how the world really is. And what your part in it might be."

Tommy made a face. "Is this that talk about babies and storks? Because I have to be honest, Silky Sadie who works the corner told me that what really happens is—"

Ma laughed despite herself. "No, it's not that."

Tommy had been holding out on me. "What did Silky Sadie tell you?" I asked him.

"Never mind," Ma said. "We'll have **that** talk soon enough, I imagine." She scooted me off and stood up. "As for the other thing, that'll have to wait till tomorrow. Time for supper now, and then off to rehearsal. Mr. Booth will throw a hissy fit if it starts late. Go wash up, you two." We ran off to the basin and the soap. As we did so I heard her say to Romulus, "Be extra careful this evening. I have a terrible feeling that they've found her. And tonight...things... will be abroad."

* * * * *

Ford's Athenaeum started out as a Baptist Church. When they'd moved on to a new place, John T. Ford had taken over the 30 year-old building and made a music hall out of it. He owned several such theatres, here and in Maryland. Folks trusted him as being wise in business affairs and as honest as a saint. That meant something in Washington. Mr. Ford had even been acting mayor of Baltimore once. When he decided to do a thing, it got done right. I'd seen evidence of that firsthand. The theatre had just opened in March, after an expensive remodeling. Popular from the first, President Lincoln had even attended a play there, only three weeks before. It'd turned from a house of God to a house of Art, but you could still sort of tell that it had been a church once. It had that feel, like ancient forces throbbed beneath it.

I finished stowing the last piece of scenery, Duncan's throne, backstage. Helping to stow it, anyhow. It took four of us to move the over-built thing. Booth, both the star and the producer, had gone all-out on this show. We half-expected a stage full of horses for the Act V battle scene. Nearby, Tommy and Ma dressed actors in papier-mâché armor and wigs. I wouldn't see much of them once the play started, as my duties were mostly on the other side of the stage. After giving them a wave, I weaved my way through the crush of performers and stagehands to the up right corner, where I'd wait until they needed me to help shift a flat or adjust a bush.

Ducking under one of the half-raised drops, I smiled at the fly operator next to his bank of ropes. It amazed me that all of this chaos—flats, curtains, trapdoors, smoky fire-prone gas lights, racks of costumes, tables full of greasepaint—could result in something as wonderful as a play. Even more amazing, some of the flightiest people you'd ever seen managed the bedlam. Booth, as full of himself as any man who'd ever lived, impressed me as a paragon of sense compared to most of the actors who shared the stage with him. Lady Macbeth loved laudanum a little too well. Our doddering King Duncan didn't always know what play he was in. Sometimes he'd burst into a song from some music hall performance he'd done as a young man. Banquo seemed well-cast as a ghost, because he frequently became invisible (well, actually he had to be fetched from the basement maintenance closet, where he'd be romancing one of the witches). Despite all of this, the play itself proved a marvel. Only Shakespeare could have made so artificial a thing into such a scary, dreadful event. The jaws of our opening-night audience would drop. That I could guarantee.

It felt hot as Hades in the stuffy theatre. All of the gas lamps and limelights seemed to double the temperature. It made me real glad I didn't have to wear any of the heavy costumes Ma had made for the actors. My flannel shirt and overalls had me sweating enough without adding velvet to it all. The boots they forced me to wear whenever I worked in the theatre chafed my toes something awful. Bare feet are ever so much better in summer. I started to count the minutes till I'd be free of this torture.

The play started. Booth chose to have his performers act out the opening battle scene while the sergeant described it. That sure took my mind off of the heat. Watching swords and shields crash into one another, I moved in my little corner as if onstage myself, weapon on hand. Johnny Lee Harper, the actor playing Macduff, had planned all of the fight moves. A lot of them seemed too repetitive to my eyes, nothing like what real soldiers might do. I began to wish that I'd been allowed to swing a sword in this play. Then they'd see something.

Be careful what you wish for, the old sayin' goes. You might just get it.

My first scene change came up after that. I placed my bench and retreated back to the corner. *There it is, I thought. My glamorous career in show business.* You need a chair moved? Call Verity. Artificial shrub placement? I'm your girl. Carry a flat and lash it to another one? That Sauveur kid's a whiz-bang at that. No wonder I started to daydream between scenes, inventing stories that me and Tommy could act out later.

Lady Macbeth—Emily Thatcher—poked me in the ear. I about jumped to the moon. It took both hands over my mouth to not let out a holler. If an opium-addled over-the-hill ingénue had surprised you, could you do any better? She whispered that she hadn't intended to scare me, but could I go and find Banquo? He'd be on in two minutes and nobody had seen him.

She added that a delivery of props that day had filled the basement with hazards, so I should watch myself. Sighing, I set off on my next grand adventure.

I expected to find him down in the basement again, rutting with Witch Number Two. *Ick!* Having seen cows do the same on our Maryland farm, I couldn't see the attraction. Seemed downright undignified to me, especially in that heat. But all of the grown-ups seemed to think it great sport, so there must be something to it. I reminded myself to find Tommy and get the lowdown on what Silky Sadie had said to him.

The stairs tended to squeak, so it took a long time to go down them. I had to walk on the sides and tiptoe, candle in one hand, the other on the rail. Behind me I could hear Booth booming out a speech, but the basement walls muffled the words. My light made spooky shadows on the wall, like goblins dancing. Smells of sawdust, mold, and cat poo tingled my nose. The dark didn't normally scare me much, but something in Ford's basement always got to me. It felt for all the world like something old and weird lived down there.

At the bottom I took a look around. A plump gray mouse crawled out from under a pile of boxes and looked at me like I owed him a toll. Plump little Ernie. That's what I called him. He always patrolled there. For some reason, the theatre cats wouldn't go near him. I just ignored the little guy and kept moving, not being one of those girls who jump on chairs when rodents show up. The walls looked dirty but cool. Cobwebs covered them, but I couldn't see any spiders. I spotted the maintenance closet just ahead. It held spare parts for rigging, oil for lubricating hinges, and tools for fixing anything that might break. A cot sat in there for the handy man to use if he needed a nap after a long day. I pictured Gus Shepherdson, our Banquo, showing Daisy Melville, his witch, how handy he was with tools. *Yuck.*

Tapping lightly on the door got me no answer. I rapped a little harder. No light showed beneath the door, but that didn't mean much, considering the circumstances. I gritted my teeth. *Darn these fool actors!* Though tempted to leave them both there to face the wrath of Booth and Mr. Ford for missing their entrance, my hand grabbed the door handle and yanked. It screeched open and I jabbed the candle in. Nobody home.

With a roll of my eyes at the wasted trip, I turned around to go back up. Looking to my right, I noticed all sorts of new stuff. Lady Macbeth had been right in saying that a delivery had cluttered things. Just a quick glance showed me baskets, picture frames, old makeup tables with busted mirrors, teapots, a moose head. *When're we ever gonna need that?* Even a harpoon. Turning to the steps, the candle light revealed something shiny in a far corner to my right. A full suit of armor. Boy howdy! I'd never noticed that before. Must've just arrived today. Picking my way carefully over packing crates, under false trees, and through a maze of other assorted stage junk, I made it to the antique. Somebody had painted it in gold, most likely for a long-dead play. It even had a fancy leather belt around its waist. No sword, though. *Oh, well. Can't have everything.* A tap told me that I felt real iron, not plaster or any other pretend material. It looked very old, maybe even as old as King Arthur. They said that knights were short back in the olden days, and this suit made me believe it. I could just about wear it. Maybe tomorrow I'd sneak back down and have Tommy help me try it on. *Verity the Valiant, Savior of Mankind.* Backing up to admire it better, I discovered that the floorboard beneath my right foot was probably as aged as Camelot, too. It groaned and gave way, sending me straight down like a condemned man dropping through a gallows trapdoor.

I only fell about eight feet, but it felt like eighty. Crashing through the pitch-black, I didn't know where the bottom would be. Ending up on my rump, I sat there panting from the surprise. A quick check told me that nothing seemed hurt much. Due to some miracle, the candle lay within arm's reach and still burned. I grabbed it and held it up to see how I could get out of my predicament.

I knew I stood below the basement, of course. That meant that I must've landed in some old root cellar or the foundation of a building that pre-dated the Baptist Church. Turning in a slow circle, I saw that the walls of this new space were cut from solid stone, carved smooth by somebody a very long time ago. I spied no door, so the original entrance had to have been from above. But I made out no steps, neither. They might've been made of wood and been removed. *Is this some ancient Injun temple, maybe? Do they even do that?* I couldn't make out any of their markings or pictures, though. What, then? No furniture, no paintings, nothing at all. Just a bare stone room. And how could I manage to get out of it?

Since it appeared that I might be stuck there until somebody came down to the basement to hunt for me, I decided to take a look around. It paced out at maybe twenty feet square. Although the walls were solid and smooth, cut from living rock, the floor wasn't. It had big inlaid tiles, but like no tiles I'd ever seen. Not square, but odd-shaped. In fact, they looked just like...my Legacy Stone.

"Huh," I breathed out loud. I squatted down and held the candle close to the floor. Hard to tell in the sputtery yellow light, but I took the tiles to be made of the same red stuff as my Stone, too. Huge arrow-shaped blocks of solid red jasper two-yards-across. They even had the same hole in the center. *What on earth is this?*

I crawled all around the room, looking at every tile. Identical, with something like black marble filling in the joints between them. And every tile faced the same direction, with the point of the arrow facing one particular wall, angled so they aimed at a single spot. I scooted up to it and gave it a look. Faint carvings crawled across it, in an alphabet I'd never seen before. The letters looked a little like the Viking runes I'd spied in a history book once, but no, not exactly the same. More swirly than Norse.

I noticed something else as I stood there. My Legacy Stone burned a hole in my chest.

Grabbing the cord from around my neck with a yelp, I yanked the whole necklace off and held it out. The Stone...glowed. A dull reddish light came from deep inside it, like a beaker of blood on a sunny windowsill. Worse, the letters on the wall began to do the same thing, shining out from the surface as if they'd been heated in a forge. *Okay, Verity, you hit your head when you fell and this is some crazy dream. You have those all the time. Don't worry.*

Things got even spookier when the letters on the wall began to move.

I shrieked. Yep, like a girl. I admit it right here in front of the world. The only other time I'd ever made that sound had been when Tommy had dropped a wriggling slug down my back. My heart bass-drummed and my head answered with a banshee solo. Not good. I preferred a dream that I could wake up from. Not this overheated nightmare.

Just as I started to holler for help, not caring whether it interrupted the dress rehearsal or not, the letters stopped moving. They rearranged themselves into a shape that I knew well. One that I could understand.

A sword.

The same fiery molten-iron color as the letters that formed it, the sword had a nearly yard-long, single-edged, slender recurved blade that swelled a little bit toward the end, looking like a slender crooked willow leaf with a wicked point. Its crossbar swirled in an S-curve with a leafy vine twisting around it, the bottom part extending back to protect the knuckles. At the end of the handle the large pommel, sort of resembling an acorn, was almost as big as my fist. The whole thing still clung to the wall, the way you see old relief carvings in museums. But somehow I just knew that if I grabbed it, I could snatch it right off.

Real smart, Verity. Put your hand on a red-hot piece of steel. Dream or not, that'll hurt. Only a lunatic would try that.

So I did.

It didn't feel raging-lava hot, but warm, like bath water. The grip seemed to be birch bark wrapped with wire but felt like supple leather. No, not leather...skin. Human skin.

I yanked my hand back as if it had been burned after all. Glancing down, I saw that my palm looked fine. My imagination must've been affected by the fall, the tiles, the letters. And now I could smell a tangy odor, easy to recognize because everyone in Washington spent the summer with it.

Sweat. Maybe from somebody who worked hard in a small space...like in a stone cavern under the ground.

To top it all off, I felt a buzzing vibration. At first I thought it lay under my feet, or in the wall. Soon I understood that it just *was*. It came from everywhere around me at once, like the very air I breathed throbbed from a close lightning strike. I started to have trouble thinking straight. *This must be what the grown-ups feel when they drink whiskey.* Fearing that I might faint, I grabbed at the sword again. This time I ignored every sensation and clenched my fist around the sword hilt. With a wrench I hauled the glowing weapon free of the wall and crashed backward onto the tiles.

Lying flat on my back, I could see that the candle had gone

out. I could *see* that, in what should have been total darkness. *Oh, this is a much better dream than the ones I usually have.* Not only that, I could hear the *Macbeth* actors reciting their lines upstairs, as if I stood right beside them. Before now the stone chamber had blocked all sounds. I could also make out a slithering sound, like a snake on the move.

My new sword, now a three-dimensional object, had stopped glowing. The blade was blackened steel, the hilt and pommel bright gold. That vine was now green and moved around the crossbar like a living thing. My new toy had no more weight to it than a silk handkerchief. Its grip felt exactly like I held the hand of a living person. I could even feel its pulse. Most upsetting of all, the blade had curled around my neck so that the point stared at me like a spitting cobra about to strike. Then the tip sort of melted until it was a toothy metal smile.

"Hi, Verity!" said the sword in a pleasant cheerful voice.

*"If I turn into a giraffe and start
bumpin' my head on doorways,
you're in big trouble, mister."*

4 / Jasper

A giant mouse squeaked and the sword clattered across the tiles. *Mouse? Where's the mouse? Is it Ernie?* No, Ernie could never be that loud. *Must be me.* I skittered backward into a dark corner. Dark? Yep, couldn't see a thing. But a second ago I had eyes like a cat. And now...

Shivering, my mouth as dry as sand, I huddled into a little ball, feeling even younger and more scared than ever. *This ain't real. I hit my head fallin' into this hole. Just a horrible dream as my brain swells. I've had worse. Pretty soon I'll wake up and...or maybe not. Maybe they'll find me dead down here after the rehearsal. 'Poor Verity. What a tragedy. But there's a war on. Thousands die on battlefields every day. Life goes on.'*

I felt my heart and my breath slowing. Not a sound audible except that. No actors' voices filled my ears now. The wonder-senses that I'd enjoyed when holding the sword had left me. Sword? Where did it go? Don't see a talking sword every day. *Get movin', Verity. If this is a dream, time to enjoy it. Life goes on.*

The Legacy Stone still glowed faint in my fist, as did the letters on the wall. By the Stone's dim light I crawled toward the middle of the room, groping along the tiles. It took quite a while, but eventually my fingers bumped into the big pommel and felt for the hilt. With a nervous swallow I grabbed the sword and lifted it, still on my knees. Well, to tell the truth, it grabbed me. Honest. I felt a hand clutch mine. Good thing, too, because I squeaked again and tried to throw it away. This time the sword would have none of that. Warm dry fingers hung on, squeezing tight. Now I could see in the dark again. The blade was glossy black, like obsidian, and the crossbar, pommel, and wire wrapping on the white grip were gleaming gold. Looking at the handle of the sword, I saw only my own fist. No other hand to be seen. But I could still feel it.

"Pleased to meetcha!" the ghostly sword's voice said. The weapon rose and fell as my hand got shook hard, as if by one of the enthusiastic salesmen who would come to the theatre to hawk their wares. "I've been waitin' for you forever. Really forever, I think. No watch or calendar, but I'm pretty sure 'forever' fits the bill." The voice filled my head but not my ears, somehow.

"Uhh...," I said, if that counts as saying anything.

The sword giggled. It sounded like a kid, a boy about my age. That made it even weirder, but also calming at the same time. "That's great. Verity Sauveur, ordained savior of the world, can't put a simple sentence together. Got my work cut out for me, I do." The voice adopted a snooty accent. "Here, try 'Hello, I am enchanted to make your acquaintance.' It's easy. Just put your lips together and—"

"Uhh...," I repeated, ever so clever.

The sword heaved a disgusted sigh. "I thought you got top grades in school! Your teacher thinks you're so smart you're unnatural. What would Mr. Ford say if he were here to see you stammerin' like a drunk?"

That woke me up. "How do you know—?"

"Hey!" The blade tip melted again until it looked like a steely thumb. Pointing back at itself it howled, "Magick sword! Yep, I can read your mind. You can accept that I'm talkin' to you but the mind-readin' is where you draw the line?" With that it snapped back to its former shape.

"I...I..."

"OK, let's try charades. Sometimes we have to take baby steps before we can run." Now the blade became an index finger. "First word. How many syllables?" The finger flowed into the shape of an ear. "Sounds like?"

At that point it struck me that: 1) I was being made fun of by a talking sword that sounded like the class clown at my school; 2) I stood in some old religious shrine underneath a Baptist church that was now a successful theatre; 3) just above me they performed a Shakespeare play about witchcraft and murder. Call me a sissy, but I just broke down and started sniffling. "Where's my ma?" I blubbered. "I wanna go home! Help! Get me outta here!"

My new sword's blade wrapped around my mouth and shut me up. It didn't feel cold, like steel, but warm and moist like someone's palm. "Hush!" it whispered. "They'll hear you."

The thought galloped through my panicked mind that hearing me had been what I'd wanted. How else could I be rescued from this dungeon if no one heard my cries? Boy-sword seemed to hear that without my being able to speak it. "I can get you out of here without their help. In fact, it's better that way. There are …people…up there who don't really want to help you." He said 'people' in a way that made me feel cold as a January swim.

Peeling the obstruction away from my face I asked, "What is all this? It can't be real. These things don't happen."

"These things happen all the time. People just explain 'em away as coincidences, dreams, or fantasies. Or else they look the other way and convince themselves that they saw nothin' out of the ordinary. People are stupid. I know. I used to be one of 'em."

Sneaky sword. Get me curious and nothing else matters. Wiping my nose on my shirt sleeve, I said, "Used to be?"

"A long time ago, maybe forever, like I said before."

"Do you have a name? Can't just call you 'Sword'."

"How about Blade of Destiny?"

"Excuse me?"

"Too showy? Cleaver of Retribution, then?"

"I don't think so."

"Edge of Vengeance?"

"Get serious."

"Dread Hand of Reprisal? Bitter Steel of Punishment? Savage Sword of Sorrow?"

Now I laughed despite myself. "Maybe somethin' without a preposition?"

"Oh, sure. Stifle my creative urges. Crush my artistic aspirations. Trammel my hopes of literary fame into the heartless dust of cruelty."

I gave the sword a frown. "Have you been readin' dime novels down here?"

"No!" The blade drooped, as if hanging its head in shame. "Wrote a couple, though."

I snorted. "Did not!"

"Okay, you caught me. But I could if I wanted to."

"Jasper!" I blurted, inspired.

"Say again?"

"I'll call you Jasper. It suits you, somehow."

My Legacy Stone flared up into its full glory at that. "The Stone approves," said Jasper the Magick Talking Sword. As he spoke the letters on the wall where I'd found him brightened until they filled the whole chamber with their orangey light. "As does my Master."

"Who's that?"

The wall runes shifted again, like bugs scampering across the stony surface. As they flowed amongst one another, rearranging into a new pattern, more letters sprang to fiery life on all of the other walls. It felt like I'd been dropped into the middle of a blast furnace, except that I felt no heat, just...love, somehow. That warm vibration I'd felt when the letters and sword had first appeared filled the chamber again and hugged me like a grandfather. I thought I could smell bread baking and hear puppies yelping. *If I'm still dreamin', then don't wake me up.*

"You ain't dreamin', Verity Sauveur," said Jasper. "You know you ain't. Because the dreams you've been havin' are awful."

True. While the letters continued their journey around me, I saw flashes in my dizzy head of the dream I'd been having off-and-on for two months. I would fall forever down a long hole, like a well, and land in a dark place. Unnaturally beautiful children, all with pale faces and blonde hair, clutched at me with skeletal fingers, led by a sweet-seeming old lady who tried to eat me with her shark's mouth. A golden-skinned man and an enormous floppy-jowled black dog came to my rescue, fighting them off as I made my escape to the sea. At that point I always woke up.

Just that brief reliving of the nightmare made me shiver. Jasper wrapped his warm blade around my shoulders until I stopped shaking. By then the letters had stopped moving and taken their final positions. They filled every inch of wall space, starting at the place where I'd removed Jasper and wrapping around clockwise. I stood in the center of the room, slow-spinning to my right, and read them.

A contract. In Britannic too.

Most of it read like lawyer-babble about the Rights and Responsibilities of the Stone Warden (me, I figured), who shalt blah-blah-blah until such time as she wilt yap-yap-yap or unless both parties agree to jabber-jabber-jabber... It seemed to be an agreement that I would undertake a quest to use the sword of the Grand Mage (whoever the heck he was) in order to lead the Marshals of the Equity (ditto) against the Esteemed Gentlemen of the Honourable Merchantry (double-ditto) and return the world to its state of Accord and Harmony. All it required was a drop of my blood as a signature and the Great Battle Against the Shadows could commence.

Uh-huh. Who did they think they were kidding?

Me. I'm the only kid in the room.

"Are you crazy?!" I shouted, which just made Jasper cover my mouth again. Unable to speak, I had to think the rest at him. "First off, I don't what any of this is about. Who are all these people? I live in the capital city of the States United and have never heard a word about any of this stuff. Second, this sure sounds like you want me to fight a war and kill people fer real. I don't think so. Third, I'm only twelve years old! Can't you get some general to do this? Washington's crawlin' with 'em. Can't swing a cat without hittin' a dozen. And fourth, I'm gettin' outta here and goin' back to Ma and Tommy."

I dropped the sword at my feet and ran toward the hole where I'd fallen into the chamber. No unseen hand clung to mine to prevent it. Jasper's voice didn't invade my head to try to talk me out of leaving. Strange mystical forces didn't take over my soul and imprison me. My downfall was much simpler than that. I fell on my face.

To this day Jasper won't admit it, but I know he tripped me. I swear I felt an armored foot stub my toe. Crashing hard onto the tiles, I broke my fall with outstretched hands. The russet stones scuffed them and I winced. Not because of the pain, but because of what I felt in the palm of my right hand.

Blood. The wound was not so deep as a well...*but 'tis enough. 'Twill serve.*

A hot wind swirled around me, peeling the letters from the wall and making the cavern look like it was filled with angry fireflies. Far-off voices chanted in a harsh language I'd never heard. I smelled a strange bitter perfume. Brimstone. Brimstone and lily filled my nose. Swallowing, I tasted something hot and coppery. The sparking letters fluttered around my head like innumerable little bats, then flew straight into Jasper's blade, which sucked them up into its blackness. Then they began glowing on the blade, and moving, the letters constantly changing. While that happened I spasmed with what felt like an electric jolt, then fell panting onto the floor.

Total silence. Total darkness. Total despair.

Had I just made a deal with the Devil? Or with something else?

Oh, I felt more alone at that moment than I ever had before or have since. With the sword out of my hand I couldn't see or hear anything. It was just me lying in the gloom with the feeling that the happy life I'd had up to that point had just ended. I still hoped that the whole experience was my hallucinating while unconscious from the fall. But that wish began to feel like a scared kid's vain delusion. Curled up in a ball like a wood louse (feeling like one, too), I cried till my throat hurt and I choked on the tears.

They say that having a good cry makes you feel better. Maybe, but that night all it did was make me mad. If this wasn't a dream then it was a nasty joke to play on a little girl and this little girl wasn't laughing. Aching from the fall into the chamber, the scuffing tumble onto the tiles, the magical jolt, and the bawling, I felt around for that miserable sword. When I finally found it I grabbed the hilt in both quivering hands, fiery runes bursting back into life, and cursed at the blade for what seemed like three solid minutes, using every awful term I'd ever heard a soldier or sailor use. When I had run out of breath and swear words I stopped, panting.

Nothing. No Jasper. No chatty wiseacre talking sword. *Is this really a dream after all?*

Growling, I stomped over to the hole in the basement floor where I'd fallen through. I squinted up at it. The opening seemed too high for me to jump up to and the walls were too smooth to climb. My revived 'sword senses' let me see that the chamber sat as empty as a banker's heart. There was nothing at all that I could stand on to get up there. I blew frustrated air through my lips and considered what to do. Far above, the distant sound of the rehearsal reached me loud and clear. One of the murderers of Banquo explained that he lay in a ditch with 'twenty trenched gashes in his head.'

"Ain't that a lovely thing to hear while you're stuck in a dark hole?" I muttered.

Should I yell for help again? Jasper had said that it was a bad idea, that there were harmful folks up there. But what did he know? Those were my friends, or at least friends of friends. Nobody dangerous. *Stupid sword. Prob'ly just a figment of my imagination anyway.* And even if he wasn't, did I plan to let a talking sword that sounded like a bratty kid tell me what to do? *If I'm the contracted savior of humanity then I need to start makin' my own decisions.* Jaw set, I opened my mouth to scream so all of Washington City could hear me, if that's what it took.

Before any sound could come out I went blind and deaf again. *But I'm still holdin' the sword. What happened to my cat's eyes?* It was hot and stuffy. My breathing echoed in my ears as if I was in an ironclad's turret. *What the—? Did somebody drop a bathtub on my head?* With my left hand I reached up to touch my face. I couldn't. Metal stood in the way.

Turned out I really was in a turret, in a manner of speaking. Somebody had slipped a medieval helmet onto my shoulders. And they'd done it in the blink of an eye without my knowing it. Now who did I know who could have done that?

"Jasper!" I snapped, wincing as the sound deafened me. I lowered my volume. "Jasper!" Yanking on the helmet got me nowhere. I stamped my foot. "Jasper! Get this thing off me. I can't breathe."

"I don't know," the boyish voice said, sounding pouty. "You called me a lot of horrible names just now. Fairly rude if you ask me. I can see this relationship is something we're all gonna have to work on. Were you brought up in a barn?"

"Next to one, if you must know. On our farm. Come on, let me out of this miserable brain-bucket. It's hot."

"Are you gonna scream? Can't have that. Alert the nasties."

"What nasties?!"

He took on an elevated hurt tone. "I won't talk to you if you're gonna take a hostile attitude."

"I'm not hostile! I'm way past bein'—!" I caught myself, took a gulp of air, counted to five. "Jasper," I went on as if sitting in a library, clipping my words between my teeth, "won't you please be a dear and kindly remove this exquisite example of a twelfth century great helm from my poor little face?"

"Delighted, my beloved Verity. Glad to be of service!" he chimed. Fresh air—as fresh as could be had down in the sub-basement—cooled my nose. That awful helmet vanished. It wasn't removed or lifted from my shoulders, it just ceased to exist. *This magick thing will take some gettin' used to.* Now I could see through the gloom once more. The helmet melted away into Jasper's blade, like water running back down a drain. My sword took on its normal shape again and the headgear was just a bad memory. *Gonna have a lot more of those, at this rate.*

"Thanks," I said, rolling my shoulders to unkink them.

"Not at all."

There was a long silence in the underground room. Sighing at last, I said, "I don't think I can do this."

Jasper's voice was gentler than it had been before. "Nobody

ever does."

"That's just it. I'm a kid!"

"So you keep sayin'. How old do you think I was when they put me in here?"

"No!"

"Yep. Just shy of my thirteenth birthday."

Funny how shared misery really does make you feel a little bit better. "How'd that happen?"

I heard a sad laugh inside my head. "Someday I'll tell you. No time now. You only have a few minutes to learn the ground rules, I expect. You can bet the Stone has tingled every Merchantry agent for ten miles."

That made me frown. "Ground rules?"

"The fine print in the contract. You didn't exactly read it too careful-like, I noticed. See, all magick has limitations and responsibilities, just like everything else."

"Is this gonna be like them stories where the genie grants wishes but there's always a horrible catch? Will I turn into a giraffe later on?"

Jasper chuckled. "No."

"That's good. 'Cause if I turn into a giraffe and start bumpin' my head on doorways, you're in big trouble, mister."

The blade reared up like a horse. There was a strange pause, as if my sword sniffed the air. "We're already in big trouble."

"Really? What?" I had hoped that those ground rules would've been explained before I had to start saving the world from whatever might be wrecking it. This magick stuff was kind of fun but so far it'd been awful vague on the why's and wherefore's.

Jasper's voice interrupted my thoughts. It now sounded ancient and weary. "The Bullies have found you. And Venoma is with them."

The Evil Ones talk like bad Shakespeare?
This gets weirder and weirder.

5 / Venoma's Threat

We had bullies at school, but I felt dead sure that Jasper talked about something I couldn't just wrestle down and Dutch-rub. And it went without saying that anyone going by Venoma had to be bad news. "Sounds like you mean trouble with a capital T, huh?"

"'Fraid so. Time to get outta this hole."

I almost whooped for joy. "Now you're talkin'! You got a magick carpet?"

Jasper sniffed. "I'm not a djinn. I have to do things my way. First ground rule: you're my Mistress and have to command me. I'm not allowed to affect you on my own except to save your life in a dire emergency."

I thought about that for a minute. "That's why you could slap that nasty helmet on my head, to shut me up so I wouldn't bring them down on us?"

"Right. Your command can be just a glimmer of a thought That's all I need. You may not even know it's a command. That's okay. I will. We magick swords are smart that way."

"Whoa! We magick swords? There's more of you?"

"You bet. Sorry to say, they ain't all as charmin' as me. The Honourable Merchantry has some that are downright rude."

"Yeah?"

"Yeah. One has a sawtooth edge that spits the Black Death into the wound. I'd say that's mighty discourteous."

I shivered at the thought of that. My sword stretched toward the ceiling until it became a fireman's pole that reached all the way up through the opening. Come on. Climb up." He took on a cheery doorman tone and sang out, "Glad to be of service!"

I shinnied up the pole quick as a squirrel. Climbing things has always been easy for me. Of course, sometimes I fall down after the climb. That's how Tommy once had to carry me and my busted ankle home for two miles. At the top I looked around, but the basement still lay empty, except for Ernie. The plump gray mouse stood on his hind legs, looked at me for a second, then bowed. I swear to you, he bowed like I was royalty. My jaw bounced off of the dusty floor.

The sword shrank upwards into my hand until it resumed its normal self again. Between that and Ernie I'd about hit my limit for grasping strangeness. I pointed at the mouse. "Did you see that? He bowed to me!"

Jasper had a smile in his voice. "Why shouldn't he? Ernie served as a Beefeater at the Tower of London for Queen Bess before the Merchantry condemned him. He knows quality when he sees it."

"Wha—? That mouse is a couple hundred years old? And his name really is Ernie? I've been callin' him that as a joke."

"No, you haven't. You've been callin' him that because you've always known it's his name."

"How's that possible? I'm not a mage."

That earned me a sigh of impatience. "Everybody's a mage, in a way. Magick's as natural as breathin'. It's just that most people have no idea what they're capable of. They get overwhelmed by what they call real life and never learn to use their gifts."

"So you're sayin' understandin' animals is my magickal gift?" I looked at Ernie, willing him to turn somersaults. Nothing happened.

"One of 'em, maybe. It's common enough. Every horse doctor has a bit of it. Most magick ain't throwin' fireballs, you know. But your gifts are many, Verity. That's why you have the Stone. And me. We make your gifts into powers. Or did you think this is happenin' to you completely by chance?"

My eyebrows went up. "It's not? This is some kind of destiny thing? Like King Arthur?"

"If you wanna call it that."

Ernie sat atop an old thread spool and drummed on it with a tiny paw. He seemed impatient about something. I made a sour face at him and said, "What's your problem?"

"You're me problem, ducky," the mouse replied in a working-class Britannic accent that sounded a little overdone to my ears, like a hammy old actor.

If my jaw had dropped earlier, it positively plummeted now.

"You talked!"

"What? The bleedin' sword jabbers on half the night and yer don't bat an eye. The mouse says four words and yer wanna call the bloody *London Times*. Morph, yer sure this is the one? Seems a bit dim to me."

"Just gimme a chance to get my bearings," I protested.

"We'll, yer better get 'em quick. Trouble's comin' our way."

I shook my head, which started to ache from all of this. "I'm talkin' to a rodent."

"Your mind gave me a command," said Jasper. "You wanted to speak to him, so I boosted your gift."

"Just like that? No, 'oh, mighty sword of sorcery, grant me this wish'?"

"We can do it that way, but to be honest, it wastes a lot of time."

"We don't have a lot of time," grumbled Ernie. Apparently he could hear Jasper, too, at least when the sword wanted him to. "Me network says Venoma's on the way. Be here in just a tick. Not in strikin' range yet, miss."

I felt I should contribute, being the Anointed One or whatever they thought I was. "How will we know when they're that close?"

Jasper told me, "The Stone'll let you know."

Hmmm. I guess bein' vague is just somethin' that comes with magick. I unbuckled the belt from the suit of golden armor and fastened it around my waist. Jasper fit nice and snug into the frog on my left hip. There was a roomy pouch on the other hip. "What now?"

"We needs to scoot upstairs and get outside without bein' seen by any of the actors or stagehands," Ernie said, hopping off of his spool.

That confused me. "Why? I know 'em. They're okay."

"Lovey, if you're gonna be our mighty leader, listen to your Uncle Ernie. The so-called Honourable Merchantry has turncoats watchin' everybody. Don't let your trustin' nature get us all transmogrified. Once is plenty fer this old coot." He began climbing the stairs up to the stage, grunting all the while. Stopping three steps up, he said, "Oh. And don't talk to the cat. He's a bloody traitor. Works for fish scraps, that's the shame of it. Too bad, really. Used to be a nice chap. Grocer in Ipswich. Would give me missus first pick o' the brisket on Thursdays."

"Got it," I whispered, finger to my lips. "No cat chat."

"You bet your arse," the mouse said, nodding for emphasis and resuming his climb.

We arrived at the top of the stairs without making them squeak too much. I tucked the sword behind me so no one would spot it and start up a curious conversation. Didn't want it banging against a wall, either. I needn't have worried. Nobody looked my way. They were all too enthralled by Macbeth's rantings about Birnam Wood come to Dunsinane. *Whoa! I lost two whole hours down there? Seemed like two minutes.*

Tommy watched over Ma's shoulder from the other side of the stage. I stopped, too. Booth may have been an arrogant puffer pigeon on the street, but on stage he had something special. You couldn't help but pay attention when he spoke. *Is that his magick, his gift?* I told myself to be careful around him. As Ernie had said, you couldn't trust anyone. And he seemed a mite too knowledgeable about the Merchantry for my liking.

Funny, then, how I so trusted a talking mouse and a shape-shifting sword and their story about evil Bullies coming to take me away.

The great battle scene began. Blades, shields, and spears slashed the gaslit air, their sweet noise even louder than usual because of my Jasper-enhanced ears. I dearly wanted to stay for it, but Ernie kept tugging at my overall cuff to keep me moving toward the fire exit. We slunk past a couple of stagehands who were admiring the Shakespearean carnage and then eased out the door, being careful not to let it slam. Drawing the sword, I started to look for enemies. After all of our careful slinking I nearly undid us by almost stepping on Ernie. That made me jerk my leg back. Unbalanced, I hopped on one foot, Jasper clutched in one hand, feeling for the wall to steady myself. Instead I fell full-length through the half-closed door.

And stopped in mid-air.

Well, this sure seems magickal. I'm floatin' like a Hindustani fakir.

I looked down. A huge iron hand, standing on a single metal foot, held me like a baby. Balanced horizontal, as if flying. The stage door bumped against my shoulder, trying to close. No one in the theatre had noticed me yet, so I eased back down off of Jasper's new form and gently shut the door. He melted like quicksilver back into his sword self. After letting out the breath

I'd been holding, I turned away from Ford's Theatre into the alley.

My vision became so sharp that it almost seemed like day. Just a slight bluish haze and shimmer gave away the magick. The medieval fight on the other side of the wall sounded near as loud as it had when we had stood in the wings. A light breeze itched my skin like tiny lizards clawed their way across it. Unlucky for me, my sense of smell now grew many times better than before, too. I stood in the wrong city at the wrong time of year for that to be any fun. It occurred to me that wandering the streets of Washington carrying a glowing sword was bound to attract attention. Jasper sensed my question before I could think of it.

"Here, let's make us less conspicuous," he said in a whisper, which struck me as funny since nobody could hear him but me. The sword shrunk down. I thought for a second it would vanish all the way, but it stopped when the blade folded into the hilt. Now I held a simple rusty tin cup. But it felt warm, with a pulse.

Shaking my head, I said in a hush, "Don't think I'll ever be able to get used to that."

"Wait'll you hit puberty," Ernie snickered, next to my ear. He'd climbed up me while Jasper had been shifting. "That's somethin' that really takes some gettin' used to."

"What's puberty?" Jasper asked.

"Search me," I said, almost shrugging the mouse off of me. "I thought you knew everything."

"I'm only twelve, too, you know. My Master just gave me the

knowledge he thought I'd need to help you. The rest I have to find out on my own."

"Can you tell the future, then?"

"I think no one can. Not with certainty. Some great mages can see several possible futures and guess which is most likely. The Grand Mage sure seemed to foresee this night, though. At least so far."

"So this has all been foretold?"

"Except for the part about yer bein' a whiny pain in the backside," grumbled Ernie.

I protested with feigned outrage. "Hey! I'm standin' right here."

"Right, lovey. You're standin' instead of walkin'. We need to get to the river. Let's go."

"Okay. Hang on."

The alley would take us onto 10th Street. From there we could move west to the Potomac, much like me and Tommy had done that afternoon. This time I didn't plan on cutting through St. Usher's. In fact, I expected to take a twelve-block detour. If these Bullies were as scary as they seemed then we sure didn't want to add Horace and his loonies to our troubles. To tell the truth, between falling into the chamber, getting zapped with magick, and trying to understand all of the impossible things that had started happening to me, I felt near to falling over in a dead heap.

Just as we were about to leave the alley we ran smack into Mad Molly. She popped up out of a niche in the wall of Clemens'

Dry Goods store, offering me a flower and muttering something that made no sense. Her dark rags and smudged face made her hard to see, even with my new eyes. I had no trouble sniffing her, though. The stench could've knocked a buzzard off a privy. Did she smell that bad all the time? Like something dug up from a festering graveyard? Molly's smell didn't distract me for long because something new happened.

My Legacy Stone became cold as a January icicle against my chest.

The Stone'll let you know, Jasper had said. But this is harmless old Molly. We've known her ever since we moved here. How can she be a —?

The inner debate ended with a violent jerk on my right ear. Ernie yanked hard on it, hauling my head and shoulders in that direction. *Ow!* Just as he did so, the ancient withered face distorted. Its jaw unhinged like a hungry snake's and three rows of jagged teeth shot forward to snap at the air where my head had been. I felt the thing's steaming drool graze my cheek, leaving it numb. Molly Monster slashed at me with a clawed backhand. I brought up the tin cup in a sad effort to protect my tingling face. She moved quick as a panther. Her talons bounced off of a round metal shield two feet across. *Thanks, Jasper!* Stumbling backward, I tripped over something and went down, scraping my rear end on broken glass.

"Bloody cat!" Ernie snarled. He leapt off my shoulder onto the animal's head. "I told yer he was no good!" I heard a terrible commotion of screeching and spitting, commingled with sturdy

Britannic cursing. *There's one kitty who won't relish catching his mousie.* That was all I had time to think about, as my attacker tried to pounce on me while I lay sprawled on the ground.

My boot met her belly, which felt solid as a block of armored plate. The shock went all the way up to my hip. That foul thing flew above and beyond me, bouncing off the brick wall. I turned to see where she'd go next while scrambling to my feet. My eyes widened to see her launch herself across the alley and crash into the opposite wall, her claws digging into the stone and holding her there like a fly on a window. Yellow-green eyes with vertical pupils glared at me, smoke bleeding out of them. A mouth the size and shape of a coal scuttle held those deadly teeth now and they clicked with excitement, slime dripping from the lower lip. No hair to speak of grew on the unnaturally long skull. Of course, the giant ears were pointed. I'd have been disappointed otherwise.

The assassin creature climbed the wall to get more height for its next pounce. What had remained of Molly's tattered rag dress fell off. Seeing the whole body of the monster didn't make me love it any more. I could now see that it was definitely female, in an unsettling and misshapen way. *Ick!* It had leathery lumpy skin like an alligator hide I'd seen in the Smithsonian. A bony ridge ran along the middle of its broad back. Her belly hung swollen and pulsing, like she'd just swallowed a large dog...or worse. All of the thing's limbs were longer than they should have been. The huge feet had splayed toes with four-inch black claws. An awful, curved spike grew from each heel.

Right then I really wished that they'd made Jasper into the Righteous Revolver of Retribution, instead of just a sword. *Sheesh, this is 1862, fellers. Modern times.*

The hellish gargoyle on the wall hissed, its black forked tongue slithering out of that disgusting mouth. *How could I not know that such dreadful things are loose in the world? And what else is waitin' for me that might be even worse?*

I saw the haunches bunch up for what I just knew would be a fatal leap. My mouth dried up and my knees shook. I knew that the shield I held couldn't protect me forever. But I also figured that this thing had grown used to overcoming its prey with fear and not having to work hard. Maybe I could rattle its cage.

"Jasper," I whispered, "what is that ugly thing?"

"Venoma," he told me with disgust. "A dearth-demon from the other side. The Bullies use her for their dirty work, to soften up their enemies."

"Soften up? How tough are their enemies if this is just their skirmish line? Who can stand up to this monster?"

"Don't worry. She has a weakness. Everything that lives has one."

"Yeah? Good. What's hers?"

Jasper laughed in my head. Somehow that simple sound steadied my nerves. "Me."

My shield melted down and stretched out until I held the gold-hilted sword again. The same blazing symbols danced down the length of the dark blade. As soon as Venoma saw this she shrank back up the wall. That made me feel ten feet tall. I hoped that would be big enough, but I couldn't be sure.

"You've seen this sword before," I said to her. "And you're afraid of it."

Venoma's voice rasped, hissed, croaked, all at the same time. It felt like hearing a dead thing while it rotted, complete with worms. Now it was my turn to shrink back. "Thou puny man-spawn, dost thou ken how to wield yon blade?"

Scared as I was, I burst out laughing. *The Evil Ones talk like bad Shakespeare? This gets weirder and weirder.* "It seems simple enough. I swing it as hard as I can and your head falls off."

The oozing thing on the wall laughed right back. At least I thought so. It sounded more like a post-mortem knife cutting into a corpse. "Only one mortal canst claim the Morphageus. 'Tis bitter death to all else."

Morphageus? No wonder he wanted to be called Jasper. I pulled the Legacy Stone out of my shirt and held it up for her to see. White frost covered most of it, but the muted burgundy glow still shined through. "Then this mortal claims it, bitch." *Yeah, this girl's feelin' saucy!*

Venoma cocked her head in silence, as if listening to something I couldn't hear. It seemed I'd flummoxed her. This kid wasn't what she'd been told to expect. Maybe the enemy, this Honourable Merchantry, didn't have all of the answers, either. That made me feel a little better. Not getting eaten by this fiend in the next few moments would be good, too, because she bunched her ugly body up again and made ready to jump.

Sucking in a panicked breath, I raised the sword in front of my face with both hands. Braced for her attack, every muscle trembled. When the pounce came, I flinched. *Great, Verity. Close your eyes and hope she lands on your sword point. Why not just go hide under your bed?* I must've looked real fearsome, because Venoma didn't come at me but instead flew across the alley onto the roof of the next building.

"Another time, man-spawn," she hissed. "Now my master shalt dole out thy pain."

Just then the stage door opened and Tommy skipped out.

"Who's a pet? I'm a freedom fighter!"

6 / Marshals of the Equity

I jerked my body to face the door. *Tommy? Tommy's one of 'em, too?* Things were spinning out of control. While deciding if I should whack him and run for it, I felt something odd. The Stone, warm and dark. Every bit of the frost had melted away, thawed by his heart of gold. *Tommy's okay! You'll never walk alone, Verity.* That breath I'd been holding forever leaked out of my nose. All my muscles sagged and I almost fell over.

"Hi, there," Tommy said, shuffling toward me. "Where have you been? Rehearsal's over. You missed a boatload of scenery shifts. Everyone's—hey! Swell sword. Where'd you get it?"

Oops. I'd forgotten to hide it or have Jasper shift into a cup again. Before I could dream up a good explanation for why I stood in a dark alley with a flaming sword, Venoma settled the whole problem. Her claws ripped a chunk of tile out of the roof she crouched on. Hunks of clay clattered onto the ground next to Tommy. He hopped aside and looked up just in time to see a 400-pound monster leap across the alley to the next roof and disappear.

"What's the—? Did you see that?" he yelled, pointing at where she'd vanished.

"See what?" I hoped that the gloom would make him think his eyes had played tricks on him.

No such luck. "Teeth. Claws. Eyes. Big," he babbled, still pointing.

"Alley cat. A tom."

He didn't buy it. "Alley cats don't have teeth like a shark. And they aren't twice my height. What's going on?" He squinted. "And why is there a mouse on your shoulder?"

I hadn't noticed that Ernie had returned. Perched near my right ear again, he waved a cheerful little paw at Tommy. "This is Ernie."

"You have a pet mouse now? Since when?"

Ernie snorted. "Who's a pet? I'm a freedom fighter!"

Tommy made a sour face. "And why is he squeaking at me?"

I'd forgotten that others couldn't talk to Ernie. "He says he likes you. Any friend of mine is a friend of his." I mentally rolled my eyes at that.

"Whatever you say. What's he holding?"

Turning my head as far as I could, I peered at Ernie. He held up his trophy with a smile. "Looks like a bloody cat's ear."

"Yuck!"

Ernie stood up to his full four inches. "Behold!" he cried. "The traitor of Ipswich has paid for his crimes!"

"You killed the cat?" I asked, amazed.

"No, lovey, but the miserable wretch is wishin' he were dead right now."

Tommy grabbed my shoulder. "What gives? You're talking to a mouse. You've got a sword like no one's ever made. Monsters are jumping around."

Ernie tossed the ear behind us and tapped me on my cheek. "The monsters are still out there. We need to get to the river. Now."

"What about Venoma?"

"Miss her already, do you? Don't yer worry your pretty little head, ducky. She'll be with the others by now. Givin' a full report on us, she is. But if we can beat 'em across the river we'll be right as rain."

"You keep sayin' we have to get to the Potomac. Why?"

"'Cause their magick don't work on runnin' or deep water, that's why."

"Does ours?"

"Sometimes. Hit or miss, it is. But that won't matter if they catch us. We has to run."

I pulled off my icky boots and took Tommy's hand. "Trust me?"

"Sure," he said, squeezing mine back. "But you're having a conversation with a mouse. Tell me what's going on."

"I will as soon as somebody tells me. Right now we have to run."

"All right." As I took off at a dead sprint he hollered, "Oh, you mean really run?"

I used the lead I'd gained to think 'cup' and shift Jasper down while Tommy couldn't see. He'd find out about Jasper real soon, but I couldn't stop to explain. Ernie kept hollering like the hounds of hell were after us, and for all I knew that was no exaggeration.

We dashed through the alley and out onto 10th Street, looking every which way for enemies. *But how can you tell who's an enemy if they're shape-shifters?* As we passed my house I skidded to a stop and ran inside. Ma would still be at Ford's, hanging up costumes. I wished I'd remembered that. Didn't like going off without saying good-bye. Who knew when we'd be back? Or if. But I could scratch out a quick note. Besides, we needed some supplies for the trip. After all, we were going to Virginia. The Confederacy. Enemy territory. Seemed kind of funny to be escaping one foe by running toward another, but it had been that kind of night.

"Be careful," Jasper said. "They know where you live."

I kept my hand tight on Jasper and crept into the flat. Everything lay as dark and silent as a Halloween graveyard. So did my Stone. Seemed safe. I lit a lamp and told Tommy to gather some food from the pantry while I rounded up other things. We had a couple of old oiled haversacks that some soldiers had given us to play Army with. Tommy stuffed them full of bread, bacon, and leftover chicken. He filled two canteens with water. I gathered up matches, paper and pencil, and a map of Virginia that Ma'd cut out of *Harper's Weekly*. As an afterthought I grabbed a couple of flat caps and both of my light wool jackets.

"You're packing like we're going on a long trip," Tommy said.

"We might be. I don't know." I sat at the kitchen table to write a note to Ma to not worry about us. Silly. She'd go crazy. Still, I couldn't do anything else.

"Why? No one acts like this unless they've done something wrong. Is the law after you?"

"No. The opposite, actually." I focused on my writing. *"Dear Ma, by the time you read this..."*

He put his hand on mine to make me stop scribbling. "Verity."

I sighed and told him everything. Just let it spill out like grain from a torn sack. Falling through the floor, seeing the letters on the wall, watching the Stone glow, taking the sword, meeting Jasper and Ernie, fighting Venoma. All of it. I showed him how the sword could change its shape. I even blew out the lamp and proved I could see in the dark by telling him how many fingers he held up. Not once did he laugh, snort, or make any other sign of disbelief. Name me a grown-up who could've done that.

"Boy," he said after a long silence.

"Yeah," I answered. Sometimes that's all friends have to say.

"Guess you'd better finish your letter then." He lit the lamp again and left me alone, moving over to the front window to watch the street.

I knew that time grew short or else I might've written twenty pages. How do you tell your ma that monsters are coming and that you're the savior of humanity? That you, her only child, were going into a war zone where thousands of men were dying? That you loved her and would see her soon? I settled for the last bit and stood up.

"Anybody out there?" I asked, throwing my haversack over my neck. I stuffed paper, a pencil, and some matches in my belt pouch.

"No," Tommy said. "We should go out the back anyway, though."

That made sense to me. Didn't want to be out in the open any more than necessary. We pushed open the kitchen door, me in the lead because I could see and hear the best. It felt a little silly to be holding a battered tin cup in front of me as if it were a cannon, but an enemy would laugh at it, too. That might give us the split-second we'd need to react. Ernie moved into my haversack. He claimed it would leave me free to fight, but my wonder-ears picked up munching sounds.

"Leave some for the rest of us," I whispered.

He peeked his snout out of the bag for a second, a bread crumb falling out of his jaws. "Child, a famished battle-mouse is no good to anybody. Press on with your quest."

Our intrepid band of mighty warriors slid down the steps into the alley. Turning right, we headed west, hoping to get to the Potomac before the moon rose much higher. After about five minutes we began to relax a little. No matter how bad things get, it's hard to keep yourself on total alert for long. It drains all the energy out of you. And I'd just about used mine up as it was. I found myself leaning on Tommy's arm for support as we stumbled along.

Which is why the giant surprised us. Two blocks from home

an enormous dark mass rose up out of the ground. Seeming as wide as it was tall—and it looked plenty tall, believe me—it blocked our way as if somebody had dropped the Rock of Gibraltar in our path. It growled at us and brought up its brawny arms. I had just enough time to register Ernie screeching "Blimey!" before things went crazy.

Tommy yelped and froze, hunkering down. Somebody hollered "Whoa!" Me, I suppose. The giant's growl struck me like an ocean wave. I punched my pathetic little cup at the thing. All that went through my mind was the picture of a fist. That proved to be enough. I felt a small tremor up my arm. With a *woof* as the wind got knocked out of him, the Goliath crashed back head over heels and lay still some ten feet away.

"Did you kill it?" Tommy asked, recovered from his fright.

"Dunno," I said. "Is it breathin'?"

"Well, go look."

"**You** go look."

Tommy raised an eyebrow at me. "You're the one with the ferocious fist."

I looked at Jasper. Sure enough, the tin cup had sprouted a steel cartoon mitt almost two feet square, extending out over six feet on a funny-looking scissors-joint thing. My own eyebrow went up, because Jasper's weight hadn't increased. This magick stuff could almost be fun. Well, except for the screaming, running, and perhaps dying horribly part.

"OK, you win," I said with a shrug. "Jasper, sword, please." The big silly hand shimmered and shrank into Morphageus again. I crept up to the fallen giant with as much stealth as I could manage. For all I knew he just shammed to draw us closer.

"He's movin' a little," I said. "Boy, he's a big cuss. I think—whoa! Tommy! Come here and help me!"

I knelt next to the tree I'd felled, the sword a cup on my belt again. With Tommy on the other side of him we managed to haul on him till he sat upright. It took a lot of effort and energy, which I had in short supply, to hold him there. He smiled at me. My Stone returned a rosy hello. *This is no enemy.*

"You packs a mighty punch, Miz Verity," said Romulus, rubbing his sore chest. Giant knuckle marks still lived on his shirt. "How do, Mister Tommy."

"We thought you was gonna eat us," I said, hugging him. My arms didn't reach anything like all the way around him.

"Child, that's the first time anybody said that to ol' Romulus since—"

"Since he almost ate me that one time," Ernie said, hopping out of my haversack and onto the big man's belly.

"Why, Mister Ernie! I'm sho' glad you's here to look out for these here chil'n."

My eyes bulged. "You can understand each other?"

"Course we can. We's both Marshals of the Equity."

Great. One more thing I don't understand a lick of. If the monsters don't get me, sheer ignorance will do me in.

"Will somebody please tell me what's goin' on! I'm at my wit's-end here."

Romulus touched the top of my head with his giant paw. It

amazed me how gentle it felt, like a baby's breath. "We been yo' bodyguards, Miss Verity. Lookin' out for you ever since you got to Washington. Keepin' you safe."

"From what?"

Ernie turned to look up at me. "From the Hon'rable Merchantry, of course."

That didn't help me any. "And just who is this Merchantry? Evil bankers and railroad men and such?"

"Oh, no, miss," said Romulus, standing with a groan. Ernie scampered up his bulky body and onto his shoulder. "The Honourable Merchantry is sorcerers. And they runs the whole world."

"You mean...like black magick?"

"The blackest, lovey," Ernie nodded. "And they want to get hold of you and your Stone."

"You a threat to them," said Romulus.

There was a long pause while I thought about this. I could hear gunboats swooshing through the Potomac half a mile away. An owl hooted from atop the Smithsonian's turret and at St. Usher's the clock tolled ten. My nose caught the scent of flower beds a block distant, even when competing with the gagging smell of the Canal. All this I could accept, no matter how unbelievable. But the thought that wicked magicians were bent on pursuing a twelve-year-old tomboy to the ends of the earth because of her daddy's gift? Too much.

"This is all some kinda mixup," I protested. "A mistake."

Jasper's voice piped up inside my head. "Do you know what

would've happened if anyone but you had tried to take me off the chamber wall?"

"Nope. An alarm bell would've rung, maybe?"

"Their bones would've collapsed into ash and their skin would've fallen to the floor like an old gunny sack. Then their brains would've run out of their ears like warm custard."

I winced. "No mistake, then."

Romulus shook his head. "Oh, no, miss. You's the Stone Warden, that's certain."

"The Anointed One," added Ernie.

"She who will restore Accord and Harmony," said Jasper.

"But," Ernie scowled, jabbing a paw at me "you're still a pain in me arse."

My shoulders fell. "I still think there's been a howlin' mess made by somebody. But as long as the Merchantry thinks I'm their girl, we still need to get outta here."

"That's sho' 'nuff true," sad Romulus. "Time's a-wastin'."

This time Romulus led us. Seemed like he could see in the dark almost as well as me. We took a meandering course, avoiding major streets and lit buildings. I followed second, Ernie back in my haversack, and Tommy brought up the rear. Every now and then our guide would get down on all fours to sniff the ground.

"Why does he do that?" I wanted to know.

"Habit, mostly."

"Habit? Waddya mean?"

"I mean that me old mate Romulus used to be a dog, before

the Merchantry...disciplined him."

"You're pullin' my leg."

"'Fraid not, missy. That's how they punish people who cross 'em, by shape-shiftin' 'em into a lower form of life."

"And somebody thought a colored man's lower than a dog?"

"You're bein' naïve, Verity, dear. Just about everybody in these parts thinks that."

I shuddered, and not just because we were skirting St. Usher's. For some reason what had been done to Romulus struck me as more awful than Venoma's stench. Had Ma known? Might she be one of the Marshals of the Equity? Was that how Romulus, of all...people...had been hired on at Ford's? *Have I just been a stupid blind kid all this time?*

"You're not stupid," said Jasper. I'd forgotten that he stayed my head. "Just human."

"Like you, once?"

"Sorta, yeah."

"You said you'd tell me about it."

"And I will. But not now. You got bigger things to think about."

"Oh, right. Savin' the world."

"Savin' yourself first. They've caught us."

I ran smack into Romulus, who crouched down, unmoving. Tommy bumped into me. *This is like some bad minstrel show. The world's dependin' on us?* Focusing my sharpened senses, I felt for anything out of the ordinary. Nothing I saw, heard, or smelled caused any alarm. *Is Jasper wrong? Who's caught us?*

Then the Stone began to freeze. Turned so cold I thought it'd burn a hole through me.

Still I saw nothing. We were across the street from the southeast corner of St. Usher's. The oak trees glared down at us like angry gods who were miffed that we dared trespass on their sacred ground without due homage. Night made them even creepier than they'd seemed that afternoon. No light came from the school's windows. They were like the eyes of dead Argus, once all-seeing but now blind.

"Let's go," I whispered, stepping around Romulus. "There ain't nothin'—"

His log of an arm shot out and blocked me. "Sshh. Look."

Maybe twenty yards ahead of us stood two soldiers, a sergeant and a corporal. They were the Provost Marshal's men— military policemen tasked with patrolling the streets of the capital. Confederate spies and saboteurs crossed the river all the time to cause trouble. Or they just walked right out of their houses to do the same. A lot of Washington's residents sympathized with the South's cause, though they had to stay silent about it. That made policing quite a dangerous job.

This didn't look like a case of military necessity, though. A frail little boy of maybe seven or eight cried to the pair that he'd gotten lost and wanted his mama. They were kneeling down trying to calm him. Telling him that it would be alright, they asked if he remembered his street address. He had his hands in his coat pocket and just shrugged, while continuing to cry, head down.

"Do you have any older brothers or sisters we could take you to?" the taller of the two soldiers asked, trying to get some helpful information out of the boy.

The little tyke nodded. "A sister."

"Do you know where she is?" asked the other soldier, shifting his slung musket.

" Yes, sir. She's right there." The kid raised his head to display creepy black eyes with no whites to them. His hand came out of his coat pocket and an impossibly long finger pointed straight at me, pale as the finest china, the tip swollen like a tree frog's. And then I noticed his white-blonde hair.

And the last piece of my recurring nightmare came to pass.

I just swung a magick sword through
a shape-shifted sorcerer and
now I'm bein' congratulated
by a spellbound talkin' mouse.
What's natural about that?

7 / Hordes of Bullies

"Say, little girl," the tall soldier, the sergeant, said, stepping toward me, "this here your brother? He's been lookin' for his family. Awful scared."

Since I'd already been spotted, we had to either run for it or bluff. The former meant maybe getting shot in the back by our own nervous sentries, while the latter meant getting closer to that disturbing child than I cared to. His unblinking black eyes seemed as large and round as an ox's. Pretty and dead at the same time, they made me feel like I stared at an orchid floating in a cesspool. *Fascinatin', though. I just wanna hold that little boy's hand and go find his mama for him. Hug him and let him know that everything will be all right.* Without making my mind up to do so, I found myself walking toward the kid.

"Verity, no!" Ernie squeaked, running up my arm. I heard him but kept walking. "Romulus! She's witched!"

I'm watchin' a puppet show starrin' Verity Sauveur.

Somebody's pullin' her strings and makin' her move. Jasper chattered inside my head, but something mixed his words up. They made no sense. Ernie pounded his tiny fists against my cheek, but on I went. Reaching out, probably planning to pick me up like a barley sack and carry me away, Romulus' mitts found Tommy instead. My stage brother jumped between us, told him to stay put, and followed me.

"Excuse my sister, sergeant," Tommy said, placing himself a little in front as we reached the soldier. "She just had a fright." His hand took mine. The moment we touched, the spell blew away. I gasped and stopped dead, startled as if I'd caught myself at the edge of a cliff.

"Fright?" asked the sergeant, eyes darting about. It seemed plain that he worried about Confederate agents more than a lost kid.

"We were chased by some rowdies. They wanted to rob us, I think."

I jumped in to help him sell it. "We saw a knife and took off runnin'. They gave up about two blocks back. One of 'em upchucked into a bush. Drunk, I expect."

The soldier looked like he wanted to get on with his real business. "Well, you kids be careful goin' back home. Where do you live?"

"Just a little ways west," Tommy told him. "We were going that way when you stopped us. Folks'll be waitin up."

"All right, then. Take your brother and run along. Be careful."

"But he's not our brother, sir," I said, watching the blonde boy out of the corner of my eye. I didn't dare look straight at him. "Poor little feller's so scared, I think he's mistook us."

The face the sergeant made said that he didn't relish the prospect of being stuck with the child. I couldn't blame him. That kid made me wish I stood on the other side of the ocean. "Not your brother?"

"'Fraid not," said Tommy. "Too bad. Cute kid. Hope you find his mama."

We backed away, keeping the burly sergeant between us and that disturbing boy, who hadn't moved a muscle since pointing at me. The short corporal with him hadn't moved either, or said anything. He seemed frozen to the street. Odd, but no stranger than the rest of my day. With a grumpy sigh the sergeant turned from us and moved back toward his partner.

"That was close," I whispered when we got back to Romulus.

Tommy nodded. "Too close by half."

I hugged him. "You saved my bacon, boyo."

"Had to. Otherwise I'd have to get a new swordfight partner. They're heck to break in."

Ernie poked his snoot out of my haversack. "You two're talkin' like we're clear o' trouble."

"We're okay, now," I said. "Bluffed 'em good. Let's go."

Jasper spoke up, able to talk now that the blonde boy didn't control me. "Who's bluffed who? He wasn't tryin' to catch us, just slow us down and mark you."

"Mark me? For who?"

Romulus touched my shoulder and pointed across the street.

"For them."

I frowned and followed his finger. It aimed at the blonde kid, who still pointed at us, still not moving. Now the sergeant stood as motionless as the other soldier. The trio looked like some kind of weird stage tableau. But even weirder was what came at us from the grounds of St. Usher's.

More eerie little white-blonde kids, almost identical to the first one. At least a dozen of them, wearing blood-red school uniform coats and short pants. Some fell out of the trees like albino raindrops. Others shinnied down the drainpipes of the school, or oozed out of ditches. One slid down the flank of a sleepy horse hitched to a patent medicine wagon. They made no sound at all. My magicked hearing picked up no footsteps, no breathing, no rustling of clothing. Nothing. All of the boys had the same unnatural, long froggy fingers that the first boy had. *I imagine we shouldn't call 'em boys. I have a feelin' in my belly they're older than original sin.*

None of them blinked their beautiful eyes.

I caught myself beginning to meet the gaze of one of the advancing children. Ernie hung from my hair and poked me in the eye. "Ow!"

"They're tryin' to trance yer, missy," he said, dropping onto my shoulder. "Skedaddle!"

Romulus shoved Tommy and me down the street, toward the river, following the smelly canal. Our giant protector took up the rear, herding us like a...well, like a dog would herd sheep. We ran hard, but at a pace we could hold for the long haul to the

Potomac. Pursuing us with a strange, disjointed gait, shoulders rolling and hips following, the boys traveled at about the same speed as us, staying maybe fifty feet behind. The first one had joined them, leaving the Provost soldiers standing like blue statues.

"What...What are they?" I asked Jasper, huffing along. Anyone who saw us would have thought me just a loonie, talking into a tin cup while scampering down the road. Or maybe they'd just write me off as poor Ellen's child. 'Verity's always been pixilated, you know.'

"Bullies," he told me. "That's what the Equity calls them. Corrupted mages who do their penance by kidnappin' or assassinatin' whoever the Merchantry sends 'em after. They were caught stealin' from their masters, or betrayin' secrets."

"Secrets? Like what?" It occurred to me that I didn't have to talk, only think. That gave me more wind for running.

"Things the Honourable Merchantry would rather most people never find out. Like how they nearly destroyed the world. How they manage to profit from every bad thing that happens anywhere. That they scheme to make those awful things occur."

I checked over my shoulder, worried about the Bullies. They were keeping the same distance from us. Why?

"What things?"

"Wars. Plagues. Revolutions. Storms. Earthquakes. Economic panics. You name it."

I couldn't believe it. "One group of people causes all that, over the whole wide world?"

"Most of it. When that stuff happens on its own, the Merchantry encourages it, makes it worse, keeps it from stoppin' too soon."

"Yeah?"

"And they don't want people to know they're behind it all."

"Don't folks know anyhow?"

"Some do. Very few. Most of 'em get bought off or warned off and don't say anything. The rest get visits from the Bullies."

Our Bully visit made me suspect that something wasn't right. They didn't get any closer or farther away, even if we slowed down for a ditch or a fence. Whenever we changed direction, sped up, walked instead of sprinted, the horrible squad of boys altered with us. What were they up to?

"Ernie, what gives? Why don't they attack? They outnumber us four-to-one. I know they have magick. Are they just playin' with us, wearin' us out so we'll be easy to take down?"

"P'raps," said Ernie. "But that's not how they usually operate. They prefers a quick vicious assault out o' sight o' pryin' eyes."

We were getting tired. Big and strong as Romulus was, he had too much bulk to be able to move it fast for a long time. His breathing sounded rough. Though Tommy had more stamina, even he drug his feet. I didn't feel any worse than I had before we'd been jumped, but that might've been Morphageus' power holding me up. If we didn't get to the river and whatever safety it offered, standing and fighting might be forced on us. Two kids, a man, and a mouse weren't the kind of odds I liked in a scrap with those witch-boys.

Bursting out in the open, our little band could see light from the crescent moon glittering on the wide Potomac where the canal emptied into it. *OK, so this is our goal. Now what?* The Bullies didn't miraculously stop because the river lay in sight. In fact, they now sped up a bit, spreading out in an arc so we couldn't move but in one direction. More had joined them. And I realized just what had been going on. The idea made me sick at my stomach.

"Romulus!" I hissed. "They've herded us here, just like Injuns do to buffalo."

"Don't I know it, chile," he nodded, backing up to keep the bullies in sight. "They's got theirselves a plan."

"But what is it? There's nothin' here." I waved the cup in a circle. "Just open ground, the river, and—"

That sinking feeling got worse.

"—And Washington's Monument," said Tommy and me together, skidding to a stop.

Washington's haunted Monument, some folks said. All those stories we'd heard about spooky happenings at the half-built tower skittered through my mind again. Guess I shouldn't have laughed so hard at the kids who'd told us those tales. Because now I saw that I'd have a ghost story of my own to share.

'*Once upon a time, twelve sinister little boys crept out of Washington's Monument. Their hair the color of a burial shroud and their fingers like those of decayed skeletons...*'

We were surrounded by the Bullies.

Close to two dozen of them now. They had us backed up

against the foul canal and were creeping in, constricting their line like a noose. Dark as it was, we could still see them. The sliver of moon picked out their hair and pasty translucent skin as if they stood under gaslights. But their silence disturbed me more than their appearance. It would have been easier to deal with them if they'd said something, anything. At school, the bullies I'd grown used to fighting made all sorts of noisy threats. I had no trouble turning their foolishness against them and confusing their tiny minds.

Romulus stayed out front. I hoped he didn't plan to sacrifice himself for me. The Marshals of the Equity might make that sort of grand gesture every day, but it would only delay things a little. We needed to get through the line of Bullies and make it to whatever safety the Marshals had arranged.

"Romulus, what're we gonna do?" I asked, turning my head non-stop to check the line of attackers. "Can we use the canal? Back up through it and get away? It's runnin' water."

He shook his head and reached into a shirt pocket. "Has to be deep water. The river might just do it, but not the canal."

"They'd still come after us," Ernie added in my ear. "Focus their magick and part that foul water like the bloody Red Sea."

"They can do that?" Inside I felt glad, because wading through a river of outhouse leavings didn't seem much preferable to being tranced by evil mages.

"Ducky, they can do things that'd turn your pretty red hair as white as theirs."

Romulus laughed. "So can she." He'd crouched down so low

he almost stood on all fours.

I frowned. "Huh?"

"Morphageus," he said, hefting a small flat item from his pocket. "Now."

Jasper must've been waiting for that, because the instant the word hit my brain the sword blazed into life. My shaky hand held it high for all to see. It made me feel like some kind of Roman god when all the Bullies stopped in their tracks to watch the flaming runes pulse along my blade. *Yeah, who's a tough guy now!*

My superior feeling didn't last long. All of the Bullies started laughing. A high-pitched cackle, like a flock of ravens.

"They're just tryin' to unnerve you, missy," Ernie said.

"Doin' a darn good job of it," I muttered.

"Notice how they never blink?" asked Romulus.

"Uh-huh. Spooky."

Jasper chuckled inside my mind. "Remember, everything that lives has a weakness."

With a low growl Romulus said to me and Tommy, "Follow close behind me, both you. I can make a hole in they line, but this won't work on very many of 'em for long. Run straight for the point o' land beyond the Monument. Verity, chile, if any of 'em gets too close, give 'em what-for."

Saying that, my protector snarled and strode right for the closest Bully like he planned to shake hands with him. His muscled arm shot out at the terrible tot's face. The enemy froze and stared at the Marshal's fist.

It held a small shaving mirror.

The Bully evaporated. I can't describe it any other way. In the same instant that he saw his reflection in the glass he seemed to collapse in upon himself, then poofed out in a cloud of orange and purple mist that faded into the night breeze. I saw the ghost image of a death's head for an instant before it shredded in the air. My ears picked up the faintest angry gasp, like whatever animated his shape was being torn apart. The grandest sight I'd seen in a night full of wonders. Romulus did the same favor for two others before they all learned the lesson. They covered their soulless eyes with amphibian fingers, hissed, and kept coming.

But we had a gap. A chance. Bursting through, Romulus howled a battle cry and motioned to us to run for it. We didn't have to be asked twice. Tommy and me took off as if shot from a howitzer. Surprise let us through untouched, though the crowd of Bullies recovered quicker than I'd hoped. All of us sprinted west, our tiny band pushed by fear. Rage and hate propelled the Bullies. They weren't interested in herding us anymore. Now they wanted to catch us. That didn't bear thinking about. Our legs pumped even harder.

One of the little monsters, faster than his fellows, almost touched me with one of those awful hands. Without thinking I swung the sword with a sharp wrist snap. The blade sliced through him with no physical resistance at all. As if I'd hit nothing. Yet a spasm of cold ran up my arm. The Bully exploded in a shower of the same sunset-colored fog as Romulus' mirror victims had. He vanished with a sigh into the night air as if he'd never existed. In my head Jasper giggled.

"Jolly good show!" cheered Ernie. "You're a natural, lovey."

Natural? I just swung a magick sword through a shape-shifted sorcerer and now I'm bein' congratulated by a spellbound talkin' mouse. How natural is that?

Fifty yards from the river Romulus slowed to let us pass him, waving for us to keep going. He stood like Horatius at the bridge, ready to do battle against a whole army to keep us safe. It seemed to me that a hand mirror wouldn't serve as much of a substitute for a sword and shield or, even better, a regiment of infantry, but what did I know?

"Ernie," I panted, slowing and tightening my grip on Morphageus, "go with Tommy."

The fat mouse dashed down my left arm so he could look me in the eye. "No, you'll need a seasoned fighter."

I saw a quick image in my mind of Ernie on a plate while a Bully salted him. "I don't wanna lose you in the scuffle," I told him. "Get to the river and, uh, reconnoiter. Report back, soldier."

"Will do!" he barked, snapping to attention and saluting like a crusty old sergeant-major. For all I knew, that's what he might have been once. Scampering down to my hand, he jumped onto Tommy's head.

"Hey!" Tommy yelled, brushing at his hair. "What gives? Your mouse is—"

"He's takin' you to the water. Go see if there's anybody there to stop us...or maybe help us."

"Where are you going?"

I set my jaw and turned back toward our pursuers. Romulus had vaporized a couple more of the boys, but there were too many. They were about to get behind him. "I'm tired of bein'...Bullied. Gonna go see what this sword can really do."

Horror twisted Tommy's face. "Verity, you're not a real fighter. All you can do is make-believe stuff."

Don't I know it. "Can't explain now, but the sword makes you better than you truly are." I smooched him on his beautiful sweaty cheek. "Get goin', boyo. I'll be right behind you."

He started jogging west. "Don't get yourself bewitched again. And don't leave me."

"Not a chance. No matter what happens, I'll find you."

We parted. As I turned away I mulled those final words to Tommy.

I'm still trying to make good on them.

Raw sewage bubbled up in geysers which settled into eight rude man-like shapes, about nine feet tall.

8 / Sorry, Tommy

Rushing back toward the Bullies, I felt dizzy and weak. This was no pretend fight, with Verity the Valiant guaranteed to defeat all her opponents without even breathing hard. What would I do if someone—or something—attacked me without a script? I had no training in actual battle. Awful things might be about to happen to me...things worse than getting bones busted.

"Jasper," I thought, "what do I do? How do I fight these things?"

"They'll try to spell you," he said, "so don't look into their eyes, of course. If they can't do that, they'll try to get behind you. If those horrid hands fasten on you, your soul will be bound to them."

"That sounds...bad."

"It is. Just remember, you're the chosen Stone Warden because of your natural gifts. Use 'em. Don't think too much, just move. I'll be with you."

"Thanks." I started running, sword raised.

"One last thing...don't let 'em take the Stone away from you. No matter what."

"That's bad, too?"

"Well, it'd end life on Earth as you know it and usher in a new Age of Darkness and Despair."

Ain't that just peachy? "Is there a set of directions for this thing?"

"Sure. Written on the wall of the sword chamber. You couldn't be bothered, remember?"

"Oh, right. Sorry."

Ahead remained over fifteen Bullies, swarming around the mighty Romulus. In a second they'd bring him down. The idea of those mushroomy little monsters crawling over him, doing who-knew-what, made my fear of them blow away. Instead of being all terrified of the buggers, I felt something else now.

Anger.

With a roar I cut two down two Bullies at once just as they were about to latch onto Romulus from behind. Sprinting through their death-vapor, which smelled like rotting flowers, I thrust the sword into the face of another. Each time I felt the same icy shiver in my arm. I grabbed Morphageus with both hands, swinging it like a bat. *Wow!* I hadn't lied to Tommy. Jasper truly did make me better, stronger. I could never have been that fast and that graceful otherwise. He was having a fine time, filling my head with silly tavern songs and cackling. Another Bully went down minus a leg. His life leaked out through the wound as he lay on the grass, then a few seconds later he exploded into the usual colored cloud. The other dozen attackers backed away from me and Romulus, staying just out of reach. I stood next to my friend. Both of us took a moment to catch our breath, standing back to back. I gasped, he panted.

"Sho' glad to see you, chile," he said, grinning despite the circumstances.

"I don't think these fellers are so happy about it." *Verity the Valiant, always ready with a snappy quip. This hero stuff ain't so hard.*

Right then something invisible smacked up the side of my noggin. It felt like I'd been kicked by a whole team of mules. I flew ten feet and landed hard, the wind knocked out of me. Rolling to a knee, I saw that the same had happened to Romulus. Several of the Bullies had joined hands. A sort of bluish shimmery bubble surrounded them, then faded. *Must be that magick-focusing that Ernie warned me about.* Why hadn't they done that before now?

"Magick's like havin' a bank account," Jasper told me. "You can draw on it, but it depletes your funds until you can make a deposit. They were savin' theirs for when they had to have it."

"What about me? I've been usin' your magick non-stop tonight."

"Your natural soul-store is huge. That's why you're the Stone Warden, remember. Plus, my master put me into the chamber with a great store of force. We're okay for a while yet. Go get 'em."

"I have an idea about that."

"I know, I can see your thoughts. Let's do it."

I helped Romulus to sit up. We had to hurry, the Bullies were advancing again. They might blast us one more time, just to make sure. Another one of those and I might not have a clear enough head to resist. And who knew what else they were able to do? Ernie had hinted at some very scary things. We couldn't give them time for that.

"Your job's done," I told the Marshal. "Get to the water."

He shook his head. "I's sworn to protect you."

"And I'm the Stone Warden, givin' you an order, Marshal."

Romulus jumped up and nodded. "Yes'm." With that he ran off full-speed after Tommy. *Well, that was easy. Hope this next bit's as simple.*

I shook my aching head. The Bullies were giving me that cackling laugh again as they rushed me. From their side they saw a scared girl in her first magick fight, out of her depth and ready to fall with only a slight push. And her bodyguard had just run away. That blue bubble built up around the six hand-holders. They were about to win.

The force blast came at me hard, but this time I expected it. Morphageus flowed across my arm into a broad circular shield again, the same as when I'd faced Venoma. But now it swelled to twice the size as that one. It hid my whole body as I crouched.

And this time Jasper was a giant mirror.

All the Bully magick sucked into the shield like water up a straw. My chest burned as the Stone turned red-hot. I slid back a step, then braced myself. With a shout me and Jasper sent the spell straight back where it came from.

I hoped that the next month's Independence Day fireworks looked as spectacular. All the Bullies who still held hands detonated in a fiery violet tornado. The others scattered like ninepins, knocked off their feet. One popped right back up, but vanished from looking at the mirror. All the rest struggled upright, covered their eyes, and charged again.

Time to go! Every muscle I had felt like army wagons had driven over it. As I ran back to join the others, sword in hand again, I seemed to run in slow-motion, like those dreams you have where you're being chased by monsters but can't escape. Boy, I can't tell you how much I wanted to wake up from that one and find Ma hugging me, saying it'd be okay.

That didn't happen, of course. The monsters were real and kept coming. Ma no doubt paced our parlor, all frantic and begging every policeman and soldier in Washington to go find her little girl. I almost laughed at the idea. *What would they do if they were here? What help could they be?* The Bullies would just trance them and make them into mindless allies who'd join the attack on us.

As I passed Washington's Monument I saw that that my friends were huddled together at the river's edge. I could hear Ernie and Romulus arguing about something. Tommy scanned the river but there was nothing to see but a lot of noisy gulls. We were supposed to get to this spot. The Marshals had insisted safety would be found here. Far to our left, the Long Bridge ran across the Potomac to Virginia, but heavy mobs of Federal infantry and artillery guarded it at both ends. Not much help there, even if we could drag our exhausted selves down to it. *What now?*

"I told you Pitcairn wouldn't show!" Ernie shouted, standing in Romulus' dinner plate of a palm. "Can't trust a bloody pirate."

"He never left us befo'," said Romulus. "Sumpin' must o' happened."

"Oh, somethin' happened, all right. Our brave buccaneer decided to take his money and run, that's what happened. Too concerned for his precious ship to be worried about our welfare."

I staggered up to them, dropping to my knees and sucking air. Glancing back over my shoulder, I saw that the Bullies had stopped chasing me. *Guess they figure they have us now. No sense in rushin'. They'll hold hands and conjure up some new nasty thing for us.*

"Who's this Pitcairn?" I asked.

Tommy said, "Blockade runner, Romulus says. Hates the Merchantry with a passion. Lives to bloody their noses. Why he thought the Union Navy would just let him waltz up the Potomac to rescue us is beyond me."

Ernie made a rude sound. "I'll have yer know that Commander Aloysius Pitcairn could sail the *Penelope's Kiss* up Pennsylvania Avenue into a forty-knot headwind if he were so inclined. Which...it looks like he ain't."

"Well, this'd be a swell time for it," I told him. I punched Tommy on the arm. He winced like he'd just taken a mule kick.

Gotta remember how the sword makes me stronger. "I remember my mythology. Ain't Penelope supposed to be eternally faithful?"

Tommy rolled his eyes. "Irony, I guess."

At that Jasper turned into a clothes iron and laughed. I sighed and shifted him back to the cup.

"All we can do is wait and hope he earns his gold," Ernie told us, gazing at the river.

Romulus plopped the mouse onto his broad shoulder. "No time to wait. If they brings help, we's stuck. Gotta bust outta here now."

"And go where?" Tommy wanted to know. "Where do we hide from these things? I'm betting there are more of them, if this Merchantry you're all so afraid of is as strong as you claim."

"Has to take that chance. They's pinned us here. Pretty soon they'll—"

'Pretty soon' became 'now.' All five remaining bullies linked hands and started building their magick. As their hazy glow sprang up I threw out my mirror shield. I sniffed a sharp odor, like after a lightning strike. A tremor bumped our feet, but nothing smacked into us this time. *Okay, now what? Did they miss?*

"You know more about 'em than I do," I said to Ernie. "What's up?"

The mouse spun around in all directions, looking for signs. "Don't know, duckie. Usually by now something's happened. Fireballs from the sky or meltin' skulls or—"

Tommy tapped me on the shoulder, pointing north. "Or manure monsters."

We all snapped our heads around and looked. Boiling and smoking, the Washington Canal, which had offended my nose ever since I'd started carrying Jasper, now brought out a new indignity. Its raw sewage bubbled up in geysers which settled into eight rude man-like shapes, about nine feet tall. The things started staggering and stumbling toward us, their oozy arms outstretched. A just-visible blue aura, and lots of flies, surrounded them.

Oh, so that's what was tryin' to crawl out of my privy. "You know, I thought this night already stunk about as bad as it could get," I sighed. With a dopey chortle, Jasper hopped onto my nose as a clothespin.

"Tryin' to get us away from the river," said Romulus. "They mus' still be 'fraid we's gonna cross."

"Then they know something we don't know," grumped Tommy.

"Romulus, can we fight them things?" I asked, pulling the clothespin off and making it Morphageus.

He shook his bald head. "Nothin' there to kill. No life. You can cut 'em up, but they'd just re-form and keep a-comin'."

"Have to break the spell, then," Ernie said. He pointed at the Bullies. "That means chargin' 'em."

I frowned. "Won't they just blast us?"

"No, they can only discharge one witchery at a time. The Proprietor don't trust 'em with all of the skills of a true battlemage. If they abandon the animation to defend themselves, the muck'll just plop onto the ground."

Shifting the shield back into a sword, I said, "Let's go, then. Only five of 'em left."

Romulus gave me a dark chuckle. "Only five Bullies! That's like sayin' they's just five brigades."

Tommy stepped up next to me. He had the same look in his eye he'd had that afternoon when he'd drilled his dagger into the stage. "If Verity says go, then we go."

With a shake of his little head Ernie said, "Warrior children. Strange times we live in."

Romulus joined us, mirror in hand. "That's true enough."

"Anyway," I mumbled, "I'd rather get covered in spells than poop."

Sure enough, no sooner had we begun to march toward the quintet of Bullies than they began to creep back. As we hadn't attacked them yet, they kept their magick up. The foul things from the canal still pursued us, lurching along like something from a touring show of *Frankenstein*. No miraculous pirate ship appeared on the wide Potomac to rescue us from our fate. Why did they want us away from the river, then?

I broke into a trot, eyes down to avoid their gaze. Romulus and Tommy did the same, staying even with me. Our enemies front and rear changed their speed, too. I wondered how fast magickally-animated manure could move. The whole bizarre scene—evil blonde children, intrepid heroes, and loathsome muck monsters—moved as one unit up the small rise where

Washington's Monument stood.

Ah. That's what they're doin'. Figures. Be careful. They have somethin' up their tiny sleeves.

Jasper and I had been having a silent discussion about the best thing to do, and now came the time to try it. The idea popped up from something I'd seen in a South Seas exhibit at a museum. If it worked, we'd have the bulge on the Bullies. If it failed, I should still have a chance to try something else. Yelling and whooping like an Injun, I sprinted at the blued line of Bullies, throwing Morphageus with all my might.

My magick sword melted into a new form in mid-air. The sharp-toothed boomerang sawed the head from the nearest mage. As he disappeared into smoky lavender flame the spell collapsed. So did the stinky things behind us. All of them smacked into the ground with a single wet thud. *Somebody's gonna come out here in the mornin' and wonder, 'What the heck went on last night?'* We were upon the other four Bullies before they could react.

No longer holding hands, they were vulnerable. Romulus mirrored one and kicked another. It thrilled me to see that a boomerang really would come back to your hand. *Now that's magick.* Jasper was shouting for glee in my head and begged me to toss him again. Tommy found a crowbar from the pile of old construction material at the Monument's base. It didn't kill the Bully he hit, but the shrimp's face turned into a squashed toadstool. Re-armed with Morphageus, I sent him to whatever villain-afterlife he had to look forward to. The pair of remaining

Bullies scampered for the rusty iron door of the Monument. I caught both of them with the boomerang at the same time and away they went. Because they'd been so close to the door, the weapon had no room to turn back to me. It clattered against the marble wall and fell to the ground.

While I rushed to pick it up my friends whooped and hollered. One moment they'd been staring at capture, or worse, and the next they'd wiped out their foes. Not bad for two kids, a former pooch, and a stout mouse. They slapped backs, shook hands, hugged, and howled at the moon (okay, nobody but Romulus did that). Bending down to pick up the boomerang, I wanted to feel the same way. When I stood up I held the sword again, but I also held worries. The Bullies wanted us here for some reason. None of the ideas that first popped into my mind were at all good for us.

After sheathing the sword, I tried to shush the cheering bunch. It took a lot of grabbing, poking, and nagging, but I got them to be quiet. "We're not outta the woods yet," I reminded them.

"What do we do, then?" asked Tommy. "Stay at the river and wait for the ship or find some other way to cross?"

"Longer we sits here, mo' likely the Merchantry send more Bullies," said Romulus. "Or worse."

Ernie shook his furry head. "Can't believe I'm sayin' this, but we should wait for that low-life Pitcairn. Romulus told the truth. He's never stranded us before."

"He's too late," I said, looking around. "We're out of time.

They know we're here. More trouble will come." I stared up at the Monument. It loomed up about 150 feet tall, of white marble. Temporary wooden stairs led up to an iron door in the base. When finished it would be a jaw-dropping 500 feet, folks said. The war and stupid grown-up arguments over money had stopped construction. For more than four years it had stood silent, no work being done. My magicked eyes could see all the way to the top, to the raw edge where rusty frames and derricks jutted into the summer night air. I could make out something else, too, something that made me catch my breath.

Venoma plummeted toward us.

The toothy drooling thing shook the ground when she landed, flat-footed, twenty feet behind Romulus. Taller and broader than him, she seemed to have grown since I'd seen her at Ford's. This might've been her true form, freed of the need to pass as Mad Molly. She bounded forward with a mighty leap and batted Romulus aside before he knew she was there. I watched him roll across the grass and lie still. No sign of Ernie, but I could hear him cussing a blue streak, so I knew he must've been all right. Ignoring Tommy, who had fallen to the ground, still clutching his crowbar, Venoma bared her triple row of fangs and leapt straight at me.

But she hit empty air. The instant she'd smacked Romulus a wish had flashed through my mind, that I could jump as far as her. Jasper's cheery "No problem, girlie!" was followed by the Morphageus flowing down my body like quicksilver again. Metal coiled into huge steel springs around my feet. As Venoma jumped at me, I boinged a good twelve feet into the air, coming to earth behind her. Those springs gave me a soft landing, changed back into the sword, it and flipped into my hands. My leathery attacker turned with cobra-like speed to see where I'd gone. That saved her head, for the mighty cut I aimed at her neck missed, zinging through empty air.

I barely remember our battle. Just a blur. She proved to be every bit as quick as Jasper and the Legacy Stone made me. All my thrusts and cuts bit into nothing. Her every counter-attack with tooth and claw got parried by the small shield that Morphageus would become in an eye's blink. What kept me in the fight, despite every muscle crying in pain and fatigue, was knowing that my friends were doomed if I failed. That and the magick power of the Stone. Jasper laughed like the little kid he'd once been. You'd have thought we were watching a funny puppet show at the county fair. *At least somebody's havin' fun.* While he did that he also showed me visions of several possible strikes that Venoma might make next, guiding me to defend the most likely. My parry arrived each and every time.

The demon, or gargoyle, or whatever she was, broke off and squatted just out of sword range. Cocking her head, she croaked, "Surrender yon Stone, and thy valiant self, man-spawn. I must needs take thee to the Proprietor. If thou dost this, thy companions shalt live."

Those companions now stood behind me. Romulus woozy but upright, Ernie back on his shoulder. Tommy stood tall beside them, ready to start swinging his crowbar if I gave the word. "I don't know who this Proprietor is," I said, trying to sound more confident than I felt, "but if you work for him, I'll have to decline the honor. As for my companions, you'll have to earn their lives." *Ooh, Verity the Valiant, givin' as good as she gets!*

"I accept thy challenge," she said, almost with a laugh. A gob of foul yellow slobber shot out of her horrible mouth with a sickening steamy hiss and hit Tommy dead in the face. His every muscle seized up and he dropped like a felled tree. Before I could react she'd slithered past me, scooped him up, and bounded onto the Monument's stairs.

"Thus thy choice," she said, holding the limp Tommy in one hideous hand like a rag doll. "Present thyself to the Proprietor before the turn of the full moon, if thou desirest ever to see this child alive."

One enormous foot banged open the enormous iron door behind her. A sick greenish light came from inside the Monument, silhouetting her. Venoma backed up into it. As soon as the swirling radiance touched her, she and her prey vanished.

The light blacked out. So did I.

Tommy was gone.

I tried to imagine a fierce pirate with a
tough-talking parrot for a girlfriend.
It gave 'henpecked' a whole new slant.

9 / The Dread Pirate Roberta

Next thing I knew I lay sprawled face-first on the grass, my throat so raw from screaming that no sound came out. I'd thought that my muscles couldn't have hurt any more than they already did, but that turned out to be wrong. From straining to move the whole world to get Tommy back, I'd reduced myself to a giant mass of pain. My hands felt broken from pounding the ground. Dirt filled my fingernails from clawing at it, too. Goo from my nose and eyes ran down my face. A roaring in my ears drowned out everything my friends seemed to be saying to me.

Somebody gripped me from behind in a bear-hug as I tried to stand and rush the Monument. It had to have been a friend because Jasper made no move to defend me. That didn't stop me from kicking his shins and biting his fingers.

"Lemme go!" I tried to shriek. It came out as a whisper. "We gotta help him!"

"He gone, chile," Romulus said with amazing gentleness, as if quieting a panicked horse. Despite his bulk, he could barely control me. "When Venoma gets 'em, they stays got."

"I don't care! We gotta try!"

Ernie cleared his throat and hopped from Romulus' shoulder to mine. "The ostium's closed. As soon as they disappeared it shut down. It's designed to do that, so nobody can follow."

Curiosity started calming my rage. "Ostium?"

"A sort of gate that lets the Honourable Merchantry travel between worlds. No one can use it but them buggers. Step through one and it takes yer where yer wants to be in the blink of an eye."

I began to breathe a little easier and felt my bunched muscles relax a bit. "Travel between worlds?" *Seems like every time I get the answer to one question tonight, three more pop up in its place.* "How many worlds can there be?"

Romulus let go of me. I slumped back down to the sun-baked earth, but didn't let my eye off the Monument door. He said, "The Comp'ny's magick's made ev'ry nation into its own world, miss."

I thought of the odd stories folks told about the Monument, how people in antique clothes would walk out of it. We used to laugh at them. "So if I was to go to, say, the Papal Fief, what would I find?"

Ernie and Romulus traded glances. They seemed to be having some sort of unspoken debate. After a long pause Ernie said, "Fer starters, it ain't June 1862 there."

My tired mouth managed to make a *pthht* sound. "Ain't polite to tease kids."

"I only wish I were teasin', ducky. No matter where yer go there—Rome, Florence, Venice—it's June 20 of 1508."

Just when I'd started to accept that there were magick swords, horrible toothed monsters, and Bullies in my world, this new thing hit me. "1508? Like Michelangelo and Leonardo da Vinci 1508?"

"Exactly like that."

"What about Imperium Sacra? Iberion? Gaulle?"

"1642, 1488, and 1804. Same month and day as here."

I gave him another *pthht!* "That's crazy!"

Romulus nodded. "We ain't sayin' otherwise, chile. The Hon'rable Comp'ny's ten diff'rent kinds of crazy."

"What? You expect me to believe that every country in the world lives in a different year? How come nobody knows about this?"

"Some do," said Ernie. "The ones that work for the Merchantry know it. Others, like us in the Equity, have found out but keep it a secret until we can undo it all. Some people suspect, but refuse to let their minds accept it."

Romulus stuck his mirror back in his pocket. "And some folks tries to tell. They's the ones that gets Bully visits."

I still couldn't buy all of this. "Impossible! People travel between countries every day. Even if you could make this happen, it'd all come apart in a week."

Ernie shrugged. "Every country has a glamour spell. When yer go there, and the Merchantry strictly controls travel now, you're made to think that you've stayed in your own world and time. Yer do your business, have a holiday, and so forth, seein' and hearin' only what you expect to see."

"How can the Merchantry control travel? Or anything else? I've never even heard tell of these people and you're sayin' they have charge of the whole shootin' match."

Swooping Ernie off of my shoulder, Romulus said, "Have to school her later. More trouble comin'." With that he nodded east. I turned my head, afraid of what new horror might be heading our way. *What now? Can't they just be happy with the misery they've already spread on me?*

Since no work was being done on the Monument, the government had decided to use the wide grassy space around it to pasture army cattle. When we'd made our way west while being chased by the Bullies, we'd come in from the north. The herds had been penned up farther south and east, so we'd not run into them. Now they were about to run into us.

Cows...we were being charged by a thousand mooing cows.

On our farm in Maryland we'd had cows. It had been four years since we'd moved, but I still remembered their fuzzy flanks and sloppy snoots. Our cows had been like cute puppies the size of hay wagons, content to munch on grass and submit to my clumsy milking. But the cows coming at us now must've been the ones who'd had enough. Maybe they were Confederate cattle, in the pay of Jeff Davis. Whatever the reason, they ran at us as if we were the cause of every bovine indignity ever suffered by a cud-chewer.

"Are they witched?" I asked, backing up as fast as my wobbly limbs would take me.

"No," said Jasper, "just whipped. There's men behind 'em. The Honourable Merchantry never uses magick except when it must. Too valuable to waste."

"Nice of you to wake up," I mumbled, heading for the Monument stairs.

"You're not the only one tired around here."

"I thought you were the all-powerful magick blade of destiny?" I could see that we weren't going to make it to the safety of the Monument stairs. The cows had surprised us. *Now there's an epitaph.*

"Nothin's all-powerful, especially in magick. You really didn't read your contract, did you?"

"Sorry, I was too busy havin' an attack of the heebie-jeebies."

Romulus pulled me back against the Monument wall, hoping that the herd would bend around us. I had no such hope. There were too many sharp horns sticking out of the oncoming mass to miss us. Back a ways I could see the men that Jasper had told me of. They were rough-looking soldiers. At least, they wore Union uniforms. Who knew what their true occupation might be? Their paychecks most likely came from the Merchantry somehow. Whips in hand, they were driving the cattle straight at us, without a doubt.

I brought up Morphageus in its shield-form, but I knew that it would just stop the horns. It couldn't protect us against the enormous weight and momentum of that many beasts. We'd be crushed flat. One of those men would pull the Stone from my dead neck and deliver it to the Proprietor. My great world-saving quest had lasted all of two hours.

"Looks like this is it," I said, hugging Romulus and nuzzling Ernie. We hunkered down, all tensed-up and waiting, while the ground shook with our imminent destruction.

But the crush never came. At the last moment, the mooing mass turned aside and headed north. I opened one disbelieving eye to see what had saved us.

Seagulls. Dozens of screeching seagulls. *Could this night get any stranger? I oughta write a book.*

The flock of birds darted into the faces of the drovers and the lead cows, beaks slashing at their eyes. Some of the gulls tore the whips out of the men's' fingers. Others fluttered their wings at the animals nearest us, forcing them to turn away in panic. It looked like the birds knew just how to herd cattle. While the rest of the flock chased the men east till they were out of sight, their leader dipped a wing and glided over to us. It landed on the railing of the stairs we'd never managed to get to. This bird sure stood out from the other gulls, mostly because it wasn't a gull at all.

Nope... a large scarlet, yellow, and blue parrot.

Perched with a proud air, it cocked its crested head at us, opened its hooked white beak, and said in a salty feminine voice, "Ahoy, Ernie!"

"Oi, Roberta!" my mousie friend said with a wave. "Yer a sight for sore eyes."

"Had a bit of a headwind or I'd have been here sooner. Like tryin' to tack against a gale."

Ernie grinned and looked at me. "Told yer."

I frowned. "Told me what?" I still worked at absorbing this new development. Talking parrots I'd seen, but never one that spoke in full sentences and sounded like Captain Kidd.

"That Pitcairn would show. Well, his lady, at least."

My eyebrows went up. "His lady? It's a parrot."

That parrot gave me a sour look. I now noticed that it—she—wore round gold-rimmed spectacles. "Who's the rude shrimp?"

Romulus chuckled. "This be the Stone Warden."

"This kid? She has Morphageus? Well, waddya know! We're doomed! Abandon ship!"

"Hey!" I said, hands on hips.

Ernie jumped in. "Lady Roberta, dread pirate of the seas, meet Verity Sauveur, dread slayer of Bullies."

"That ain't sayin' much. Any fool with a mirror can—"

"And she just fought Venoma to a standstill."

Roberta shook her head so hard that her glasses almost flew off. "Well, shiver me timbers!" she crowed, thrusting out a wing to me. "Put 'er there!"

I reached over and shook her feathery 'fingers.' "Pleased to meetcha, ma'am."

"Ma'am!" Her eyes widened, making her look like a snapping turtle. You have thought I'd called her a dirty name. "Let's have none o' that. You just call this old bird Roberta, or Bert, or Bob in a pinch. First Mate o' the *Penelope's Kiss* I am."

Romulus snorted. "Pitcairn's first mate, you means."

"I better be his only mate, or I'll have his guts fer garters."

I tried to imagine a fierce pirate with a tough-talking parrot for a girlfriend. It gave 'henpecked' a whole new slant. "Well, Roberta, thank you kindly for comin' to our rescue. Don't know what we would've done otherwise."

"Think nothin' of it, shipmate. Aloysius would've come himself, but the Yankee blockade's tighter than a virgin's knees. Even worse now, on account o' McClellan's so-called offensive. Cap'n's got the *Kiss* stowed down the coast, close by Cape Charles. It'd take a keen eye to spy her. We towed her up an inlet, far enough so's the navy won't spot her easy. Then he sent me to find you. Good thing, too, seems like."

The seagull flock wheeled around from the cattle herd and floated just over our heads, making a horrible racket. Now I could tell that what I'd taken for typical seabird squawks was actually some of the rudest language I'd ever heard outside of an army camp. To make it worse, they had women's voices. I started to wish that the Stone hadn't made me able to understand animals.

"Have to pardon these ladies," said Roberta, "but they spend too much time around sailors. A shame, really. Most of 'em was hatched in the better sort o' nests."

"Oh, I've heard worse," I fibbed. "Can't complain after the service y'all did us."

One of the gulls fluttered down next to the parrot. Her wingtips and the ring around her yellow bill were a rich black.

"Our pleasure," she growled. "The Merchantry's been no friend to our kind." She turned her beak to Roberta. "The drovers are runnin' so hard they may not stop till mornin'. I spoke to the head cow and she said she was sorry and that if she'd know'd that these folks was our pals she'd have run the other way."

"Right kind o' her," said Roberta.

"I told her so. I pointedly didn't tell her what the army plans to do with her and her friends. If things've calmed down here, I'll take the girls back out to the bay. Fish're runnin' about now."

Roberta turned her head in all directions. "Seems safe enough. Merchantry may send somebody else, but we plan to get movin', so p'raps they'll miss us. Thank ye kindly, Matilda."

With more profane screeches the gulls flapped away to the river, then turned to follow it south and east toward Chesapeake Bay. They'd fly right over the two great armies which were about to duke it out near Richmond. When they did, the average of civilized discourse in that region would drop in the worst way. Imagining the comments Matilda and her friends would make as they looked at how humans settled their disputes brought a smile to my face. I hadn't done much grinning that evening.

"Bert's right," Romulus said. "Merchantry'll keep the pressure on. More folks comin' fo' sho'."

Ernie agreed. "True enough. The blighters want Verity to come to them, that's why they snatched young Thomas. But they won't want to depend solely on that. We can expect their other blasted agents to try to capture her, just to make sure."

"Then let's get movin'. If the *Kiss* is at Cape Charles, we got's a long way to go, most of it through Confed'rate territory."

I could see that the prospect of crossing the river and traveling through slave-holding Virginia didn't set well with Romulus. He'd only been free for two months. What colored man would want to willingly enter Rebel land, no matter how vital the mission? Heck, I didn't relish the thought myself.

"Do we have to go through Virginia?" I asked, hoping that a better plan would present itself. "We wanted to put the river between us and the Bullies, right? Since that didn't happen and we already fought 'em off, why go into more danger than we have to?" Even as I said it I knew what the answer would be. *Because Tommy needs us.*

"Don't we wish there was a better way," Ernie said, hopping into my hand. I raised him up so we could talk face-to-face. "But the Merchantry's base is in London, so it's to Europa that we have to get, ducky. To the Scepter'd Isle. That's where the Proprietor will be, and where they'll take Tommy."

Romulus sighed. "And the only way we can get there is on Roberta's boat."

"Ship," she squawked, correcting him.

"Ship, then. Merchantry has mos' other civilian ships under they control."

"So you're tellin' me," I said in a glum tone, "that our one choice is to cross over two hundred miles of Confederate territory, hunted by both Rebels and the Honourable Merchantry, with no money, no horses, no friends, and pretty near no food. We have to find our way between two huge modern armies that're about to fight the biggest battle in the history of Northern America, then cross Chesapeake Bay through a naval blockade. Once we do that, we get on a pirate ship, run the blockade again, hopin' we don't get sunk by the Merchantry's private navy, and sneak into the Scept'red Isle, which is protected by more magick than you can shake a stick at. Then we have to somehow find Tommy, probably in some horrible dungeon guarded by ogres and trolls, and steal our way back out the way we came, all without bein' witched, shot, stabbed, or drooled on by Venoma."

Ernie smiled, I think. "That's why you're the bleedin' Stone Warden." He turned to Romulus and Roberta and winked. "Mind like a steel trap, she has."

"I just hope's we don't end up in a steel trap our own selves," said Romulus.

Roberta flapped her scarlet wings. "I say we all shut our traps and get outta here. Brace for action, clear the decks, and run up the bloody flag."

I sighed. "This is it, then. We're off for Virginia."

And here's hopin' Tommy's still in one piece...and that he's still human.

A chaos spell.
Every country in a different time,
Irlann filled with literary characters,
Scandia hip-deep in fairies and dragons and trolls.
Total lunacy.

10 / Honourable Merchantry

Before we took a step towards Virginia the argument started. I wanted to go home first, to check in with Ma and make sure she was okay. The others considered that a real bad idea.

"They be waitin' fo you," said Romulus, shaking his big bald noggin. "Comp'ny knows where you live. Ain't worth the risk."

Ernie agreed. "You'll be strollin' right into an ambush, missy. Bullies right and left, I'd imagine. Better if we just head for the bloomin' river right now."

I sighed and looked at Roberta. *Might as well give everybody a vote.*

The parrot peered through her spectacles at me like a snippy schoolmarm. "Never sail into a blind cove. You'll take a broadside sure as shootin'. Riggin' gone and rudder blown away."

Just as I opened my mouth to give my opinion on the matter,

a fourth voice interrupted the thought I'd formed. "Since you're takin' a poll, kiddo," Jasper volunteered, "I think that they're all of 'em right. Even the silly mouse."

I swallowed a giggle. Ernie couldn't hear Jasper now. "So there it is. Four votes to one against swingin' by home. Just leave my poor ma to her fate. She could be turned into a cockroach and hidin' under our kitchen stove, but we just ignore that and move on."

After a pause, I got a chorus of, "Yeah, that's about how we see it."

"Besides," Ernie added, "I happen to know that all the bugs in your kitchen work for the Equity."

"That cat's a dif'rent matter, though," Romulus growled.

"Do you speak of the pathetic one-eared creature which imagined itself immune from chastisement?"

The giant Marshal's eyes widened. "One-eared? I got's new respect for you, Master Ernie."

Ernie bowed. "I accept your merited acclaim. Don't worry about the traitorous feline. By now he's shoppin' for stickin' plaster."

"So," said Roberta, flexing her wings. "Are we off?"

"We are," I announced, stepping out with a bold stride.

Fifteen minutes later we were passing as close by St. Usher's as we dared, heading east. *It's good to be the Stone Warden.*

Jasper whined. "Did I misunderstand how the votin' thing works?"

"No," I thought to him, keeping my extra-sharp eyes peeled

for Bullies. "You just misunderstood that we actually held a vote."

"Oh, so this is like when the President has a Cabinet meeting and then ignores all of their sage advice and worldly wisdom?"

"Somethin' like that."

"What's that make me, then? Secretary of Shut-Up-You're-Just-the-Magick-Sword?" He turned into a mouth with a padlock on it.

I snorted. "And Ernie's Boastmaster-General."

Gliding back from her scouting trip, Roberta circled over me and said, "Clear sailin'. No sign of Bullies or anythin' else," before landing on Romulus' outstretched arm.

That sounded good to me. And the Stone felt toast-warm against my skin. But if Horace and his cronies, maybe with reinforcements this time, lurked about St. Usher's, we might not know it till they were on us. Romulus had handled them that afternoon, and Jasper could scatter them like chaff in the wind, but I preferred to get home with no trouble at all. We were all tired, me especially. Tired people made mistakes, and that we couldn't afford.

St. Usher's sat on our left, looking like a bulldog ready to charge. No Bullies dropped from its trees, but just the memory of that sight proved enough to make me grit my teeth and grip the handle of tin-cup Morphageus. I scanned the soot-stained old building, alert for anything odd. *And what might that be? What counts as 'odd' now? Witches on broomsticks? A troop of Headless Horsemen? Countless cobras spittin' lightnin' bolts?*

All I noticed was a single candle in a top-floor window. Nobody could be seen in its light.

"Ernie," I said to my tiny friend, who rode atop my haversack like a sultan on an elephant. "What gives with this place?"

"What gives? It's Honourable Merchantry headquarters for Washington City, that's what gives."

"Yeah? Why a school? Why not some government building? Heck, why not the Capitol, come to that?"

"The Merchantry works behind the scenes as much as they can. They have a real and legitimate presence in London as the Honourable Merchantry of Esteemed Gentlemen. That's the tradin' company they founded way back in Good Queen Bess's time."

My eyes widened. "They've been around that long?"

"Oh, dear me, yes. But then it was just a shippin' business, for the spices. Nutmeg, cloves, cinnamon. Worth more than gold. All of the Merchantry men got rich as Croesus. Had their own navy and army and courts, to enforce their private law on the islands. Paid off members of Parliament and the Crown to keep things that way. Long as the money flowed and they kept their political meddlin' to just trading matters, no one complained."

"But?" I asked, sensing I might be getting some of the answers I'd been looking for all night.

"But about fifty years ago, things stopped goin' their way. Some of 'em backed Bonaparte, for a start. Hedgin' their bets, they called it. That ruffled some feathers in Whitehall when it got out, I can tell yer. Heads rolled. Literally. Some things money can't cover up. Spice trade wasn't the gold mine it had been before, neither. The plants themselves were bein' cultivated all over the world, from stolen seeds and whatnot, in places the Merchantry couldn't always control. The Proprietor and his Council saw that their ships alone weren't gonna keep the company in power."

"So what did they do?"

"Started usin' that money o' theirs to buy influence. Very subtle, they was. And patient. Helped their kind o' men to get themselves elected here and there, to smooth their way with the law and with governments. Bought all the right companies in every country to help 'em control its commerce. Did most of it through third parties so most folks didn't know what they had their hand in. That's still how they work, for the most part. The magick came later."

Now this is gettin' interestin'. "So the Merchantry is a real company, then? Folks go to work in regular offices and have jobs, like?"

"Oh, absolutely, duckie. Most of what they do is all legal and aboveboard. It just goes deeper and darker than people know."

Ernie stopped and cast his beady little eyes about, as if he feared that spies were going to swoop down and catch him spilling the beans to me. I couldn't blame him for it, after what I'd seen so far that night.

"Go on," I urged. "Don't leave me hangin'."

"Like we said before, they run the whole world now, indirect. Everyone thinks that elections matter, and judges are honest, and there's real competition in trade. It looks like that, at first glance. But it's the Merchantry that manipulates things, like a puppeteer, to its advantage. And its advantage lies in misery."

I frowned. *Doin' a lot of that lately.* "Misery? How so?"

"Well, look at wars. Very profitable. Their shadow firms can sell to both sides. So it's just good business to encourage those sides to keep fightin'. A little sabotage at a peace conference, a few ships flyin' the wrong flags and attackin' a convoy, that sort of thing. And economic panics. Make a country's stock market plunge, and plenty of money-makin' schemes come to mind. Buyin' cheap shares, for one. Land prices go down, too. Then bring the economy back up, sell what you bought for a premium, and there you are."

"They make all of that happen, everywhere?"

"Not always. Some things happen naturally and the Merchantry just takes advantage. But they don't mind helpin' things along, that I can tell you. The cholera epidemic in Naples? They caused that, sad to say. And there's plague in the Caucasus right now, courtesy of the so-called Honourable Merchantry."

"So where does the magick come in?"

Ernie puffed out his furry cheeks. "That's a point of considerable debate, don't you know. They've kept that under wraps as much as they could. But we do know that on the spring equinox of 1850, twelve years ago, everything changed. Our sources have found out some of it, but not all."

This is startin' to worry me now. That's my birthday.

"Seems they found a magick source, a power never known

before. Magick's always existed, of course, though most people denied it. That made it nigh invisible. Your average man doesn't want to believe that his neighbor can witch him into the sky. So he puts the evidence down to 'coincidence' or 'mass hysteria' or what have you. Magick stayed low-key, like the major practitioners preferred. Power never likes to share.

"Anyway, the Merchantry found a magick power of some kind. We don't know what yet. And in March of 1850, they used it...and the world changed overnight."

"What happened?" I shuddered at what the answer might be, but just had to know. That'd be my situation for months to come.

"They cocked it up, that's what happened. Too greedy to think about what they were doin'. Remember, 'can' and 'should' are two very different things. Instead of the spell givin' 'em easy dominion over the earth, it twisted things round most awful. They'd been manufacturin' chaos, keepin' the world as violent as they could, and by jiminy, that's what they got. A bedlam spell. Every country in a different time, Irlann filled with literary characters, Scandia hip-deep in fairies and dragons and trolls. Total lunacy."

My jaw swung down around my knees. "This is all just a stupid mistake? A bunch of greedy idiots played with fire and that's how I got burnt?"

Romulus spoke up for the first time since Ernie'd began his story. "That's how we all gots burnt, miss. Don't go thinkin' you's alone in all this. The whole wide world's in flames."

"And you're holdin' the only hose," Jasper said, turning

himself into a fireman's nozzle.

I stamped my foot. "Golly Moses! Are all grown-ups imbeciles and villains?"

"Pretty much," Ernie chuckled. "I invited a Merchantry lord to take a flyin'...uh, jump at the moon. Now look at me, four inches of holy terror."

Roberta ruffled her feathers. "My ship got ambushed and sunk by a Merchantry man-o'-war. Their captain offered me a choice of hangin' from the yardarm or...this."

"All I did was piddle on my owner's rug," Romulus said. "How's that make me an imbecile?"

"By volunteerin' for the Equity, me bucko," explained Ernie, climbing up onto my shoulder so he could speak straight at his partner.

Romulus laughed, then realized how loud he sounded and hunched down. "Cain't argue with you there, mister Ernie."

"You two need to learn a thing or two about inspirin' confidence in your young charge," I told them. "This fireman is about ready to hide in a hollow tree till this whole thing goes away."

Ernie bit my ear. "Ow!" I squealed. "What the—?"

"Don't say that, even as a joke," the chubby mouse barked. "You're the sole hope for millions and millions of people who've just about given up."

I stopped dead in the middle of the street, not a block from home, so upset that I hardly noticed the pile of horse dung my foot was parked in. "You and Romulus and Jasper keep sayin' that, but I don't see that you or the Equity have thought this through. Look at me! I'm a tall bony girl who likes to play-act that I'm a great hero. Verity the Valiant! Who in their right mind decided that I could be the one to overthrow the Honourable Merchantry and set things right? What kind of sense does that make?" I sniffed. *Here I go, startin' to blubber again. Hope no Bullies are waitin' to jump us.*

"Nobody decided," Ernie said with a shrug.

"Just happened," added Romulus.

"What you mean?" I asked through my quivering lips.

"We mean," the mouse went on, "that you seem to think that they held some kind of bloody meetin' in the Great Lodge of the Equity and your name got bandied about. Didn't happen that way, precious."

"Then how—?" I blurbled.

"The Grand Mage left a prophecy. He used to say that he wouldn't always be among us, and that a black evil would come when he'd gone and we'd have to stop it our own bloomin' selves. But he'd prepared a mighty weapon that we could use to make the difference."

I wiped my nose on my sleeve. "The Morphageus."

Romulus shook his broad head at me. "No. The weapon weren't no thing. It were a livin' person."

Ernie nodded, agreeing. "He was quite clear about it. 'Take comfort not in blade of fame.' That's the prophecy. 'Trust hair of flame and truth of name.'"

A little laugh crawled out past my tears. "That's so corny."

"Most true things are, lovey. A baby's giggle. A puppy's tail. Your mama's lullabies. Don't you go discountin' things because you think they're sentimental."

"I get that 'hair of flame and truth of name' might mean me," I said, "but it could also mean lots of other folks, too."

"'Tain't the whole prophecy. It went on: 'An outcast childe of Gaulle is she; beneath an unmade dome they be."

Boy, that's worse than the first line. Who writes the Equity's prophecies? Don't they have a Scriveners' Guild for that sort of thing?

"OK, that narrows it down more," I agreed. "Ma says our people were Huguenots who came from Gaulle almost two hundred years ago, from some dinky village in the south. And the unmade dome is obvious. But Jasper insists that nobody can truly tell the future. So how—?"

Jasper's perky voice spoke up in my head. "There's tellin' the future and there's makin' it happen. Listen to the final line of the prophecy."

"Uh, he says that there's more to the prophecy?"

Ernie cleared his tiny throat and said, "Yep. 'Her mother fair shall live alone; the child will wear a russet stone'."

"Ah, so it's no accident that my pa left me this," I whispered, touching the Legacy Stone which still hung warm and dark around my neck.

"Doubtful," Roberta said with a shake of her scarlet head. "That Stone's been handed down to the most worthy for ages."

"And just how do they know who's most worthy?"

"Coin toss, maybe?" Jasper offered.

"Ha, ha," I growled.

"What?" asked Ernie.

"Nothin'. Never mind." I frowned. "Then the Equity's been around for a long time, then? Not just twelve years."

Romulus said, "Equity's existed as long as they's been inequity, chile."

"That'd be forever, shipmate," Roberta added.

"Older than the Pyramids, we is, duckie," Ernie said.

"Speak for yourself," the parrot retorted, preening.

My head didn't just swim, it was waterlogged and going down for the count. Were my folks both with the Equity? Had Pa, who I had no memory of at all, been the Stone Warden before me? Or had he just found a pretty rock and put it on a string? Could I really go up against something that seemed as all-powerful as the Honourable Merchantry? Or would I just end up as somebody's pet monkey in a London office? Heck, would we even make it that far? We were planning to go across Confederate territory and into what the papers called 'the very mouth of hell.' Everybody else was running out of there as fast as their legs would carry them.

Most important question of all…could I make it to the privy behind my house before the Great Savior of Humanity wet her overalls?

I must've looked awful brave, dashing toward what my friends thought could be certain doom. Tell the truth, I just had to answer the call of nature. Things had been so wild and crazy that I hadn't been paying any attention to what you'd call normal things. Monsters, magick, and more had pushed everything else from my mind. Ignoring Ernie's warning, and the fact that he had abandoned me for Romulus' pocket, I raced through the very same alley where Venoma had jumped us. If she'd been lurking there right then, the great quest would've been all over in a hurry. I'd even shifted Morphageus into the tin cup again, to make running easier. Verity the Valiant gave no thought to battle.

Crashing into the outhouse, I dropped my overalls and drawers as if they were on fire. I did my business with a sigh and a smile. It was the first time I'd relaxed in hours. I know it's not lady-like to say, but there you have it. Come on, even Queen Gwenivere had visited the jakes every day, hadn't she?

Right then I first started to feel real hatred for the Honourable Merchantry, the rage that I have yet to let go of. For just at that moment, with the evening breeze tickling my bare bottom and my feet tangled in my overalls, I smelled a bad thing.

No, not **that** bad thing. This was worse. Much worse.

Rotting flowers. The perfume of a Bully. Even worse, something moved. Something big and hurtful.

And it's right underneath me.

My innards twisted, caught in an orange-green tornado
that stank like brimstone and lilies.
Dull razors sliced into every inch of my skin.

11 / Mr. Pitts Barks at Verity

The Legacy Stone icicled my chest. *OK, this is about as bad as it could be.* That thought threatened to overwhelm my mind, which didn't have a lot of 'whelm' left anyhow.

"Could be worse," Jasper said in an annoying cheery voice.

"How?" I tried to slide my drawers up my shaky legs without catching the notice of whatever crawled around in the bottom of the privy.

"Door could be locked." He still acted too perky by half.

I pushed against the door. It didn't move. Something on the outside had jammed it closed. I ground my teeth till they squeaked. "Someday this Proprietor and I are gonna have a real serious conversation."

"And with any luck I'll be doin' the talkin', kiddo. But what do you plan to do right now?"

"I suppose screamin' and bawlin' would be undignified?"

Jasper snorted. "From where I sit, seein' where you sit, I'd say dignity and Verity keep little company nowadays."

Wonderful. A misquote from Nick Bottom. You would pick

that character. Ha, ha. The sword is such a card.

"You know Shakespeare?" My clothes were almost all the way up. The goopy ploppy rumblings underneath me grew louder and closer.

"Well, not personally, no. I've been wedded to Morphageus for a long time."

I fastened the last button. *Time to go!* My hand gripped the cup and aimed it at the stinky hole I'd been sitting on. A roar came out of it, accompanied by a smell that rotted, yes, but nothing like flowers. Bracing myself against the jammed door, I spread a round steel shield hard against the opening. *Boy, Jasper's gonna have plenty to say about this.*

Something heavy and strong lifted me up about half a foot. Muck sprayed out of the gap. I started to recall that afternoon's laundry session with longing. This called for a change in tactics. Morphageus became a giant armored gauntlet with eagle's talons. It dug its fingers into the wood of the seat and sealed its mighty palm against the thing trying to escape. The threatening sounds were muffled but still plenty powerful and the outhouse shook like a feather in a gale. But Jasper held firm. Nothing came through. I let go of him to devote both hands, both feet, and both lungs to escaping the shack.

Now I know I try to sound like the toughest kid in the world, but when I want to I can shriek as loud and as high as any other girl. Stuck in that privy, an angry magick-born poop monster trying to devour me, I really wanted to. Opening my mouth as wide as it would go, I let out a cry that would have done a steam locomotive proud...just as Romulus yanked open the outhouse door.

"Oww! Lordy!" he hollered, hands on ears. "What you doin'?"

"Bullies!" I cried, bowling him over and landing on top of his enormous form. I kept going, stepping on his face as I rushed away from the outhouse.

"Where?" asked Ernie, dancing away from Romulus' shirt pocket, holding the mirror in both paws.

Roberta circled overhead, squawking, "Can't spy 'em. Must be over the horizon."

I looked at our kitchen door. No gaslight or candleglow could be seen in the windows. *Ma should still be up, frettin' over me.* The outhouse still swayed and creaked. A Bully sure lurked someplace nearby. Maybe several of them. I put my finger to my lips and pointed toward my home. Romulus nodded his understanding.

"I think they're in the dry goods store over yonder," I hollered for the benefit of anybody hiding in our house. Walking back down the alley, away from our building, I signaled to Romulus to grab the mouse and for Ernie to keep the mirror. He nodded and waved at Roberta. The parrot swooped down. She grabbed Ernie in her claws and he scrambled onto her back. While I crouched down to pretend I'd gone toward the Clemens store, Romulus moved as fast as a bullet's shadow toward the kitchen door. With a mighty foot he shattered the door, jamb and all. As he whipped aside Roberta dove through the jagged opening with a cry of "Give 'em a broadside, me hearties!" Now I could see the dim blue witchlight that I'd missed before. *Bullies in my house. Where's Ma, then?* I started sprinting toward the steps, forgetting that I was unarmed. Morphageus still held the privy monster at bay.

Before I could take ten steps it had ended. My magicked ears picked up Ernie yelling, "Once more unto the breach, dear friends!" *Must be Shakespeare night.* The Bully death-sigh whooshed out behind the orange-violet flash I'd grown to love. Then silence. Roberta broke that by flapping back out into the alley, whooping in victory.

"Sent 'em both off to see Davy Jones, we did!"

Romulus stood by the steps. "Two of 'em. Prob'ly left as lookouts in case we come back. Don't think they's any more about."

I tapped the black silk cord around my neck. "Nope. Stone's warm again." Brushing past him, I burst into the flat, all frantic. "Ma! Ma, you here?!" I cried, knowing that she couldn't be.

Nothing. Dead silence. *No, no, no! Where is she?* I crashed from the kitchen to the parlor to the bedroom, noting the signs of a hasty exit. A chair overturned, cupboards and drawers left open, papers trailing across the rug. Freezing still, I cocked my head to hear if maybe she was hiding someplace. No breathing sounds, no rustling, not even to my wonder-ears. *Think...where would she go if somethin' happened?*

My breathing grew shallow from the panic. Lightheaded, I sat down at the kitchen table. Our sugar bowl had tipped over, spilling its crystals in odd dunes. I blinked as Romulus lit a pair of candles. Shadows waved across the room like ghosts. *Maybe they are. Maybe they're Ma and Tommy, tryin' to say goodbye.* Roberta hopped onto the chair next to me, Ernie astride her neck. They looked like something out of a fairy tale. 'Rodent and Parrot's Magickal Adventure.' My chubby mouse friend held one of Ma's smallest, sharpest ivory knitting needles in both paws.

"Now I have a weapon, too," he announced, waving it about like a spear, to Roberta's dismay. She wrenched her head to and fro to avoid losing an eye.

"Weapon?" I blurted, jumping up as if I'd just sat on a tack. "Jasper!"

I blasted out of the kitchen door and streaked down the steps and across the alley to the privy. Once at the outhouse I hesitated and checked my Stone. No bad guys around. The tiny building stood as solid as ever, all shaking and groaning had stopped. Its only smell was the usual awful stench it gave off in summer. *Ah, the heady aroma of Washington City in July. Mrs. Lincoln's special perfume.* Jerking the handle, I let the night air in and hollered, "Jasper!"

"No need to pretend you care about me," he whined. Morphageus still held the metal glove shape, impatient spiky metal fingers tapping on the scarred wooden seat. "Abandoning me in this foul jakes, awash in the muck of countless Sauveurs. I battle savage piles of animated dung, sacrificin' my spotless surface to the night-soil terrors, so you can ride off to glory—"

Rolling my tired eyes, I said, "Yeah, yeah, yeah. Get over to the pump, you."

"Yippee!" he sang, sounding even younger than usual. He scampered over to the steps like an awkward puppy, still in his gauntlet form. I worked the big green pump handle till clean water—cleaner than what covered him, anyway—glurgled out. He rolled around, giggling, letting the stream sluice off his smelly coat of crud. When he'd got as close to sparkling as he was likely to get, short of using a steam hose, he shook himself all over. I couldn't help thinking that Romulus must've done that, in his old life.

"Did you miss me?" Jasper asked, snaking up and around my body in his black sword shape.

I grabbed the hilt and sheathed Morphageus. "I was gone for maybe five minutes."

"Believe me, kiddo, it felt like five years from where I sat. Excuse me, from where **you** sat, actually."

"Ho, ho. You should be onstage, Mr. Comedian." We headed back into the kitchen.

"Yeah, I could star in an umbrella stand, or be a wall display..."

Romulus, Ernie, and Roberta were still in the house. Ernie gorged himself on sugar, his fat little squirmy legs sticking straight up out of the bowl. I heard disturbing gobbling sounds. Roberta shook her feathered head as if she watched some poor drunk lying in a gutter. Standing by the parlor window, Romulus kept a sleepless eye on 10th Street.

I stifled a laugh. "Now there's a sight to inspire confidence in the Marshals of the Equity."

Ernie struggled out of the sugar bowl, his twitching whiskers looking as if he'd fallen into a snow bank. "That's me. A confidence man."

"You can say that again, bucko," Roberta muttered.

A man-sized burp came out of the mouse's snout. "Trust old Ernie. I make all your problems disappear."

Giving the messy table a glum look, I said, "Somebody made Ma disappear. I can't imagine where—"

My eyes narrowed. Ernie was saying something, but my magicked-ears had closed. Every sense bent to the sugar patterns on the table. There was a word written there, scratched with a hasty finger.

CROATAN.

Croatan? Like Sir Walter Raleigh? Like the Lost Colony of Roanoke we learned about in school? That Croatan?

"Did one of you do this?" I asked.

Everyone gave me a blank look. "Do what?" asked Romulus.

"Write in the sugar."

Roberta chomped an apple she'd grabbed from the fruit bowl on the sideboard. "Been too busy raidin' the stores."

"I can't see nothin'," said Romulus, squinting at the writing and turning his head every which way to try to make sense of it.

Ma. Ma left me a message! She's gone to North Carolina. But why? And how?

"We gotta go," I announced.

"Virginny or bust!" cried Roberta, spewing fruit everywhere and flapping her blue-tipped wings.

I shook my head. "We're just passin' through there. I aim to go to North Carolina. To the Outer Banks."

Ernie pawed the sugar coating from his muzzle. "Me bloomin' ears must be clogged. Say again?"

Pointing to the word written in the spilled sugar, I said in a firm tone, "This says she's headed for Croatan Island. That's hard by Cape Hatteras."

Romulus moved to block the door. I thumped up against him. "You don't know that."

"I know she's gone. I know she wrote this message as she was leavin'. I know that—"

The parrot cocked her piratical head at me. Her spectacles made her eyes look big and funny. "You should know that the Merchantry might've written it to send you into a trap."

"Why would they do that? Venoma said they want me in London by the turn of the moon. What good would trappin' me down south do 'em?" A rushing started to fill my ears, like a flash flood arriving.

Ernie crawled up my arm and plopped into my haversack. "Maybe Venoma laid the trap. Thing yer needs to know about the Honourable Merchantry, missy...chess players all. They stick plots inside of plans inside of schemes. I think it keeps 'em from gettin' bored."

"You cain't run off without thinkin', miss," advised Romulus.

The room echoed with my frustrated roar. "What in tarnation am I supposed to do?! My whole family's gone, who knows where? Our only clues point in opposite directions." My pulse pounded and the room grew fuzzy.

"But a word written in sugar's a powerful flimsy excuse to crowd on all sail," Roberta said, preening her feathers.

"And whether or not Venoma's tryin' to snare us, we know she has Tommy," Ernie pointed out with a definitive nod.

I paced around the kitchen, confused as a duck hit on the head. "OK, here's what we'll do. I'm the Stone Warden, and my final decision is to..." No matter how hard I breathed, no air seemed to come in. Swallowing hard, I tried again. "My decision...is...we..."

My last memory of my home was of the spinning ceiling, and Ernie diving off me onto the table as I fell.

*   *   *   *   *

Foul-smelling canteen water shocked me awake. Sitting up with a scream, I felt Romulus' hand across my mouth. Seemed like a barn door smacking into me.

"Sshh!" he whispered. To my mind his low tone shook the air more than my shriek had. "They'll hear us."

I sucked in air through my nose to clear my head. Marsh. Mud. Sea-bird pooh. We hunkered down in a mass of bushes. *Must be back at the river.* My blurry eyes asked a question. Two of them, actually.

Jasper answered. *Oh, yeah. Someday I'll figure out this whole mind-readin' thing.* "You fainted. More Stone and Merchantry than you could handle for one night, I expect. Romulus carried you here like a baby. We're at the river. And we're not alone, as usual."

"Who is it this time?"

A shrill male voice broke the night stillness. "Sergeant Reilly! Take a squad further to your left."

"Yes, sir!" another voice answered, accented with the brogue of Irlann. "Corporal, bring your men this way."

Ernie crept along my arm, holding his little knitting needle like a pike. He'd sharpened it to a fearsome point while I'd been out. "Let 'em come! I'll perforate their gullets."

"Infantry," said Romulus. "Look like a whole battalion from New York."

Sounds like another great reason to cross the river. To get away from our own troops.

"Merchantry troops, you mean," Jasper corrected. "Somebody high up sent them to bring us in. Told 'em we're spies or saboteurs."

I peeled Romulus' hand from my mouth. "They've got us dead to rights if they follow that last order. We'll be boxed in with the water to our backs. "What now? I don't imagine that mirrors will work against muskets."

Romulus started easing back toward the water. "We gots to go. Now. Quiet as...mice."

It took a lot of willpower to stifle my snicker at that, with Ernie all but chanting a war-cry from atop my elbow. "Where's Roberta?"

"Scoutin' fo' a good crossin' spot. Has to be easy to get to, dark, and have a good tree handy."

"Tree?"

"To make us a boat."

The army had scoured the river for any type of craft that might be used to help spies. They tried to control river crossings and make it as hard as possible for Confederates to get help from our side. That's why our search for a rowboat, a canoe, or any other craft came up empty, as we'd known it most likely would. I gathered that we were supposed to find a tree and make a raft, but after what actually happened, I should've figured that the Stone Warden needed to expand her imagination even more than she already had.

Romulus led us along the shore, away from the soldiers. As their voices and stompings faded, I relaxed a bit. I still ached all over, and felt the kind of tired that tends to come when you're dead and buried. Roberta had swooped in to tell us that she'd found a good tree by the river, south of the Monument. It lay in sight of the Long Bridge, but it was dark enough there for our purpose. I fell behind, what with my shorter legs and being almost a corpse and all. When I caught up with the Marshal, he was talking to the tree. And it talked back.

Figures. Should've known that 'good tree' meant somethin' else to these guys.

"Is this her?" asked the tree, a medium-sized peach. It almost seemed to peer down its nose at me, though it had no visible face. His voice sounded young and educated, like the jaded university students from Georgetown who came to Ford's sometimes. All he needed was a book of Cicero's orations and a glass of beer.

"This be Verity," said Romulus. "Verity, this is Pitts."

Pitts? A peach tree named Pitts? You gotta be kiddin' me.

"No joke," Jasper chuckled in my head. "And don't let on that you think it's funny. Thin-barked, this one is."

"Pleased to meet you, sir," I said with a little bow.

"Oh, don't patronize me!" snapped Pitts, shaking his foliage. He muttered under his breath in a snippy tone. "Ten years planted here, listening to messages on the root network from all over the world, just waiting for my golden opportunity, and they send me a snot-nosed brat."

"Well, this brat's got good ears," I shot back.

"Oooh! How wonderful for you. Too bad you're wet behind them."

Something snapped in me. I'd been pushed around enough by my enemies; I didn't need it from my supposed allies. The Stone flared white-hot in my left hand and Jasper, shaped as a woodsman's axe, leapt into my right fist. "You gonna help or not? I'd just as soon carve a canoe outta you as listen to this."

The tree gasped. "She does have the Stone!"

"Stones, more like," snickered Ernie. "A pair of 'em."

"Told you," Romulus said with a satisfied smile. "Can we get goin' now?"

"Sure, sure. Does she know what's about to happen?"

Roberta, perched on one of his branches, said, "Well, we ain't exactly got to that yet."

Oh-oh, this can't be good. "Got to what yet?" I asked, eyebrows up and hands on hips.

"Send a girl to do a tree's job," sighed Pitts. He grunted and his roots pulled free of the shore mud with a long sucking sound. Like a clown with oversized funny shoes, he waddled toward the river. I was so amazed that I almost missed Jasper speaking to me.

"We're up the creek without a paddle," he giggled. "But not for long. Hold on tight now."

My innards twisted, caught in an orange-green tornado that stank like brimstone and lilies. Dull razors sliced into every inch of my skin. The bones of my face felt like they had split into a dozen new chunks and rolled under wagon wheels. Something heavy dragged my backside down to the muddy ground. While I lay there I retched. Dry heaves and dizziness fought for my soul.

What's happenin'? This is the most awful thing ever...

Turned out that shape-shifting hurt. I mean it really hurt.

I tried to stand up, but my body wouldn't do it at first. It wanted to stay on all fours. The weight still clung to my backside. *What is that thing? Feels like a wet carpet.* Bending my head to see what was going on with my tortured body, I found that my neck had shortened. The thing didn't want to move as far as it had before. My eyes were still magicked, so seeing in the dark proved to be no problem. What I saw **was** a problem.

Fur. Rusty fur. And paws with claws.

This better not be permanent or I'll turn Jasper into a commode and make use of him.

"Romulus, what...?" I tried to say. My voice squeaked out, like a giant rat spoke for me. He didn't answer. Instead, he handed me his mirror, which I trapped between my clumsy new paws. I gawked at what stared back at me. Beady eyes, buck teeth, whiskers, and a flat rubbery tail.

I'd been turned into a giant red-haired beaver.

*..the uprooted peach tree waded into the Potomac,
then slid over as if a lumberjack had felled him.
"Ooh, that's nice!" Pitts said, wiggling his shoots.
"Cools the roots."*

12/ "Safe" in Virginia

"Jumpin' Jehosophat!" I shouted. The words sounded, I don't know...beavery. I could understand what I said, of course, and so could my friends, but to somebody who wasn't a Marshal of the Equity it must've just been animal chattering. All to the good, otherwise those searching soldiers would have come running. "Jasper! What did you do to me? How'd you...Jasper? Jasper?"

No answer. No giggly smart-aleck voice in my head. Nothing.

I felt for the sword with my clumsy paws. *Gone!* What a catastrophe. *I'm a giant rodent and the only one who can maybe change me back has skedaddled.* My pudgy form spun in circles to see if I'd dropped Morphageus in the weeds near the riverbank. Nope. *He's gone, for sure. Now what do I do?*

"Sword's gone!" I barked through my buck teeth. "Sword's gone! I've lost Morphageus. We're in trouble now." I wiggled my whiskers at Ernie and Romulus. "Come on, help me look."

The Marshals were trying their darnedest not to laugh, but it wasn't working too well. Romulus howled like the hound he'd once been, rolling in the grass. Ernie held his fat sides as if they would explode, which wasn't a sight I wanted to see in my predicament. *One calamity at a time.* Roberta and Pitts snickered from the river's edge.

"This ain't funny!" I hissed. "It's a disaster."

"Oh, it's a disaster, all right," grumbled the peach tree. "Worst disaster since Bull Run."

Roberta chomped her sharp beak into the branch she sat on. The tree yelped. "Be nice," she scolded.

"Some friends," I groaned. "Are you gonna help me find the sword or not?"

"It's around your neck, duckie," Ernie said, pointing.

I groped at my throat. The Stone still hung there, on its silk cord, but I found something new there, too. It felt like a dog collar, but all made of steel. "What's this?"

"Morphageus," said Romulus.

"Can't be. He's not talkin' to me. No voice in my head."

Ernie rolled his eyes. "Of course not."

"Goes without sayin', shipmate," added Roberta.

"What do you mean by that?" I demanded, tugging at the collar.

"He cain't talk to you when you changes shape," Romulus said, as if I'd asked to be told my own name. "All his power's goin' into holdin' the spell."

"She didn't read the contract," Ernie told the others with a shrug.

"Didn't read the contract!" tree and parrot exclaimed in unison.

Romulus just shook his bald head in disappointed wonder.

Seems to me the Stone Warden ain't gettin' the respect you'd think she'd deserve. "Okay, okay! So I didn't read the contract! Do y'all feel superior now?"

They looked at one another and nodded.

"And what else might I want to know? Hmm...How's about when do I stop bein' a tree-gnawer? That'd be handy information."

"Spell just lasts an hour, matey," Roberta answered. "Better hurry up with this."

"Hurry up with what?" I notice that I spoke with a lisp. *Darned beaver teeth.* "Everybody talk plain. Jasper may read minds, but I can't."

"Crossin' the river, lovie," Ernie said.

"Finally!" sighed Pitts. With a cracking of limbs and rustling of leaves, the uprooted peach tree waded into the Potomac, then slid over as if a lumberjack had felled him. Roberta launched herself away from her crashing perch. "Ooh, that's nice!" Pitts said, wiggling his shoots. "Cools the roots, you know."

Circling overhead, Roberta called out, "Let's get goin'. That battalion's on our trail."

No sooner had the words left her beak than a bullet cracked past us. Romulus splashed into the water, clutched a large branch, and hid himself in its foliage. Our parrot guide swooped down to pick up Ernie and drop him into a knothole. I hesitated, but not for long. When more bullets started humming past us like horseflies from hell, I waddled into the water myself. The soldiers were close enough now that their voices could now be heard by ordinary ears.

"Push!" Ernie hollered.

"Huh?" I still wasn't sure of the plan.

"You're our steam engine and our screw. Pitts is the hull."

"And the lot of you are freeloading passengers," the tree said.

Now I realized why Jasper had given me this silly form. Not only was I a beaver, a natural smooth and strong swimmer, but I'd kept my Verity size. One enormous rodent, able to propel the tree along with good speed, even in the strong river current. It took a little getting used to, but after a couple of minutes of experimenting with my tail and webbed feet I had Pitts gliding through the water like a Yankee clipper. Good thing, too, because the vanguard of the infantry unit had arrived at the water's edge and commenced to blasting at us with their Springfields. It must've looked odd to anybody watching, to see dozens of blue-coated soldiers standing on the bank at midnight, shooting at a floating tree. No doubt some of the troops thought it strange, too. But they followed their orders and kept firing at the 'Rebel' tree.

Before we were halfway across, I started to believe that I had found my natural form. Being a swimming beaver just felt right, somehow. Gliding through the cool water made me think that Roberta might've had the same sensation when she flew. I felt weightless, like the hot-air balloons the Army observers used, and as powerful as a locomotive engine. My broad flat tail threw out a great wake as it propelled us along.

"Woo!" I shouted, snout popping above the surface. "If I'd known that shape-shiftin' was this much fun, I'd have done it years ago!"

"Not always so much fun, miss," Romulus said. "'Specially if it ain't yo' choice, and you gots no way back."

Ernie ran along Pitts' trunk until he could stand right in front of my nose. "That's why you'll only hold shape for an hour. It can become a cravin', like opium. Some mages get so attached to it that they have no control. They either lose themselves and can't shift back, or their power is so corrupted that they shift with no intention. Sometimes their bodies shift in a mix of forms. Then you get monsters like Venoma, or worse. So don't get to lovin' this too much. It ain't a good thing, missy."

"Then you don't feel a thrill, bein'—?"

"Lordy, no! A forced shift is a curse put on you by a twisted power. Any good feelin's are washed out by the evil that's witched you."

"But I didn't choose to take this shape, either. So then why do I—?"

"Yes, you did. Somewhere deep in your mind you decided that this would be a good thing. All Morphageus can do is boost your mind and body. Except for defendin' you from harm, everything else he does is caused by your will."

Defending me from harm would have been a great idea right

then. A monstrous geyser blew up just ahead, drenching all of us. Hard on its heels came the boom of a distant naval cannon. It looked like the Merchantry had more than just the infantry battalion in its pocket. Dahlgren guns were firing from the heavy artillery battery to the north. Two more enormous cannonballs splashed nearby, while a third skipped across the surface and threw up a tower of mud on the far bank.

"South! Turn downstream!" ordered Pitts. Two of his main branches began paddling like the arms of a human swimmer. His longest roots kicked, too, making him look like a lifeguard on a mission. We swung around in a wide left turn. The young tree's crown tried to rise up out of the water, but couldn't get high enough to get rid of the drag. I flicked my tail and swam up to his 'armpit' to add my strength to the cause. Dozens of Minie balls from the soldiers' rifles spattered sharp about us, clipping leaves and twigs. Bark cartwheeled through the night air. Roberta squawked and raced ahead, out of harm's way. The rest of us moved to the far side of Pitts' trunk for cover.

"Thanks," Ernie said.

"You're very welcome!" he snapped. "I gather that I'm just a wall to you people. A piece of lumber to cower behind. I have feelings, you know. This doesn't exactly tickle." Saying that, he rolled over and started doing a lazy backstroke. Romulus, Ernie, and I were ducked under.

"You ain't the only one with feelin's," I told Pitts. "And if you don't start bein' more polite I'm gonna try out these new beaver teeth on your hide. Make the sawdust fly."

"Touchy, touchy!" the peach tree muttered. But he shut up and continued swimming down the wide river.

We were coming up to the Long Bridge. It came by its name honest, for the Potomac must've been near upon a mile wide at that point. Made of masonry at each end, it was wood elsewhere, with two draws in it so ships could pass through. Though no boats were in sight, one of the draws had been raised anyhow, to keep unauthorized crossers from having an easy time of it. That wasn't much of a problem, since the Army had placed Fort Jackson atop Arlington Heights in case the Confederates tried to storm the capital. Filled with artillery and infantry, it strictly controlled access to Washington City. Near the open draw stood a pair of soldiers, smoking pipes and every now and then spitting into the river.

My witched ears could hear the pair talking. I shushed the others and whispered to them that we had to pretend that we were nothing more interesting than a fallen tree and a lonely old beaver. Romulus and Ernie hunkered down amidst Pitts' leaves, all but invisible in the crescent-moon darkness. I glided through the water, staying as silent as I could manage while still steering the tree toward the gap in the bridge.

The soldiers were doing what soldiers always did on guard duty in the middle of the night. They were complaining. "Blockhead gunners," one of them said in a northeastern accent. "Shootin' at a river full o' nothin."

"Yep," his partner agreed. He sounded older. "Anybody with half a brain knows that every grayback in Virginia is down at

Richmond, laughin' at McClellan."

"Aw, Little Mac knows what he's about, I expect. Mark my words. He'll turn the tables on Johnny Reb yet."

The older guard guffawed. "If he don't set the table for 'em instead!"

"Harney, I'm willin' to lay you a steak dinner at the Willard that—say, what's that there?"

"Where?"

"To yer left, 'longside that tree."

"I don't see nothin, Buck."

"You know, fer a guard you ain't got the eyes God give a mole. Right there, in the far-side fork."

"Looks like a...beaver. A big'un, too"

The younger sentry unslung his musket. "Big'un is right. That's a trophy I don't aim to pass up. Make me a whole suit o' clothes and two fine hats, he will."

Harney protested that even if he hit the beaver he'd likely never get it out of the river, but Buck had already banged away. Any other critter would've been dead to rights, but this rodent had magick ears and understood the Queen's Britannic. I ducked under, letting the peach's trunk absorb the heavy bullet. It dug a giant crater in Pitts' hide.

"Ow! Damnation!" he hollered, rising halfway out of the water. His limbs snagged the side of the bridge as we were about to rush through the draw. With a mighty wrench he hauled himself onto the roadway and glared down the astonished soldiers. They gaped right back at the dripping talking tree, mouths hanging open like beached fish.

"I do declare that I have had my fill of you hairless apes puncturing my integument!" barked Pitts. "How would you like it if I did the same to you?"

A green peach, solid as a rock, bounced off of Harney's noggin. The sentry sat down so hard he bounced. Rubbing the egg-sized knot on his forehead, he goggled at the tree and gibbered like a baby. His partner, still quicker on the draw, hauled up Harney's still-loaded Springfield and cocked it. An instant later Pitts snatched it out of his hands and tied it around the bridge rail like a holiday bow.

"That's not a rhetorical question," grumbled Pitts, punctuating his remark with another painful peach shot, this time at the soldier still standing. When Buck had plopped down beside Harney, nursing his own lump, Pitts advanced on them. They were too amazed to stir an inch. I sympathized. Typical Army drill didn't include Birnam Wood coming to Dunsinane.

"Lucky for you two I'm in a hurry, or I'd plant you deep. I reckon I'll have to settle for watering you down to the roots." With that he plucked the soldiers up by their blue sack coats and hurled them downstream close to a hundred feet. They skipped like the cannonball had earlier, landing in the shallows on the Washington side.

No sooner had Pitts made a self-satisfied nod of his crown than I heard distant clattering from the Washington City bridgehead. Troops coming at the double-quick, from the infantry company posted down there. No doubt already alerted by all the earlier shooting, they had sprung into action when the sentry had fired at me. Time to exercise the discretion that I'd heard was the better part of valor.

"Let's go!" I cried. "Their friends are on the way. More bad news for your integument."

Pitts hopped off the bridge and landed with a whoosh on the far side. I swam through the draw. Romulus and Ernie were already there, splashing toward the tree to grasp its trunk again. To make better speed Pitts let his roots drift downstream. I resumed pushing with all my beavery might. By the time the reinforcements arrived at mid-bridge, we'd lost ourselves in the river's gloom. To anyone else who might spy us we'd just be a fallen tree floating along, all innocent and natural.

Arlington Heights disappeared to our right rear. The cannon and musket fire had riled up some of the bastions up there, but no one shot at us. Either word hadn't got out to all the troops across the Potomac, or the Merchantry didn't command as many of them as I feared. I felt dead certain, though, that enemy telegraph signals were flying thick and fast ahead of us. No doubt more trouble waited for us at Alexandria.

"Won't they just wire ahead and order more soldiers to go for us?" I asked Ernie, who stood on a limb drying himself with a leaf.

"They would if they could, matey" said Roberta, landing heavy behind the soggy mouse. "But it seems that all the telegraph wires goin' south have been cut." She spit a piece of frayed black cable out of her beak. "Savvy?"

Okay, I need to remember that I'm travelin' with trained professionals. "I savvy. Good work, ma'am."

The scarlet parrot chortled. "Ma'am! Ain't you the well-brought-up child."

"Well, I am the bright shinin' hope of the free world," I said with a grin, believing none of it.

"Hah!" grumped Pitts. A flexing knothole seemed to be serving as his mouth, but I still couldn't spot anything like eyes to see with. *Guess it wouldn't be magick otherwise.*

"Where exactly do we aim to cross over?" I wanted to know.

"Need to get to Confederate territory," Ernie answered. "Beyond the Yankee emplacements. Once we get past Alexandria it won't be far. More unguarded shoreline there."

Roberta nodded while using a toe to clean bits of cable from her beak. "Jeff Davis has stripped near every one of his troops out o' northern Virginia. They're all 'round Richmond now, tryin' to hold off McClellan. Stonewall Jackson's moved out o' the Valley, too. Guess he got tired o' sailin' circles around Banks and Fremont. If he's at Richmond a Rebel attack can't be far off."

"That means we should have an easy time of it," said Ernie. "From here to Richmond should be mostly empty, if we choose our route with care."

"But then," Romulus pointed out, "we gots to find ourselves a way through—or 'round—two armies."

"I'll fly over and wait for ya, shipmates," snickered Roberta.

Ernie took her glasses off of her face. He looked around for something dry to clean them with, then gave up and perched them back on her beak. "Maybe I'll go with her."

"Y'all's doin' me a load o' no good," complained Romulus.

"Me, neither," I said. "If I stayed like this I could maybe swim around the Peninsula, but I guess I'm gonna change back soon. Fifteen or twenty minutes, maybe."

Ernie climbed onto my furry head. "Don't worry. Ol' Ernie has a few tricks up his sleeve yet."

I dug my claws into Pitts' hide with a muttered apology and climbed aboard. Now that no one took notice of us I didn't need to push. The tree steered himself and we made good time just going with the Potomac's current. Between the cool night breeze and easy gliding action of the river we could've been on a calm pleasure cruise. *Of course, havin' monsters and sorcerers trying to kill you does bleed a bit of the bliss out of the thing.*

Alexandria slid into sight on our right. It looked to be a good sized place, but a lot smaller than Washington. Most of its citizens were Union soldiers, the local populace having fled the year before. A few loyalists remained, along with those who didn't care to take sides one way or the other. Lots of spies and Merchantry men, too, no doubt. None of that was visible at one in the morning. No lights to speak of, not even in Fort Ward, the big bastion built to defend the approach to the capital. Just dead quiet. We floated past the town with not so much as an unkind word directed at us. After all we'd been through in the past few hours, I could hardly believe it.

A couple of miles past Alexandria brought us to a wide and empty patch of weeds on the southern side. I slid back into the water and helped to maneuver the tree into the shallow spot. Roberta flew up over the shore for a mile in every direction. Reporting back, she assured us that all was clear and we could safely leave the river for solid ground. Pitts rolled over, stood with much creaking and complaining, and waded to the bank. Romulus, with Ernie in his pocket, got ashore on all fours and shook himself dry. I followed and did the same. Then I stood up and peered about with my witched eyes, sure that I now qualified as the largest rodent in the Confederate States of America.

I was in Virginia.

Enemy territory.

Roberta made a rude sound
from somewhere amidst Pitts' foliage.
"Aw, bosoms ain't all they're cracked up to be, missy.
More trouble than they're worth, most days."

13 / A Brief Rest
Saturday, June 21

Enemy territory? Can't be any worse than my own house and neighborhood have been today. Not much peace, love, and joy since this afternoon.

My first act on Southern soil was to collapse on the grass. Small wonder, what with shape-shifting, swimming the Potomac, pushing a tree through the water, getting shot at with muskets and cannon, and burning up any reserves of energy I might've had after fighting and fleeing various impossible monsters. Those reserves chose that moment to get used up. I flopped face-down and lay there as if some mage had tripled the Earth's gravity. At that moment I believed it be perfectly possible.

Crickets chirped all around us. Far off an owl hooted. Something burrowed beneath us, maybe a mole or groundhog. How many of them were like Romulus, humans magicked into animal forms against their will? Had I been in carriages pulled by former schoolmasters? Was last week's beef dinner a case of cannibalizing a curator? Did we trap rats at Ford's that had once been laundresses? If I'd had the strength I might've shivered at the thought.

Romulus threw me up over his shoulder and hauled me into a clump of trees, yet set me down as if I were a treasured soap bubble. Warm but soothing canteen water went down my throat. The Marshal acted like he took care of five-and-a-half—foot-tall beavers every day. Heck, maybe he did, for all I knew about him. Perhaps they had a secret Marshal school that the Equity ran in Marrakech or Timbuktu or Atlantis or wherever. Ernie and Romulus might've been thoroughly trained in 'Enormous Rodent Hydration.' 'Bully-Slaying' and 'Talking Tree Recruitment' seemed to have been on their curriculum, too.

"I feel awful," I whispered.

"I know," he said. It occurred to me that he wasn't just saying that, if Ernie had told the truth.

"How long has it been...since...?" *Just how do you bring up the subject of when somebody had been magickally transformed from a dog into a slave? It'd never been covered at my school.*

"Oh, 'bout a year, I reckon." He fed me some bread and an apple from my haversack. "Seems like fifty."

"Is it hard? Bein' human?" My skin started to jerk on my bones. Soon I'd be human myself, and I had an idea that it'd be just as raw a change as the first one had been, an hour before.

"Most days. Can't smell nothin', can't hear nothin'. Back

hurts from walkin' on half my legs."

"Sounds like my Granny, complainin' about her lumbago. She told me to never get old."

"You took her advice without meanin' to."

"Huh?" Now my bones began to jerk under my skin. That felt worse. It wouldn't be long now.

"The Stone Warden don't feel the bite o' time, they say."

It struck me that finding out what that contract had committed me to would've been smart of me. "You mean I'm stuck bein' twelve years old, forever?"

"Not forever. Just till your quest's done."

"And if it takes thirty years?" My stomach heaved. Whether from the shape-shift starting or the idea that I'd stay a kid till I hit fifty, I couldn't be sure.

Ernie ran up Romulus' shirt and clung to his shoulder. "Then you'll have the best complexion of any matron on earth."

"And the smallest bosom," I pouted.

Roberta made a rude sound from somewhere amidst Pitts' foliage. "Aw, bosoms ain't all they're cracked up to be, missy. More trouble than they're worth, most days. Why, I once had a corset that fit so—"

Much as I wanted to hear about Roberta's unmentionables, and how or why a parrot might wear them, my body had other ideas. The spell ended at that instant. I felt like I tumbled down a mineshaft full of spiders and straight razors. Dizzy and nauseous, I arched my back so hard that nothing but my head and heels stayed on the ground. Spit bubbled out of my mouth.

I heard a faraway scream that got louder and louder, till it filled my whole aching, spinning head.

It was Jasper's voice.

"Boy, oh boy! Nothin' smells worse than wet beaver fur! Get a whiff of you. Whoo!"

I looked at my paws. I felt them, rubbed them. Skin. Good old freckled Verity flesh, all pruned from being in the river so long. Romulus held up his mirror. My snub nose and blue eyes were there. Reaching behind me, I tried to grab the beaver's tail, but it had melted away with my buck teeth. I was back in all my glory.

Jasper still blabbed. "Did you have to swim through every bit of fish poo in the river? The Canal and the outhouse episodes were bad enough, you know."

"I just kinda figured you for an expert by that point," I said aloud. "And where do you think the Canal empties into?"

"Say what?" asked Ernie, with a puzzled frown.

I tapped my noggin. "Jasper. He's back."

"And better than ever!" the voice of Morphageus announced.

Switching to internal conversation, I told him, "You know, you were only gone an hour."

"But what an hour it was! Giant beavers, talkin' trees, gunplay, swimmin' the mighty Potomac—without a paddle, I might add—"

"Hey, we had my tail. I thought it was pretty sharp work for a beginner."

"I stand corrected." With that the steel collar around my neck hopped off. My sword landed in front of me, hilt-up, its blade split into a pair of bare metallic feet. Jasper bowed to me. "Well done, Stone Warden."

I nodded back. "Thank you very much. Next time give a girl some warnin' before you transmogrify her bones."

"Can't promise anything. Circumstances may dictate another snappy response. But we'll try to develop proper teamwork." Morphageus sprang into my hand, its blade whole again. I turned it into the battered cup and it clung onto my belt with tiny metal fingers.

Roberta looked down her beak at me. "What's the plan now?"

"She needs to rest before we can take another step," said Ernie. "This is as good a spot as any." He waved his needle at Romulus. "Can you make us a hidey-hole?"

"Sho' nuff," the big Warden replied, standing wide-legged and flexing his huge arms. "Stand back."

His broad strong hands blurred as he started digging between his feet like the dog he'd once been. Grass, dirt, and rocks showered behind him. In five minutes he'd made a hole deep and wide enough to hold him and me. No normal person could've done that, not even with a pick and shovel. *Okay, one more amazin' thing for my evenin'.* We snuggled down inside it after scattering the removed dirt so as not to call attention to our hiding place. Ernie jumped in last, curling up on my neck next to the Stone.

"Roberta, give us a holler if anybody suspicious comes nosin' about," he said.

"Aye-aye," she answered, saluting with one blue-tipped wing. "I'll keep a weather eye out for enemy sails on the horizon."

The peach tree ambled towards us. "And I'll guard you all, too. It'll take a keener eye than most to spot you." All the stars disappeared as Pitts settled atop us, his roots spreading over most of the hole and wriggling into the earth. To any observers we were just one tree amidst a clump of others.

"When should we wake you?" asked Roberta. "When the sun peeks over the yardarm?"

"Not 'less trouble come," said Romulus. "Otherwise, let her sleep till sunset if need be."

That proved to be a wise decision. I didn't open my eyes till late afternoon.

*   *   *   *   *

Peeling open one gummy eyelid, I squinted at the single ray of dim sunlight that managed to slip between Pitts' roots. No sound could be heard, even with my magick ears, except for the dull rush of the Potomac a hundred yards away. *Well, that's a blessin'.* What I could hear, loud as a trumpet, was the call of nature. *Time to move.*

I took care to uncurl my legs, not wanting to wake Romulus or Ernie. They'd had a hard night, too. *Hmm. Not to worry. They ain't here.*

Pitts moved his 'feet' a bit to let me out. Standing stiff and sore in the midsummer sun, feeling older than the Blue Ridge Mountains to our west, I shaded my sleepy eyes. There was no one in sight, friend or foe. But now I could hear low voices from the other side of the ridge behind me. Not only that, I also smelled frying fish. *Food. Oh boy!* Last night's bread and water had been a life-saver, but my belly now screamed that it wanted filling on a more regular basis than every sixteen hours. Trotting up the rise, I made sure Morphageus was still a tin cup so the sword wouldn't bounce on my hip and maybe trip me. Nothing like a humiliating crash onto your snoot to ruin your reputation as the savior of world freedom.

The feast lay just over the ridge, in a cluster of high bushes, out of sight of anyone patrolling the river. A pit full of coals gave off much heat but little smoke. Romulus had found an old broken frying pan someplace and four fat fish sizzled on it. Ernie lay on a log, next to Roberta. Neither of them showed any interest in what sizzled in the pan. The little Marshal chewed on something grey and awful-looking; the red parrot just yawned. While my mouth watered at the prospect of an honest-to-goodness meal, my recent experiences made me wary.

"Anybody we know?" I asked, eyeing the quartet of unfortunate bass.

Roberta shook her head. "Don't think so. We did ask."

"And they said...?"

"Nothin'," Ernie told me. "And you know what the rule is...silence means assent."

"I doubt that silence usually means 'Oh, go ahead and eat me.' I know my silences don't mean that."

"Have to agree with you on that one," said Roberta.

"So we're sure that these fellers ain't part of an unlucky

church choir that sang out of tune at a Merchantry function?" I asked.

Romulus shook his head. "Naw. They's just fish." He turned them over with his fingers. The pan looked like it'd been abandoned by soldiers when its handle broke off. "Not sayin' it be more right to eat 'em because o' that. They's still dead, shape-shifted or not. It is what it is."

I scrunched up my nose. "Maybe I'll just eat somethin' green and leafy instead."

Pitts called up at me from his spot near the riverbank. "I heard that!"

Roberta whistled. "He's a might touchy about vegetarians," she whispered. "Says they're just a bunch of murderers and thieves."

"All in your point o' view," nodded Ernie. "I'm biased against cats me own self, but there you are."

Throwing up my hands, I announced, "I'm gonna go do my business, then dive into a fish dinner. If that makes me a bad person, so be it." I made my way past the odd assortment of allies I'd collected, needing to piddle in the worst way.

"Keep yo eyes and ears peeled, miss," said Romulus to my back. "No Bullies in the daylight, but they's plenty o' other trouble at hand."

"Don't worry," I replied, starting to skip, "if anybody interrupts my elimination, then elimination is what they'll get."

It was quick work to climb farther up the hill to another thicket, take care of things, and start back down. While up there

I peered about to see just where we were and where we might be heading. Alexandria was a distant speck upstream. I could just make out the masts of ships moored at its wharves. Other craft, both pure sail and those aided by steam, made their way along the Potomac in both directions. Washington almost seemed lovely from this distance, with the wind blowing away from me. The incomplete Monument and Capitol Dome rising above the trees looked like odd white fungi on a lush green lawn. It felt ever so much more peaceful, war or no war, to see it all in the sunlight. No monsters. Leastways, no monsters except the usual ones, those with muskets and cannon, bent on mass destruction of their friends and neighbors.

That thought reminded me that I stood in Confederate territory. I turned to look away from the water, at Virginia proper. Green fields rolled away toward the mountains, cut with a few fences, lots of trees, and the occasional road. A couple of lonely farms sat in the far distance, but I saw no movement around them. The owners had probably lost everything—cattle, horses, chickens, crops—to foraging troops of both armies. It occurred to me that we were in the ranks of the marauders now, competing for supplies with hundreds of thousands of armed men. I should make the most of what Romulus had on the skillet. Pickings might be slim for a while.

Romulus and I devoured the fish, aided by the last of our bread and canteen water, with a maximum of relish and a minimum of guilt. Ernie and Roberta preferred seeds, which might've upset Pitts but no one thought to inform him. I ate standing up, keeping my senses sharp for any surprises that might come our way. After our awful night I had already taken on the wariness of a wild animal. No matter how safe and sunny things seemed, I assumed that either the Merchantry or the war could cloud things up real quick.

"We travelin' by night or by day?" I asked the group. There were advantages and difficulties with either, to my mind.

Roberta squinted through her spectacles and said, "Day means fewer monsters. Bullies can't come out in the sun. Venoma can, but it makes her real weak."

"No ghouls, trolls, ogres, or specters till sundown, either," added Ernie, sitting on a log and burping. *Oh, ain't that swell? The whole book of Grimm's Fairy Tales is after me.*

Romulus buried the fish bones with a boot heel and commenced to put out the fire. "But we can fight a few o' them easier than we can the whole Rebel army. Sometimes it be the everyday enemies that gits you."

"At least we can see where we're goin' by day," I said, looking around to make my point. "Night time means gettin' lost or ambushed." I pulled my map of Virginia from the haversack and peered at it. The thing turned out to be too large a scale to show many roads.

My cup piped up for the first time that day, in predictable fashion. "Why don't we ask Jasper what he thinks?" whined the voice in my head. "Oh, he's just an enchanted object, what could he possibly know?" I rolled my eyes and pointed to my belt, to let everyone else know that there was another opinion being shared. "Well, perhaps the poor benighted creatures whom he serves are tragically unaware that he has a map of the whole world at his metaphorical fingertips."

My eyebrow arched up at that. "No foolin'?"

He turned into a little court jester cap. "Do I look like I'm foolin'?"

"He says he can navigate, no problem," I told my friends. "But I still think I'd like to try movin' in the light. It'd be faster, and the troubles we'd meet would at least be human, I expect."

Ernie snorted. "Keep tellin' yourself that, duckie."

"She's right," said Roberta, spreading her wings to catch the afternoon breeze. "Merchantry don't like to show its magick if it can help it. Whatever we meet in the daytime will more'n likely be humans, either paid or enthralled."

"Unless they gets desp'rate," Romulus muttered. "Then you can count on battalions of goblins and such."

"Then let's not push 'em that far," I suggested. "Keep our heads down and not rub their noses in anything."

Ernie jabbed his tiny spear into the log, almost skewering his foot. "We'll need a cover story. Something to deflect suspicion away from why a white girl's travelin' alone with a colored man in a war zone."

"I'll think of somethin' directly," I said, already going over possibilities in my mind. Jasper could help me develop them. "Then we'll all have to learn the details and keep to 'em."

Roberta flapped up into the elm tree above us. Squatting on a thick branch, she said, "Daytime it is, shipmates. I'll stand first watch."

"We can stay put tonight and head out at dawn," said Ernie, sharpening his knitting needle on a rock. "Get started after plenty of sleep. Might not get a lot of that the farther south we go."

Having finished kicking out and burying the fire, Romulus straightened up. "Best refill the canteens. They's a crick to the west a bit."

It occurred to me that a medieval-style belt on a modern girl in overalls would attract attention. So I removed the sword hanger part and kept just the belt. I had the cup grab tight onto it with tiny hands. "Why not use the river?" I asked.

"Crick water's cleaner. And the Merchantry's still lookin' for us. Best not to show ourselves that direction. They has less eyes in the Confed'racy than they does in Washington. That's why we crossed the river. They magick is considerable less across that water."

I frowned and tagged along with him as he started off with the canteens. "The rules of magick don't seem sensible to me. The Merchantry magick, the black kind, can't work on or across flowin' or deep water, right?

He nodded. "True, mostly."

"Then how can they function at all? The world's full of oceans and lakes and big rivers. And how does our magick work in water? I swam in the Potomac for an hour last night, all shape-shifted. Shouldn't that've been affected?"

"Cain't say I's an expert, but the way I understands it, strong life wants to fight black magick. And water is all life, missy. So Merchantry magick hits it like an egg against a wall. Course, not all walls is built sturdy. Sometimes they's cracks and such that let some bad spells through. Even on the sea a Merchantry ship can sometimes call on harpies or change the weather. But they avoids that, 'cause it's just as likely to turn against 'em. So they tends to use normal ways around water...simple boats or bridges to get across, guns instead o' fire spells, that sort o' thing."

An idea came to me. "Then we can use spells around water 'cause ours is life-magick, not death-magick?"

"Guess so. Our magick gets renewed by water and wind and laughter and such. Theirs is revived by hate and pain and things bleedin'. So we can work with water better than they can. Your spell held last night because it started on land. You prob'ly couldn't have shifted while you was in the river. Still can backfire, though, so you gots to be careful. Deeper the water, more dangerous to the user. Ocean's special tough."

"How does an ostium work, then? Venoma talked like she was on her way to the Sceptr'd Isle."

"Don't know. They's a kind o' shadow world that the Merchantry knows 'bout. That's where Venoma lives. Maybe it bypasses the water somehow."

"And we can't use their ostia?"

"Ernie claims he saw a Marshal do it once. He weren't sure how. Most times the place stays dead if you try. Nothin' happens."

"So if we went into the Monument right now...?"

"Just an empty room to us."

"Then the Merchantry's people must have a special charm or word or object."

"Maybe so."

We arrived at the creek, which turned out to actually be a sweet spring trickling out of a jumble of rocks. As Romulus dipped both canteens into it, making them blurble, I thought about the story we had to concoct to explain our presence in Virginia. The particulars were half-set and I was about to ask Jasper to help me edit them. I concentrated so much on it that I dropped my guard. Romulus couldn't hear over the noise of the water. That's how we got surprised.

The hammer of a pistol clicked overhead. A smooth Southern voice drawled, "Afternoon. Captain Laurence Tyrell, CSA cavalry. And who might y'all be?"

When in doubt, always tell a man he's God's gift to women.

14 / Tyrell's Pistol

"Okay, Jasper," I whispered to myself, "a stranger's pointin' a gun at us. How'd you let that happen?"

"Hey," the boyish voice in my head protested, "you're the Stone Warden here. I'm just a lowly servant. Put those wonder senses to their proper use."

"Ain't you supposed to protect me from imminent danger?"

"Don't seem imminent to me."

"He's got a gun!" I shouted aloud, before I could catch myself.

The strange voice said, "So I do. There is a war on. Can't be too careful."

My eyes rose to the top of the highest boulder to my left. Silhouetted by the setting sun, the speaker was just a long-haired shadow in a gray kepi. I shaded my eyes and edged sideways to try for a better look.

"Ah-ah," he said, scolding me with the barrel of his enormous pistol. "You didn't say 'mother-may-I.' Hands where I can see them, please."

With a disbelieving snort I pointed out that I was only twelve, and a girl to boot. That didn't wash with our new friend. "I'd be tempted to sympathize, but it just so happens that a sergeant in my troop got shot off his horse by a Federal drummer boy who was merely ten. And you're a sight bigger than him." He eyed my overalls, boots, and short hair. "Look to be a cooler customer, too...er, ma'am."

I held my hands up and turned around in a full circle. "Look. No gun, no knife, nothin'. Not even a slingshot." At a nod from me Romulus did the same. "We're harmless, sir."

"I don't know about that. Your darky there looks like he could pick up this rock and heave it to Richmond. He yours?"

"Yes, sir. Bought and paid for." *Sorry, Romulus. I'll make it up to you later.*

"Who else you got with you?"

"Nobody. Just us."

He seemed to be considering something. After a short pause he slid backwards out of sight. When that happened Romulus moved over so that he could shield me if the Reb came back shooting. I motioned for him to stop. The Marshal would have to pretend to be a slave again, submissive. Small and young as I was, I should still be the white person in charge. This stranger had to be led to believe that, or he might send for more soldiers. It seemed unlikely that he was here on his own.

Romulus got the message at once. He seemed to shrink to half his size and stared at the ground. It broke my heart to see him do it, but knowing that it was just an act reassured me. I did my part by puffing up as if I bossed around giant negroes every day. I'd seen others do it in Maryland. Though it left a bad taste in my mouth, I was stuck until we could get rid of this fellow. *At least the Stone's still warm. That's a good sign.*

Tyrell eased around the side of the rock pile as if he had not a care in the world. Now that we weren't staring into the sun we could see him clearly. Tall and lean, but not scrawny, he wore a dusty gray Confederate uniform. The coat was short, trimmed in yellow, and had three bars on its high collar. Thigh-high black boots with silver spurs clung to his long legs. At one time the kit must've cost a pretty penny. You could've said the same about its owner. He carried himself with the same haughty air that Booth did. In fact, he might've been the actor's kin, seeing as how he had a similar dark moustache and handsome profile. His face looked longer and sharper, though. More foxlike, with a clean white scar along the left jaw. Brown as fine chocolate, his eyes gave the unsettling impression that they could both read your mind and see your underclothes.

"Now, then," he said, slapping rock dust from his clothes while keeping the gigantic pistol trained on us, "you have the advantage of me. I've told you my name but I don't know yours." His voice betrayed some fine schooling, maybe in Europa. I wondered what had made him join the army. Some fool lust for excitement, I imagined, like most of them.

"Mary Williams," I answered, picking the name of one of my school friends. Giving this fellow my real name didn't strike me as sensible. I had no reason to believe he was a Merchantry man, but better safe than sorry at this point. With a nod toward Romulus I added, "This here's Jim."

Tyrell leaned back against the rock as if he was safe in his own home. "Well, Miss Williams, I can't help but wonder why someone of your tender years would be between the lines. Do you live hereabouts?"

"Oh, no, sir," I said, deciding that playing dumb and innocent might work on his chivalrous nature. In my experience cavalrymen all thought they sat at King Arthur's table. "I'm lookin' for my older brother, Tommy. We got word that he might be in Richmond, wounded. Ma sent us to go see."

The Reb scratched his ear and peered at me. "Is that a fact? Which regiment?"

I knew he'd be bound to ask that, so I was ready for him. Me and Tommy had spent quite a bit of time reading the papers and talking to soldiers. Jackson's Valley Campaign, a flat Federal failure, had been the talk of Washington that month. "Stonewall Brigade. 33rd Virginia. Company E."

"Ah, the Emerald Guard. Fine lads. From Irlann, most of them. You look the part yourself and no mistake."

I made myself look all anxious. "Are they in Richmond, do you know? We're ever so worried about him. There was some sharp fightin' in the Valley and down south. Got a letter from a cousin, we did, sayin' that he thought he'd seen Tommy in Chimborazo."

Tyrell frowned. "Lot of boys in that hospital. Easy to mistake one of them for someone else, bandaged and all. Seems a flimsy reason to send a girl child on a hundred-mile journey, even one dressed as a boy."

"He's the last survivin' man in our family," I blubbered, figuring that turning on the waterworks might help my case. "We lost Pa to a shell at Manassas and Hiram to dysentery in camp this winter. Tommy's the only one left. Ma's beside herself with worry. So she asked me to go huntin' him while she stayed to work the farm with our other two hands. I'm dressed like this because a skirt is just impractical on the road, and because if folks think I'm a boy they'll take me serious. And now I'm lost!"

Wailing like some two year-old, I feared that I'd over acted it. *What would Mr. Ford say?* Romulus shuffled over and gave my shoulder a clumsy pat. "There now, Miss Mary. It'll be alright. Ole Jim'll look out for you. We'll find Mr. Tommy, just you wait and see."

Good job, Romulus. They must have actin' lessons at the Marshals' Academy. I could see that Tyrell was buying our story. His pistol barrel drooped off-line and he seemed to be considering his options. That was fine by me because I recognized the gun and knew what it could do. Sticking out my lip and making it quiver, I gave him my best forlorn-waif look. What red-blooded Southern gentleman could resist coming to the aid of such a befreckled urchin as me?

"Tell you what," the good captain said, "I'm a bit lost myself, in a small way. Heading south to get back with Wade Hampton and Jeb Stuart. They need the intelligence I've gathered. I reckon I can take you under my wing for a spell if you're so inclined."

I sniffed and wiped my nose on my shirt sleeve. "That's a fine offer, sir. I know it'd make my ma breathe a sight easier to know that such a fine figure of a man as yourself is lookin' out for us." *Yep. When in doubt, always tell a man he's God's gift to women and girls.*

The hand-cannon dropped into its holster. With a satisfied smile Tyrell gave me a nod and clapped his hands. "Well, then! Too late to start today. Not more than a couple of hours till sundown. We should get shelter for the night and plan our route for tomorrow." He waved a hand to the west, toward the buildings I'd spotted earlier. "Already spied a likely place. There's a house yonder that looks as if it's been abandoned for some time. In fair shape, though. Not plundered too badly by either side yet. No food, but the well seems alright and the roof is good."

I beamed at him with my most grateful face. "See, Jim, I knew he'd be as sharp as he is handsome. Trust a scout to know the lay of the land. Lead on, Cap'n."

Tyrell half-turned to do just that, then twisted back around. "Where are your bundles? Surely you aren't out here with just the clothes on your backs?"

Romulus spoke up, eyes lowered. "Lost 'em crossin' the river, sir. Canoe got swamped by a steamer."

I backed him up on that. "Like to scared me outta a year's growth, it did. We were lucky it happened close to shore or my ma might be all alone right now. All I saved was this haversack.

Even lost my shoes."

"Looks like we'll have to rustle up some grub then," Tyrell said, squinting into the lowering sun. "But let's get to that house first and settle in. It's a goodly hike for a girl your age. Maybe two miles or more. Time for you to join the cavalry."

With that he gave a whistle as piercing as a steam locomotive's. My magicked ears felt like they were being stabbed with needles. As I turned away from the noise I saw Roberta take off from her tree. She flew in an alarmed way, it seemed to me. Ernie rode atop her neck, brandishing his little spear. I waved them off as well as I could without attracting Tyrell's notice. The parrot got the message and swooped low, gliding along the top of the high grass until she landed behind a bush a few yards back of us.

When I looked back to Tyrell, I saw him jog out past the clump of rocks. A vibration buzzed through the ground and up into my feet. Something came our way. My better-than-human senses told me it was big, powerful, and alive. It seemed like every time a thing like that showed up it tried to kill us. I laid my fingers on the handle of my Morphageus-cup, just in case it turned out to be something hostile.

Our new arrival came out of the red setting sun like a god in a myth. Bloody light haloed its huge head. Long lovely fair hair danced in the summer air as if it had a life of its own. The golden coat shined so much you could almost have used it for a mirror. Full of dark fire, its eyes seemed to dare you look in them for the terrible knowledge it held. Its broad chest and stout legs promised any enemy a hard time of it. This was an impressive specimen. I caught my breath as it skidded to a dusty stop in front of Tyrell.

"Nice horsie," chuckled Jasper.

"Darn tootin'," I replied silently, remembering that I needed to keep Jasper a secret.

Tyrell stroked the giant golden horse's neck and muzzle like a lover. "This is Alcibiades," he announced, as if the beast was royalty. Maybe he was, with all of the shape-shifting going around. I had read about Alcibiades in school and recalled that he'd been a famous Greek hero who ended up betraying Athens. *Prob'ly not a tactful time to bring that up.*

"Old Al's taken me safe and sound through many a battle," the captain continued. "I know he'll do the same for you." I wondered if he'd meant to imply that we'd be fighting battles on our trip. That didn't bode well. But it would also be typical of the turn my life had taken.

Before I could react Tyrell had grabbed me around my waist and tossed me onto his horse's back. It felt like sitting on a field of shorn gilded grass. That is, if you like being plopped onto the world's hardest McClellan saddle while you do it. *Ow! My bottom!* Did he expect me to ride all the way to Richmond on that torture device? Even Torquemada would've blushed at the brutality. Maybe Jasper could magick me a pillow.

"Off we go," said the handsome Rebel, striding ahead of the stallion. He didn't even bother to grab the reins or bridle. The enormous horse ambled behind him as if tethered by a harness of thought. Romulus got in step beside me, keeping an eye out for any nasty surprises. Out of the corner of my eye I saw a flash of red and blue in the sky. Roberta followed at a careful distance. Good. We were all together.

As uncomfortable as Tyrell's saddle felt, at least to my civilian backside, Al's gait turned out to be smooth as satin. Like riding on a cloud. No wonder the cavalryman seemed in love with his beast. We glided west along the rolling landscape, shading our eyes as the sun slid lower into the mountains. There wasn't much sign of war here, except for the lack of people. No burning trains, no dead bodies along the road, no signal towers, no fortifications. We could've been on a typical summer evening's stroll. I almost forgot the previous night's terrors.

Tyrell chattered as he walked, seemingly without a care in the world. But I noticed that his hand stayed near his holster and his eyes never stopped sliding across the terrain. He'd probably sprung enough ambuscades, or blundered into them, to be always on his guard for enemy action. Nothing like a nasty year of war to teach you to stay alert. I'd learned that lesson in just one day.

"I'm from Williamsburg myself," our host said, waving his left hand to the south. "Lovely old town. Founded way back in the early 1600's. Used to be the state capital. The Tyrells have been there since Hector was a pup. Now the Bluebellies have their muddy feet all over it."

Reminding myself that I was supposed to be a good Confederate, I said, "You must be right eager to get back down there and help clear 'em out. I know I would be."

He nodded with a bright smile. "True enough, little lady. I have some special friends waiting to meet me who are itching to help. We should meet up with them in a day or two."

I wanted to know who these people might be. The more folks we were surrounded by the more likely that we'd be discovered for what we really were. But prying might make him think that we were spies instead of friends. A sidelong glance at Romulus told me that he thought the same thing. We'd have to wait and see how things developed.

At first Tyrell seemed so unguarded in his talk that he might tell us what we wanted to know without a lot of prompting on our part. He mentioned his parents' names, his sister's wedding date, his dog's favorite game, and all manner of personal information. After about a half hour, though, I noticed that he gave out nothing specific about his regiment, commanders, battles, weapons, or plans. Outwardly a charming fool, our captain proved to be nothing of the sort.

We responded in kind. As Tyrell casually but keenly questioned us on our past movements and future intentions, I spun him a long fluffy story about stealing a canoe from a wharf in Alexandria, evading Federal patrols in Leesburg, getting spooked by a persistent sharpshooter around Manassas. Romulus would help me out when I'd get stuck. Whenever Tyrell tried to pry to closely for details, I managed to fend him off with funny little side stories adapted from tall tales I'd heard from actors and stagehands at Ford's.

"How'd you come to be in the army?" I inquired, to get him off of our affairs and back onto his.

"Why do you ask?" he frowned, as if it was so obvious that no one but a fool would ask.

"I mean did you join like some of the boys did, just because their friends had? Or from pure patriotism, to defend hearth and home? Did your family insist you do them honor by fightin'? Have you hated Yankees from birth? That's true of a lot of folks." I gave him a wicked grin. "Or maybe your girl said she'd never kiss you again if you stayed out of the fight?"

He threw his head back and laughed like a bronze bell at that. "Becky? Little you know of her. She's more likely to be entertaining half a dozen new beaux now that I'm riding with Stuart."

"Oops. My mistake, then."

"On the contrary, Miss Mary. The mistake was all mine, trusting that her good breeding meant that she was of high moral character, rather than being the harpy she most plainly was." He made a sour face. "Let it be a warning to you. Choose your own mate. Don't let your mother have a hand in it."

Aha. A motive I hadn't thought of. Going to war to escape the love of your life. No wonder Tyrell seemed so carefree. He was less miserable being shot at than he'd been in the arms of Miss Becky.

"Words to live by, Cap'n," I smiled, giving Romulus a look. He knew how likely that was to happen. My stubbornness came direct from my ma, both by blood and by example. It'd never occur to her to try to stuff a husband down my throat.

That is, if I ever see her again. And if I ever begin to age past twelve. This save-the-world quest has barely gotten started.

"Don't start with the self-pity and the poutin'," Jasper sighed.

I looked around in a panicked way, but Tyrell didn't react. Jasper's speech in my head always sounded like a clear voice right beside me. Every time I heard him it amazed me that no one else could. "Easy for you to say, Mr. All-Powerful Sword of Destiny."

"Ah, about that. Since you couldn't be bothered to check the ground rules, I thought I'd take it upon myself to warn you that at midnight tomorrow—that would be about 30 hours from now—my initial charge of magick will be gone."

My eyebrows shot up. *What?!* "Gone?" I yelled in my thoughts. "Gone? As in...gone?"

"Gone as in 'exhausted, emptied, spent, finished, used up, depleted.' Gone as in 'maybe it's in my other purse. Gone as in 'with the wind.'"

"This is a fine how-do-you-do! What good is bein' the Stone Warden then? I'm supposed to be savin' the world with a Morphageus that don't work?"

"Who said I won't work? You'll still have me for emergency self-defense. That power draws from you and the Stone bein' together."

"That's a relief. Wouldn't want to try to fight Venoma again with just a tin cup."

"Oh, I think you could still handle her. Fill her to the brim with your vengeance. Drown her with your righteous fury."

"Ha, ha. You're such a drip."

"But any shape-shiftin' or other exotic magicks will have to be paid for in advance."

"What on earth does that mean? You openin' a bank account? I have to bribe you to help me?"

"Somethin' like that. I'll let you in on all the rules tonight."

"Lovely. They ain't gonna be in Romish or Attic or Pomeranian, are they?"

"They are, now that you mention it, but I'll translate 'em for free."

"Thank you kindly. If I decide to use the cup as a spittoon, will you take offense?"

"Not as long as you don't take it personal if I turn into a seven-foot steel scorpion right after that."

"Oh, okay then. Tonight it is."

At that moment Alcibiades stopped moving. We'd arrived at the farmhouse where we planned to spend the night. Now I saw the war up close. The walls were bullet-pocked.

Home sweet home.

Angels...it was angels at first.
A couple dozen of 'em,
wearin' cavalry boots and spurs.

15 / Fresh Dreams

The sun had finally set, it being the longest day of the year, and a cool breeze chilled me. We all sat in the dark bare parlor, a small fire sputtering in the grate. Romulus tended to it while the bare-headed Tyrell stared out of a broken east window as if he expected every Yankee soldier in Washington to come screaming out of the murk. It turned out that the captain had been staying at the house for a few days, on and off, and had laid in a supply of hardtack, beans, bacon, and coffee. The well out back still flowed sweet, so we had plenty of water for drinking, cooking, and washing.

Crickets chirped all around us. At least, I hoped they were crickets and not poor witched farmers or unlucky soldiers. Other than the bugs, the fire, and the wind all that could be heard—if you had Jasper-boosted ears, anyway—was the upstairs whispering of Roberta and Ernie. I'd seen them soaring past us as we neared the house. A harmless-sounding question to Tyrell about horse care in wartime had distracted him long enough for my friends to land on a window ledge. As soon as I could I'd sneak upstairs and let them know what was going on. *Maybe by then I'll actually know. Miracles happen.*

"Nice house," I said, more to break the silence than to demonstrate my appreciation of Southern architecture. Actually, it was a pretty impressive place—two stories, bay windows down below and gables above, fancy-carved ceiling molding, paneled cherry doors, widow's walk on the roof. Pricey rugs remained on the oak floors. The owners must've had to flee too suddenly to have taken them. "Pity they had to leave it."

"No choice," Tyrell muttered, turning away from his sentry post. "They were tarred, feathered, and sent across the river on a rail for accommodating the Yankees."

That made me shudder. Folks tend to laugh when they hear tell about an angry mob tarring people, especially if they think they deserved it. But it's an awful thing. Often the tar was not just melted, but heated to boiling. The victim—usually stripped naked—could be horribly scalded. Even if they weren't, the cooled tar had to be torn, peeled, or cut off, leaving ugly scars for life. And a long ride on a sharp rail would strip the hide from bare legs and crotch. I'd seen it all happen in Maryland once, four years before, to a shopkeeper who'd cheated his customers. The memory of his screams had kept little eight year-old Verity awake at night for weeks.

"Tough justice," I breathed, standing and stretching. Tyrell twitched his long moustache. "Could've been worse. At least their necks weren't stretched. And this house is still standing.

Sometimes the mobs burn them, to prevent a return of the traitors. If they're feeling charitable, they allow the owners to leave first."

*Makes you wonder who decided to call it a **Civil** War.*

Stretching and yawning, the cavalryman turned from the window. He'd decided that the Washington City garrison planned no sudden rush on his position this night. The captain smoothed his long dark hair where his short-billed cap had mussed it. Half its buttons undone, the gray jacket revealed a sweat-stained white shirt. The fine tall riding boots dozed in a corner by the fire. Despite all of this relaxation on our host's part, his formidable pistol remained against his thigh in its fancy holster. I wasn't sure if this readiness for action showed a standard wartime caution or his less than total trust of us.

"We'll need to maintain a sentry all night," he announced, peering at a gold watch that looked to be some kind of family treasure. "Two hours each should do it. It's nine o'clock now. Your darky can take the first and the last. I'll take second and you take third, missy. Too many renegades and deserters to let our guard down, to say nothing of enemy patrols. Bluebelly cavalry isn't much to worry about normally, but even they can carry the day if we're caught napping."

If Romulus resented being given an extra guard shift, he didn't let it show on his placid face. It bothered me that he was so able to slip right back into his slave mode. But then, he'd only been free for a couple of months. What bothered me even more was remembering that Morphageus would lose most of its power in another day. *Have to get away to talk to Jasper about that.*

Tyrell said he should check on his horse. When he'd donned his boots again and gone out to the maple tree Alcibiades was tied to, I slid over to the hearth where Romulus fussed at the logs with an iron poker. I wanted to take advantage of our brief moment of privacy. Up till then Tyrell hadn't left us alone for a second.

"Hey," I whispered, "I have to go upstairs for a minute. Ernie and Roberta are up there. Need to let 'em in on our new situation."

The Marshal didn't ask how I knew that our friends were in the house. Either he'd heard them already—I felt sure that his canine hearing hadn't all been lost when he'd been made human—or he naturally assumed that I had. "OK, miss," he nodded. "That Reb asks 'bout you, I just say you off explorin' like kids do. Be careful now. I don't trust him much. Apart from him bein' a Reb, they's somethin' not quite right 'bout him."

"Maybe," I said, "but my Stone ain't given me a warning."

"It might not. The Stone only goes cold 'round monsters and dark magic. If he's just a normal Merchantry spy you'll get no notice from it."

"Oh," I sighed. Here I'd been thinking I had a magic villain detector all this time. *Guess I'll have to start payin' attention to things more, then.*

The stairs had been well-made, like the rest of the old house, and didn't creak a lot. I made it to the second floor without making much noise. Good thing my eyes were Jaspered because it looked gloomier than General McClellan's prospects up there. None of the firelight reached the four empty bedrooms and not much of the meager moonlight came through the windows, even though the drapes had been stripped away long ago. There was a musty smell of sadness, as if something lingered of the poor unlucky folks who'd once been happy there. A careful listen told me that Ernie and Roberta were hidden in a small room on the north side. I could hear sloppy chewing sounds.

"Boo," I whispered, closing the door careful-like behind me.

"Boo yourself, missy," Ernie said around a mouthful of reddish gooshy stuff. He and Roberta were sharing a snack. The window ledge they sat on was a sticky wet mess.

"Where'd you get a ripe peach?" I asked with envy.

"Ask your new friend. They're outta his saddlebag," the pirate parrot replied.

The mouse burped and picked his teeth with his knitting needle. "Stolen yummies always taste better. It hit the spot."

"You find anythin' else in his bags?"

Roberta shook her scarlet head. "Nothin' incriminatin'. No secret codes or maps or other such fun stuff."

Ernie made a disgusted sound. "There never is. Just once I'd like to have a spy handed to me on a silver platter like that."

His partner chortled. "Remind me to tell you 'bout the time I caught an enemy ship's surgeon smugglin' plans for a Marshals' attack in his underwear."

"I shudder to think of the circumstances that led to that

graphic discovery."

"You and me both, bucko. Three hundred pounds of Belgian lard he was. In fact—"

Tyrell wouldn't be distracted for long. I had to get moving. "Can we save that tasty reminiscence for later, please? I have to get back downstairs in a minute." While Jasper grew himself some little arms and legs so he could do cartwheels and backflips around the room, I told them about meeting Tyrell and what few clues he'd dropped about himself. "Can you poke around the territory tonight, check in with any contacts you might have, eavesdrop on Reb scouts, whatever it takes? Find out if he's on the up-and-up or whether we need to get shed of him quick?"

Saluting with her broad wing, Roberta whispered, "Aye-aye. I'll have a talk with the pigeons and the jays. They're the nosiest birds around."

"And I can sneak into the closest Confederate headquarters," Ernie offered. "Chin with the field mice. They always keep their ears open while they're rummagin' through the mess scraps."

"Great," I said. "Thanks. If you get goin' now you'll have six or seven hours till dawn. We move south at first light."

Ernie stretched and tied his needle tighter around his round belly. "South to where? To the ship or to your ma?"

"Don't know yet. Both, I hope. Have to get past Richmond and them two armies first."

"Won't be easy," Roberta said. "Couple hundred thousand troops and their baggage trains...they'll clog all the roads. Be suspicious and trigger-happy. Might want to start thinkin' 'bout a disguise and a cover story."

"Got one already."

"No, I mean a real disguise."

I shook my head. "Like the beaver? No, thank you! You got no idea how much that hurt."

Ernie laughed and climbed onto Roberta's back. "Oh, I think she does, girlie. Talk to Jasper. There's other ways to change your face without shape-shiftin'."

That was news to me. "Really? I have to sneak away later to gab with him anyhow. He's gonna explain the ground rules about how to use Morphageus."

Now it was the bird's turn to laugh. "Like to be a fly on that wall." Ernie nodded in agreement.

"Why?" I asked with a concerned frown. Did everybody know all about this stuff but me? "What's he gonna say?"

"You'll find out soon enough, missy. See you at dawn." With that Roberta eased out of the window and launched herself into the murk.

After staring after them for a moment until even my magicked eyes lost them, I re-cupped Jasper and crept back down the stairs. Tyrell hadn't returned. After looking out the front window and seeing nothing, I filled Romulus in on what our two friends were doing. Then I left him to keep an eye out and curled up in a corner to take a nap until my sentry shift at one a.m. I used my haversack as a pillow and my wool jacket as a blanket, curling into a tight little ball near the fire. Even after sleeping all day, I still had no trouble nodding off in no time.

And falling straight into a new dream.

The last time I'd slept, exhausted from my first hectic and horrifying night as Stone Warden, there had been no dreams. Not a one. At least, none that I'd remembered. All the previous images of golden men, black dogs, and creepy kids—clearly some sort of premonition—had been flushed out of my head. Maybe once a dream came true I had no need for it and the next premonition would take its place. *Is this part of carryin' the Stone? Is it a natural outcome of holdin' Morphageus? Or is somebody sendin' me dreams like a telegraph operator? Who could do that? And why?*

My new visions came like pictures in a scrapbook. Sometimes they were written words, like the kind you cut out of a newspaper and paste in. Other times they were realistic images, as you'd get in a normal dream. Once the words turned into a face, but it was of no one I knew. Not a lot of sounds seemed to accompany the visions, just some weird singing voices in a strange language in the background.

Angels...it was angels at first. A couple dozen of them, wearing boots and spurs. They flew over country that looked like the part of Virginia we were passing through. One of them held me in his arms. We dodged giant letters in the sky, all jumbled up and not spelling any words that I could make out. In some of the letters were people in strange foreign-looking outfits. Other letters held Bullies. On the ground below us somebody led the black dog from my old dream, now with a spiked collar, toward a large purple-and-gold ship that sat on a beach made of skulls.

Standing tall on the shore were three figures with swords and other scary-looking weapons I didn't recognize. Facing them stood a young woman in a fancy hooped dress and wide-brimmed hat. I couldn't see her face. She held the armed figures at bay with a whip. Then the angel dropped me. I fell forever and landed hard on the skull beach. Ma picked me up, smiling, then threw me through the air onto the ship. Roberta caught me in her beak before I could hit the deck and handed me to Tyrell. Farther out to sea, a giant whale swam toward us like a rocket.

I woke with a gasp just as the whale was about to ram the ship. My whole body shook. Blinking, I looked around the room. Romulus snoozed beside the last faint embers of the fire. Leaning next to the front window, Captain Tyrell stared out at the wide and empty lawn, arms and ankles crossed. When I sat up and stretched he turned his handsome head in my direction and smiled.

"A fine alarm clock you have in your head, Miss Mary," he said, unlimbering his feet and ambling away from the window. "It's just one o'clock. Time for your guard duty."

"Fine by me," I told him, rolling my head to uncrick my neck. "Weren't sleepin' too well anyhow."

"So I gathered. You were twitching something awful. Bad dreams?"

I struggled to my feet, which seemed to be asleep still. "Maybe a little."

"Can't say as I'm surprised, you being away from home on such a difficult quest." Tyrell had brought in his saddle and blanket. He lay down on them as a makeshift bed, the same way I imagined he'd done every night since the war had started. "Well, you keep a sharp eye out all around the house for the next couple of hours, then wake your Jim to do the same. Make certain you don't fall asleep now. Endanger us all if you do. Haven't seen anything out there yet, but you never can tell. Every now and then take a stroll around the house. Do it at irregular times, so your movements can't be predicted if there are scouts about. Make sure Alcibiades is secure and can reach his water. Toss some rocks into the trees to see if anything moves. You see or hear anything that's not a mouse, you run and wake me, hear?"

"Yes, sir," I answered, smiling inside at his talk of the mouse. I'd almost corrected him when he'd called me Mary. *Better get my cover story straight in my head and keep it there.*

"Good girl. See you in the morning." With that he rolled over and started in to snoring, dead asleep in a second as only veteran soldiers can do.

I waited a few minutes to let him get full asleep, taking a look out the window and still seeing nothing. Putting my coat and cap on, I made my way out the back door to do as he'd told me. Behind the house I found the well, a trampled garden, and a couple of sheds. One looked like it had once held tools and the other had been the carriage house. Both were empty now, stripped bare by vengeance and common wartime looting. In the trees beside the tool shed I came across Tyrell's golden horse, looming even larger at night than he had in the light of day.

Alcibiades munched the grass at his broad feet while giving me a look that seemed to demand I genuflect.

"Hey, there, Al," I whispered, keeping my ears peeled for anyone who might be lurking in the trees. I rubbed his velvety muzzle. Al checked for an apple in my hand as a matter of course. When he came up empty, he turned away with a snort.

"Sorry, fella. Maybe next time." A tour around the house showed me that we were still safely alone. I saw no sign of Roberta or Ernie, so they were still off spying. I hoped they made it back in time and without running into any trouble. I knew that they'd been taking care of themselves for years, but my new dream had me spooked, not least because I had no idea what any of it meant. For all I could tell the whole thing foretold disaster for them.

After going back into the parlor to check on Tyrell, who slept like a righteous man or a very comfortable villain, I tiptoed out back again. Finding Al still okay, I crept into the windowless tool shed, the farthest building away from the house. I didn't want any surprises while talking to Jasper.

"Wake up, sleepyhead," I said in a semi-loud voice, tin cup in hand. I preferred speaking aloud to him when I could. It made me feel like Tommy, or something resembling Tommy anyways, still stuck by me.

"You're a fine one to talk," Jasper said, the tin cup flowing out into the black shape of Morphageus. It sprouted cartoony hands and feet, then hopped out of my grip to do pushups on the dirt floor. "Have any good dreams lately?"

I scowled at him. "Was that you?"

He held up his cute little hands in mock outrage. "Me? Oh, lordy no! How you wound me, child!"

"What was it, then? I can tell it's like the other dream. That one came true, near as I can tell. What does this one mean? Where does it come from?"

"Dream interpretation's somethin' you'll have to work out on your own. I'm **in** your head but I'm not **of** your head, if you catch my meanin'." As he spoke he leapt up to the rafters and started swinging while humming a playground tune.

Sighing, I grit my teeth, then tried to relax. "Well, what about where they come from? Are they just dreams that come with the Stone, or is somebody makin' 'em happen from the outside?"

"The Stone doesn't cause dreams or visions by itself. It only magnifies the Warden's natural gifts. That means you already have the Sight, even if it's so slight that you ain't aware of it, or you have the talent for receivin' the thoughts of others."

"Which is it most likely to be?"

He dropped from the rafters with a back-flip and wrapped himself around me as if we were about to waltz. His blood-warm hands probed my skull like a phrenologist. "Hmmm. Offhand, I'd say the second one. You're gettin' messages from somebody who has the Sight."

"You can tell that from gropin' my head?"

"No. I can tell that from the fact that you have no idea that a few dozen men are about to attack the house."

He pointed his giant pistol right at my face.
Like staring into a railroad tunnel.
Any second I'd see the bright light of the locomotive.
Then I wouldn't see anything else.

16 / Hellfiend Legion

I crossed my arms and raised an eyebrow at Jasper. "Uh-huh."

"Would these lips lie?"

"You ain't got no lips."

"Well, read 'em anyway... 'a-dozen-men-are-about-to-attack-the-house!'"

I sighed. "I was just out there, you know. Didn't see nothin', didn't hear nothin'."

Jasper's blade spread out into a big eye, then an ear. "And that logically means...what, Miss Stone Warden-for-a-day?"

After scrunching up my face and thinking, I said, "They were waitin' outta range. Maybe somebody in the house called 'em in when me and you came in here."

The sword clapped its adorable little hands. "Clever girl!"

I smacked my palm to my forehead. "I knew we couldn't trust that Reb!"

"What now?" asked Jasper. He acted like he was my tutor or

something.

"We sneak out and see what's up. Romulus is still snoozin' in the house. Don't want to let him get caught nappin'." I felt the Stone, but it lay quiet. "No magick or monsters so far. Are they just ordinary men? Not Bullies?"

Jasper jumped into my fist, his hands and feet disappearing in mid-air. "Let's go find out."

After a couple of long deep breaths I opened the door and my ears. Grass rustled outside, to the north and east of the house. Since the shed sat to the southwest, that meant that we were covered by the building for the moment. No sound or movement came from inside except Tyrell's snoring. *Is he fakin' that after sendin' these guys to us? Or is there somebody else out here helpin' 'em?* Since I hadn't spotted anybody yet it made sense to be cautious, so with a thought I made the sword into a black shield and held it in front of me. Whoever advanced on the house had discipline. No one spoke, laughed, coughed, or otherwise betrayed themselves. If they carried weapons, and times being what they were I had to believe they were armed to the teeth, they were all careful not to let any metal noises give their positions away. If it weren't for my magicked ears I'd never have known they were there.

Easing behind the shed and sidling to my left, I crept behind the square stone well and peeked around the corner to get my first look at the attackers. Three of them were in view now, tiptoeing through the apple orchard just north of the house, about thirty yards away. They wore pieces of Federal blue and

Rebel gray uniforms, mixed with civilian shirts and hats. Not a single one of them looked liked he'd bathed or shaved in weeks. All carried muskets with fixed bayonets and all had the hard look of professional soldiers on a do-or-die assault.

"Renegades," I said in my mind to Jasper. "Deserters from both armies. They mean to cut our throats and take whatever they think we have."

No time to warn Romulus. I could see another three following twenty yards behind the first bunch. Beyond them, a bit further from the house and on the side we'd first come from that afternoon, six more were coming on. This was all up to me. No help would come from Marshals or seagulls or anybody else. And I had to do it quick and quiet or they'd all rush me at once. I had my doubts that even Morphageus could beat those odds.

"Jasper, listen real careful to what I want to do." I laid things out for him in the few seconds we had while sneaking around behind the first six attackers. He agreed that it was not only possible, but would be fun. *Easy for him to say, he won't end up dead if things go wrong.* I swallowed hard, broke into a run, and did it.

The only warning the three in the rear had was the *boing* of the giant springs on my feet as Morphageus bounced me into the air like he'd done against Venoma. By the time they'd turned to see what went on behind them, the springs had flowed up my body to my arms and shaped itself into honest-to-goodness bat wings. My belly lurched. *Jiminy! This is crazy! I'm flyin'! We're higher than our hayloft back in Maryland. Maybe this is a really stupid idea.*

With Jasper's aid I shakily glided down onto the renegades from twenty feet up. As I landed without a sound, every muscle tensed for a crash, one wing thumped into a head, another into a neck. As the third turned to see what had dropped his comrades, the hilt of Morphageus laid him low with a one-two to the belly and skull. Whipping around to crouch behind a tree, I tried to stop my terrified panting and my stomach churning. This wasn't like Bully-fighting. I'd just hurt real people. I'd felt their bones crunch. The other three had turned around at the sound of my assault. As they came toward me I reminded myself that they couldn't see me in the dark, but I could see them. *Okay, then. No time to whimper. Let's go.*

The nearest one went down with a surprised gasp as the boomerang bounced off his noggin and returned to me. When the man beside him crouched down to check on his condition, a metallic fist flew out of my hand and boxed him to sleep. By this time, the last renegade had realized that he was under attack and had raised his musket. But I was beside him in the gloom now, and Morphageus cut his gun in two like a dry twig. When he tried to run, the magick blade snaked around his throat to choke him into dreamland.

All of it had happened in thirty frantic seconds. I dropped down into the tall grass at the edge of the orchard. Six down, six to go. I knew that later I'd upchuck from the terror of it all, but right now the Stone seemed to protect me from the worst of normal feelings. Good thing, too, because now the other deserters knew that something had gone wrong with their careful plan. Their leader, a bulky fellow with a heavy cavalry saber in one hand and a Colt revolver in the other, looked straight at me and froze. *So much for hidin' in the grass.* With a hiss he snapped the sword in my direction. All of his men turned as one unit and rushed me, silent as death. Pretty good simile, considering the circumstances.

I should've been in a total panic, me a little girl and them hard desperate killers. But it felt like the Stone put out a calming energy that slowed things down and gave me time to think. What I thought of was to run into the thickest part of the orchard, a new longer shield hanging off my shoulder. It covered every inch of me from head to toe while weighing less than my coat did. Up till now the renegades had valued silence over anything else, but there was no telling when they might abandon that in favor of shooting.

No bullets came my way. I was lighter than they were, and in better physical condition, since I hadn't been living as rough as them and had witched legs. Scampering into the woods like a bunny, I put a little distance between us, zigzagging between the trees. *I need the perfect tree, preferably one that don't talk. Hey, this'll do.* It had a dense coat of leaves, but also had a strong horizontal branch about eight feet off the ground. Heavy footsteps pounded behind me, sounding closer than they really were because of my wonder-hearing. I'd already let Jasper know about the new plan and he was ready. My arm tugged the shield from my back. By the time my hand flashed forward and up

Morphageus had become a thin steel cable with a grappling hook on its far end. It snaked around the branch and bit hard. My momentum and lots of pulling jerked me up onto the limb in a flash. *Good thing me and Tommy climb trees all the time.* Wiggling against the trunk to hide in the foliage, I waited for my pursuers.

They came at a trot, in a skirmish line, several yards apart, two to my left just below me and three farther to my right. The one who'd sent them after me stayed about thirty feet back, weapons ready. In a normal battle that arrangement made sense, since a cannon shell would likely cause a single casualty, instead of wrecking the whole formation. But in this situation all it did was put them too far apart to gang up on me. Before they could become aware of that, I took a deep breath and struck.

My metal bullwhip snapped down, wrapping around the closest soldier's arm. I yanked with all my might. He crashed hard into the trunk of my tree. Shaking the whip loose, I boomeranged his companion and then looked to my right. Things had happened so fast that all they knew was that two of their men had vanished. They threw themselves onto the ground. Now I heard the unsettling sound of muskets being ratcheted to full-cock. *Guess the silent treatment's about to end. Now what?*

Still choosing to make no sound, their leader pointed up at my tree. He crouched back far enough that he could see everything that had happened. Good night vision, too, it seemed. I couldn't let his men react and start shooting. Three bullets at once might be more than I could defend against. Springing up and out of the apple tree, I bat-winged again, soaring over the tree closest to the trio. The instant I landed Morphageus flashed in both hands, angry scarlet runes glowing along its blade. With every bit of strength my body could muster I swung the magick sword. It bit into the lower trunk of the twenty-foot tree. I felt no more resistance than from cutting a cattail. With a snapping creak it fell over like a lady fainting from a too-tight corset.

Right onto the three alarmed renegades.

Lots of panicked yelling commenced. Silence was no longer golden. From the sound I guessed that one of the attackers wouldn't be talking for a while but that the other two more than made up for him. They clawed at the branches that pinned them to the ground. One caterwauled that his shoulder had been broken and the other screeched for help from his sergeant. *Sergeant? Oh, their leader. Where's he?* I whipped around to where the sword-wielder had been a moment before, my shield up and ready to take a pistol ball.

Nothing. He was gone.

I spun in all directions, using my magicked sight to see if he was trying to flank me. Nope. He rushed back north as fast as his legs could get the job done. In a second I lost him as he crested a low ridge and disappeared, probably heading for the nearest tavern. I imagined him drinking half a bottle of whiskey and telling some barkeep about the tiny monster that had bested eleven grown men with guns.

"Whoo!" Jasper hollered. Good thing only I could hear him. "Verity the Valiant! You are the Stone Warden Extraordinaire, girl!"

I sagged down into the grass like a soggy rag, all my battle-born strength sapped. Shivering, I curled up into a ball, hands over my ears to block out the yells of the men under the tree. Other voices joined them, as most of the renegades I'd clobbered struggled into wakefulness. They groaned about their injuries and started moving north. Some crawled, some stumbled to their feet. None paid me any mind or even looked like they knew where I was. They just wanted to get away from the awful nightmare that had laid them low. Me, too.

"I don't wanna do this," I moaned to Jasper and to anybody else who might be able to read my thoughts. "Monsters, magicians, runnin', fightin', flyin'—**flyin'!**—hurtin' people...I wanna go home." I blubbered into my dirty coat sleeve, Morphageus on the ground in front of me, a tin cup again.

Jasper's voice managed to sound young and ancient at the same time. "That's why it has to be you. No one who wants the Stone, who desires its power, can be allowed to have it. No one who craves the Sword and glories in its destructiveness can be trusted. That's why all such mortals who try will be slain trying to wield it."

"I might've killed somebody here. That ain't me. I just play-act with swords. It's make-believe. Give this to some war hero, some strong man who wants to charge the enemy and save civilization. Give it to Mr. Lincoln and let him find a real Stone

Warden."

The cup melted into a hand. It felt as warm and giving as a real human hand. Running along my cheek in an almost paternal gesture, Jasper said, "It doesn't work that way. The Stone finds its own master, and it's never wrong." Standing on two fingers like a tiny person, the hand jabbed its thumb at me and added, "If it makes you feel any better, all Stone Wardens have felt this way. It's a sign that you're the right one for the quest."

I sat up. The pained voices had all but faded away. All three deserters pinned by the tree had been freed. A light breeze cooled my cheeks where tears had wet them. "All Stone Wardens? I'm not the first?" Somehow that made me feel better. Misery really does love company. *And my enemy, an evil company, really does love misery. Oh, ain't I clever in adversity?*

"A few. The Merchantry's not the first bunch of lunkheads to try to run the world, you know. They're just the nastiest, and the best at it."

"And the lunkheads always lose?"

"So far. Don't ruin our record, okay?"

That got a smile out of me. I held out a palm and he hopped onto it. Clasping that shimmery hand hard, I felt better. Almost like holding Tommy's, or Ma's, when I'd felt down. "Thanks."

"My pleasure." He jerked my arm around to the north, turning into a telescope for an instant. A goofy eye bulged out of it, then I held Morphageus again, runes all fiery. "Oh-oh!"

I leapt up, heart pounding. "Oh-oh? Oh-oh's usually bad. What's with the oh-oh?"

A finger flowed out of the sword tip, pointing to where all of the renegades had gone. I made a pained face. Partly because I ached from fighting, partly from seeing that they were coming back, most of them. In front jogged the guy with the saber. He didn't have a happy look on his face. Neither did I, I felt sure of that. Because the ten or so reinforcements he'd hidden behind the hill had now joined the rest. Close to twenty angry armed men were running at us, guns raised to fire.

"Time to go, I think," I muttered.

"Wise decision, Venerable Savior of Mankind," Jasper snickered. "They don't look like they're about to export any love in your direction."

I didn't bother answering. I was already sprinting for the house. Raising the sword to my lips, it became a giant bugle just as I started blowing. A raggedy but fierce cavalry call blared through the still Virginia night. That made me glad I'd watched so many army drills around Washington City. After doing it a second time, I chanced a look over my shoulder. My pursuers had stopped, expecting horsemen to charge them. When that didn't happen, they commenced their advance again. *Oh, well.* It'd bought me a few extra steps. And maybe Tyrell and Romulus were awake now.

With Jasper now covering my back as a shield, I swerved to the rear of the house. If Tyrell started shooting from his window, I didn't want to be in his line of fire. It was possible he was working with the onrushing enemy. I knew he had the one pistol and his sword. He might have more weapons on his saddle that I hadn't noticed, but that still didn't change the fact that the odds, with Romulus, were still seven-to-one. And though I might've been able to take down quite a few if left to myself, I didn't dare risk showing Morphageus to Tyrell until I knew for certain whose side he was on. No good winning a battle just to have a horde of Bullies show up at his call, if he turned out to be a Merchantry agent.

My change of direction proved a good decision. No sooner had I darted to my right than a swarm of leaden bees slammed into the side of the house. It sounded like someone with an enormous arm had thrown a handful of rocks against the hardwood panels. Glass flew everywhere from a shattered window. *Whoa! Close! Run, run, run!* I skidded around the corner of the house, noticing that Alcibiades had disappeared. Did Tyrell run off and leave us? Or did the musket volley spook his mount? Not likely, since he was a war horse. But in my experience, the bravest horses could still shy at their own shadows for no earthly reason.

A kick opened the back door for me while I used both hands to pull the shield from my back and make a cup out of it. *You're innocent cowardly little Mary Williams, remember. No magick, no fightin' unless there's no choice left.* I shrieked like the dainty girls at school would do whenever they saw a bug.

"Cap'n! Cap'n! Help!" I screeched, the door not yet closed behind me. As if he were a genie I'd just called by rubbing the lamp, the Reb officer appeared at the other end of the kitchen. Unlike a genie, he didn't seem ready to do my bidding.

He pointed his giant pistol right at my face.

It was like staring into a railroad tunnel. Any second I'd see the bright light of the locomotive. Then I wouldn't see anything else. *Oh, you're stupid, Verity Sauveur. Dumb, dumb, dumb! Delivered yourself right to 'em you did.* Figuring secrecy didn't matter much now, I started to bring up the cup to make a shield of it, but it was too late. My eardrums split with the pistol's crack before my hand got halfway up. Teeth gritted and shoulders hunched, I waited for the end.

The end came, but not for Verity. Tyrell had fired over my shoulder at a target behind me. Thick white smoke wrapped around my head as I felt the bullet *zizz* past my left ear. Somebody gurgled near the back door and fell heavily against the jamb. The captain dashed past me, blazed away at someone else, then slammed the door. After throwing the bolt he ran back toward the parlor, grabbing me by my coat collar. Half-dragging me with him, he growled, "Are you mad, girl? What did you do to bring them down on us?"

I shook myself loose and crouched in a corner. "Nothin', sir. I was only makin' my sentry rounds like you told me to. They commenced to rushin' the house just as soon as I turned the corner."

"Well, we're in for it now. Must be almost a whole platoon out there. They won't try the back door for a bit, not with two men down on their first try. They'll go for the other door, or more likely a window. We can't watch them all. If they assault several places at once then we're done for. Have to hope we guess right and make them pay dear for whatever choice they make."

Romulus kept watch at the front door, which stood open a tiny crack. He lay on his belly, peering out across the front lawn. "Nothin' this way yet, sir."

Tyrell reloaded his gun, which I recognized earlier as a LeMat revolver, using the ramrod built onto it. I'd seen one displayed by a Union sergeant. He'd taken it off a dead grayback, or so he claimed. They were the only ones who tended to use them. It held nine .42 caliber bullets, bad news for any renegades who got close. If Tyrell stayed patient and picked his shots with care he could cut our attackers down to half-strength in a hurry. But I doubted that these seasoned fighters would be foolish enough to rush through a doorway and let him mow them down. My ears told me that they were coming from at least three different directions now.

Pulling a small ivory-gripped pistol out of his boot, he handed it to me butt-first. A four-shot pepperbox, it was scarcely larger than my palm. It amounted to a revolver with no barrel. After every shot you had to turn the thing to line up the next chamber. No accuracy at all, I'd heard, unless you jammed it right up against somebody, but better than nothing, especially since I couldn't use Morphageus.

"What's this?" I asked.

"In case they get by me," Tyrell replied in a preoccupied voice.

"I can't shoot somebody," I whined in my best poor-little-

Mary voice. "Give it to Jim." I pointed to Romulus, who turned his head halfway, keeping an eye on the front.

You'd have thought I'd asked Tyrell to boil himself alive. "Are you daft, child? Arm a slave?"

"He raised me from a babe," I shot back, stamping my foot and pouting like I'd seen spoiled rich plantation girls do in Maryland. "Taken care of me all my life. I don't think he's about to kill us and join them renegades."

With a shake of his head, the Confederate sighed, "Fool modern notions." He unhooked the saber from his belt and slid it across the wooden floor to Romulus. "There. That's as far as I can go."

Romulus closed the door, stood, and drew the sword. It looked like a toy in his huge mitt. The heavy steel scabbard stayed in his other paw as a handy club. "They's goin' 'round the back, sir. Front's clear."

With a sour laugh Tyrell said, "No it's not. That's what they want us to think." Hammering almost drowned out his words as musket butts pounded on the back door. "I've seen this bunch before. Hunted them, in fact." He picked up his saddle and headed for the hall. "Hellfiend Legion, they call themselves. Bounty jumpers and deserters. The scum of both armies. They leave no prisoners as a matter of policy." As two windows on opposite sides of the house were smashed in, he opened the cellar door and tossed the saddle down. "Land pirates, that's what they are. Scum, yes. But clever scum all the same. There's an ambush waiting us out front, I'll bet my mother on it. No escape that way."

Tyrell half-cocked his pistol and shoved me down the basement steps. He hollered at the top of his lungs, "Upstairs, everyone! We'll sell our lives dear from up there!" Booted feet stomped across the floors of the empty house. Motioning for Romulus to follow me, he whispered, "That should buy us time to secure this door. Going upstairs is a death trap for us and they know it. They'll look there first and they'll be careful about going up the steps." He pushed us down the steps, swept our footprints from the floor with his hat, and closed the door. It boasted a strong lock on the inside. I wondered why. If they'd sealed up slaves in the cellar as punishment, or while waiting for a sale, the lock should've been on the outside. Determined men would make short work of it, but then they'd have to fight their way down a narrow stair, one at a time, silhouetted in the doorway with no place to hide from that awful gun.

With the door shut it was black as Hades. Our well-prepared guardian struck a match, though, and soon an old oil lamp that had somehow survived the looting showed us our new refuge from a ceiling hook at the base of the steps. The basement looked a mess, but not as clean-picked as the rest of the house. An old mattress, boxes of rags, a broken pitchfork, spare bottles of lamp oil, a rack of spoiled pickles in jars, and other assorted junk items cluttered the lumpy dirt floor. No windows, even the usual tiny ones most cellars had, were in the upper walls. Somebody had wanted this place to be tight. And it was...a nice tight prison for us.

"What now?" I whispered, pausing to listen as heavy feet clumped above us. "Once they see that we ain't upstairs after all, they'll have only one other place to look."

Nodding in agreement, Tyrell murmured, "Don't I know it. But this is the best of a lot of bad choices. No way out for us means no way in for them. They won't be keen to come down those steps one at a time to be picked off. They're raiders. That means they prefer easy takings and running to fighting skirmishes. If they were lovers of battle they'd never have left the army."

"But won't they just wait us out?"

"No point. Come dawn they'll be at risk of being spotted by a cavalry patrol from either army. That volley they fired at you will have piqued someone's interest, this close to Washington. When the sun comes up they'll want to be hiding in a patch of woods someplace. The Legion is badly wanted by both sides." He started tearing rags into long thin strips, indicating that we should do the same. "Besides, they'll have already noticed that we have no loot worth the fight. Tactical logic dictates that we aren't worth the casualties they'd take." He tied a rag strip across the railing of the stairs, a few inches up. I saw what he wanted and added mine. Soon we had a tangle of tripwires ready for anyone who came at us. Romulus soaked the treads in lamp oil to make them slippery, as well. We piled the heavy wooden rag boxes up in a wall at the bottom of the stairs. Throwing the mattress over it, we took shelter behind our barrier. The second we did so the cellar door exploded from a series of mighty kicks.

Musket balls splintered the front row of boxes. Crazed voices screamed doom at us and shadowy figures clattered down the steps.

So much for tactical logic.

I dove for the room's opposite corner
as my Marshal bodyguard
took the head from the nearest foe.
It bounced into my lap, blood splattering my face.

17 / Pickles

Explosions, gun smoke, and curses pretty near overwhelmed my heightened senses. Tyrell took down the first three men with as many shots. *Guess they drew the short straws.* One fell near the door and got hauled back up by his fellows. The other two rag-dolled down the steps to crash into our box wall, scooting it back a foot and demolishing our careful tripwires. I squeaked, and not just to stay in character as pitiful Mary. Men had been shot dead in front of me, their hot red blood pooling near my foot. I scrunched back. This wasn't like skewering Bullies, who most likely weren't alive the way we'd think of it, or muck monsters. Real red murder was being done in this small space, to protect me. I hoped I'd prove worth all the slaughter.

As soon as the door had been cleared another pair charged us, hoping that the first wave had undone our defense. They found out different, as both went down to the captain's deadly aim. A quarter of the Legion had died already, heaped at the foot of the stairs. I thought of the awful battle at Shiloh in Tennessee two months before, where the dead in the Hornet's Nest were said to have been stacked like cordwood. My young mind boggled at the thought of hundreds, even thousands, being massacred like this. *No wonder men desert the army, if they're exposed to this sort of thing on a regular basis.*

Tyrell had four shots left, by my count, and so did I. Our enemy still had around fifteen men to throw at us, if they had the stomach for it. Maybe they didn't. The cellar door banged shut and for a few moments we sat in silence, ears ringing. Whispers and scratchings above told us that our foes hadn't chosen to retreat yet.

"I guess five was enough to lose," mused Tyrell. He turned to rummage in a pouch on his saddle. "Time to reload. If they try again it'll be with something different."

Truer words had never been spoken. While his back was to the door it snapped halfway open. Something round and heavy bounced down the steps, sparks spitting out behind it. They'd tossed an artillery shell at us! Before I could think of what I was doing I'd shoved Tyrell face-down into the filthy floor and kept him there with my foot. Ignoring his outraged grunt of surprise, I squared off to the shell, tin cup swinging as it bounced one last time, clearing the barrier. By the time I made contact with it Morphageus had answered my wish. A steel tennis racket swatted the cannonball back at the door, flying through the diminishing opening as the renegades yelled and tried to close it.

The instant the door shut a sharp crack split it down the middle. Screams of pain and fear, muffled by the damaged door, told us that somebody—several somebodies—had been hoisted with their own petard. Stinging smoke snaked through the cracked door. Our odds had improved some more. Maybe now they'd decide to cut their losses and go bother somebody else.

"What happened?" asked Tyrell, dusting himself off and looking up at the demolished door.

"They threw a shrapnel shell, sir," said Romulus, eyeing my bat in warning. I shrank it back into a cup before Tyrell could think to look my way. "Miss Mary shove you aside and throw it right back at 'em. How 'bout dat?"

Giving me a long, hard look, one eyebrow up, the Reb said, "Well, Miss Williams, there's more sand in you than I first judged to be the case. Well done. But perhaps you should leave the real fighting to the men, hmm?"

It took a lot of effort to not roll my eyes at that, my experiences of the last couple of days being what they were. But blurting out something like 'When was the last time **you** battled poison-spitting demons, Mr. Smarty-pants?' wasn't going to help our cause any. Besides, right then another shift in our fortunes drew my attention. While we'd been focused on repelling the assaults down the stairs, our enemies had been flanking us. A hole appeared in the ceiling with a tremendous screeching of nails.

"They pryin' up the flo'!" Romulus hollered, launching himself behind us to where a filthy hand waved a Colt revolver in our direction. The saber slashed at it. Just as the gun fired the hand, still clutching the weapon, flew into a corner of the cellar.

Its owner yowled and fell back from the hole. Somebody else jammed a Springfield musket barrel in his place, only to jerk away when he felt the sword's point in his face. I hoped they were out of cannon shells or our brave defense would have a sudden end.

"Lunacy!" Tyrell shouted, aiming up at the opening. "This makes no sense. Why do they want us so much? What do they think we have?"

Before he could take that thought far enough to start asking direct embarrassing questions of me, the door crashed open again and more renegades fired muskets at us. They missed as we hurled ourselves against the walls, but that just gave those above their chance. More boards wrenched free and three snarling men dropped amongst us.

Tyrell shouted for Romulus to deal with the falling attackers. I dove for the room's opposite corner as my Marshal bodyguard took the head from the nearest foe. It bounced into my lap, blood splattering my face. Kicking it away, I lost my meager dinner beneath the pickle jars with a sour belly-lurch. The captain's pistol roared four times. From the pained sounds that resulted it must have hit as many targets. Then I heard the hammer hit nothing. Reinforcements skidding down the oil-stairs shouted with malicious glee. *Oh-oh.*

Another of the enemies from above went down, smashed into a wall by Romulus. That left one more, but another pair dropped down to his aid. All were armed with Bowie knives or hatchets. A ferocious four-way fight commenced, almost too fast for me to follow. Romulus, his eyes ablaze with the eerie light I'd seen at St. Usher's, snapped the knee of one man with a vicious whip of the scabbard, then used the shrieking fellow as a shield while he fought the other three. Blades gleamed in the weak lamplight from thrusts parried and cuts dodged. No one spoke taunting words like you read in novels. They only grunted from their efforts. Jasper, though, sang "Dixie" off-key in my noggin.

At the base of the stairs Tyrell defended himself with the old pitchfork against two attackers with bayonets. His new weapon lacked a tine and over a foot of its handle, but was serviceable. The Legion fighters weren't used to close-quarter bayonet work and kept interfering with one another, to the Reb's advantage. He managed to grab the barrel of one musket. When its owner tried to jerk it back, Tyrell pushed as hard as he could. The unexpected shove, added to the enemy's own force, jabbed the musket's butt into his belly. He sat down with an *oof*. Tyrell tried to take the gun from his stunned hands, but just then the other man lunged at him and he had to leap away.

While the vicious fighting continued I tried to think what I could do to help. Scurrying farther back into my corner was the first genius tactic I came up with. I bumped hard into the pickle rack. Luckily, none of the jars fell on my head. In fact, they didn't budge an inch. One of Romulus' opponents flew past me, his arm opened to the bone by the saber. More legs appeared in the ceiling hole and in the upstairs doorway. We were about to be overwhelmed. I gripped my pepperbox harder and thought about how best to use it, much as I didn't want to shoot a man.

Its legendary inaccuracy would make it as dangerous to friend as to foe.

That was when it registered that the pickle jars should have moved...at least a little.

I peered hard at the rack they stood on, then wiggled it. *Hmmm.* All of the jars were pinned to their shelves with angled nails at the base and copper wire at the top. My fingers traced up the side of the rack, feeling behind it. *Ah, a latch! I thought so.* With a quick jerk I freed the catch. The whole rack swung open on a well-oiled hinge. I peered in with my magicked eyes. A tunnel. An honest-to-goodness tunnel. I could see food stores and smell fresh air. *So that's why the locals hated you folks so much. I bet this used to be an Underground Railroad station. Good for you, whoever you were. You've just saved our bacon.*

"Hold!" a deep harsh voice hollered. I turned my head to see who it was. At the top of the stairs stood the leader of the men I'd bested earlier. His face was unexceptional, but scarred and cruel. The oil lamp swung back-and-forth from being bumped during the fighting, making his features even eerier. He wore a Union general's hat, a Confederate artillery major's shell jacket, and heavy civilian pants like I'd seen on teamsters. At his rough command, the renegades ceased fighting. They had us all dead to rights anyway. Muskets poked through the doorway and through the ceiling gap. Our brave defense had failed.

No one looked my way yet. I closed the secret door until it just about latched again. A quick yank would open it. Romulus lowered his sword and Tyrell dropped his makeshift weapon.

His pistol pointed straight at the leader's face. The man didn't blink. In fact, he grinned. It wasn't one of those happy grins, though. More like the ones boys at school make just before they dip your pigtails in an inkwell.

"Nice try, but we all heard your hammer hit air. Drop it, if you please."

With a shrug the captain gave him a little 'Oh, well' smile and tossed the LeMat away, about three feet in front of me. Romulus did the same with the cavalryman's saber. *Now. Do it now.* I jumped up and ran to Tyrell, hugging him tight from behind and whimpering.

"Mister! Mister!" I blubbered, "whatever will happen to us now?"

His eyes grew wide for a split-second as he stared at me. I tried to send him a message with my own eyes, but couldn't be sure it'd worked. He ducked under the swinging lamp, which nearly thunked him in the head.

"Mind the lamp, sir," I added with a wink. *Think, Tyrell, think.*

His mouth twitched as if holding back a smile. His hand squeezed mine, then his face grew nasty. "Stupid brat! What do you mean 'us'? Look at the trouble you've got me into!" He shoved me away from him.

Right onto the LeMat. I rolled hard as if he'd pushed me with great force, which he hadn't. I ended up near the pickle rack, Tyrell's gun beneath my jacket. I howled in feigned misery. Romulus moved like he'd step to my aid, but I stopped him with a waggled finger. Then I looked at Tyrell. I read it in his eyes. He'd seen me take the gun. I just hoped he knew what happened next. And I was beyond glad that he hadn't yet used his gun's little surprise feature.

"Trouble!" said the enemy leader, not moving from his high vantage point. "Trouble's right. I've lost better than half my force because of you. Bested by a Reb, a darky, and a little girl. Good thing the reward's worth it."

Tyrell frowned. "Reward? For me?"

"Don't flatter yourself, grayback. Fer her." He nodded toward me. "Somebody wants that brat real bad. And they're payin' a chest of gold to whoever gets her."

Oops...now I knew why they'd fought so hard. Should've known this was no accident. The Merchantry sure had a long arm.

Tyrell gave him a shrewd eye. "And my people will pay just as much to get me back in one piece."

His people? Who were his people, I wondered. His rich family in Williamsburg? The Confederate government? Or somebody else?

The Legion commander laughed like an executioner who'd been offered a penny to just forget the whole thing. "Oh, I hardly think so. Any other time I might oblige you, but I've lost too many men. The boys here are itchin' for a bit o' retribution. Though fer you I might make it quick, fer a consideration. Call it professional courtesy." He glared at Romulus. "Afraid this buck ain't gonna get off so easy. Darky that size'll make fer fine sport in the woods. We'll hunt him like a bear the rest o' the night. Might wear his skin fer a while. That'll make an impression at our next raid."

Everyone except Romulus thought that was mighty funny. While all of them laughed and pointed at him, I took advantage of their eyes being elsewhere. I stood, reached under my jacket, and pulled out the pistol. A quick glance confirmed what I'd suspected about it. It felt heavy as an anvil in my little hands.

"No!" I barked, aiming the gun at the leader. "You won't!"

Dead silence fell on the whole group. You could've cut it with the proverbial knife. Then the guffaws roared back into life again.

"Kid, you should leave fightin' to the professionals," the hard man at the top of the stairs warned me, wiping away a tear of mirth. "There ain't no bullets in that gun."

I pulled the trigger for effect, knowing that nothing would happen. The loud click sent them all off into giggles again, but it also served to distract them while I thumb-flipped a lever on the hammer to its lower position and cocked it again. The Hellfiend Legion was about to get a lesson in Rebel weaponry...and in overconfidence.

"And y'all should pay more attention to Confederate pistol design." Tyrell inched backwards, knowing what was coming. "This here's a LeMat revolver. Clever-designed gadget, it is. See, this here gun revolves around a tube, instead of a pin like you have on a Colt. And that tube happens to be, in this instance, a 16-guage shotgun barrel."

With that I pulled the trigger. The kick nearly knocked me off my feet, despite my enhanced strength. The explosion of oo buckshot made my sensitive ears ring, as did Jasper's shout of "Yee-hah!" I hit my target dead center...not the man who'd taunted me, but the blazing lamp hanging just above the last stair. Flaming oil splashed onto the steps, setting the oil we'd spread on them alight. Fire swooshed up, along with black smoke. White gun smoke also filled the cellar. Together it all blinded and panicked the renegades. That was all the help we needed. Romulus dove for the saber, rolling up to a knee with it. He pushed me toward the pickle rack and began swinging the heavy blade at enemy shins. Men swore and howled. Guns fell to the floor.

While I yanked open the secret tunnel door, Tyrell whipped out the pepperbox I'd jammed into his waistband when I'd hugged him in pretended distress. One shot snapped out at the ceiling hole, hitting a musketman. The weapon dropped amongst the mass in the center of the room. His next shot searched for the leader, but he'd already dashed out the door and vanished upstairs. Both remaining bullets dropped men who'd recovered their wits and were aiming at me. *Thanks, Cap'n!* Pocketing the little gun and snatching the LeMat out of my hand, Tyrell kicked a renegade onto the blazing stairs, tapped Romulus on the shoulder, and followed me into the tunnel. The Marshal grabbed two of the spare bottles of oil and hurled them onto the steps. A wall of fire shot up, engulfing two more renegades. Screams split the hot air as all our enemies rushed for the ceiling hole, begging to be pulled up by their comrades. Flames swirled onto the walls and rafters. I choked on all the smoke. Soon the whole house would go up. We had to move quick.

An instant later we were on the other side of the pickle rack, securing three heavy bolts and catching our breaths. I wanted to hoot and holler about whupping up on the entire Hellfiend Legion, but remembered that I was supposed to be a frail Southern blossom and settled for crying instead. While playing my role I still managed to scout things with my Stone senses. Fresh cool air told me that an exit lay ahead, but quite a ways off. Tyrell led us toward it, putting as rapid distance between us and the burning house as he could while feeling his way in the total darkness. I pretended to be as blind, though to my eyes the tunnel looked about as bright as dusk on a summer evening.

Smoke had already begun to seep into the tunnel, which looked to be a good quarter-mile long. We seemed to be moving west and north, though it was hard to tell being underground. I hoped that the Legion didn't know about the tunnel, or we might be blundering into a trap. Tyrell anticipated my worry.

"Be careful when we get to the end," he said, reloading on the move. I noticed that despite everything that had happened in the melee, the cavalryman had remembered to grab his saddle. Romulus carried it for him while he rammed powder and ball into the LeMat, all without being able to see a blessed thing. "I don't imagine our friends know about this passage, else they'd have used it against us instead of tearing through the floor. But caution seldom slays a soldier."

The tunnel stood six feet tall, impressive to me but Romulus still had to stoop way over to get through. Its width was about the same, though every now and then that doubled to make a chamber for food or sleeping pallets. All the walls had been smoothed and the ceiling reinforced with railroad ties. Someone had gone to a great deal of labor and expense to make it. I wanted to ask Romulus about the Underground Railroad, but figured that Miss Mary Williams wouldn't be the sort of snooty Southern belle who'd speak of such things in front of a Confederate officer. *Have to keep in mind that I'm supposed to be for slavery.*

After around fifteen minutes of shuffle-footing we came to a slight bend. I could tell from the smell of the air that an opening waited just ahead. Tyrell held up a hand, then a finger to his lips. Why he thought anyone could see either gesture mystified me. To maintain my act I ran into him as if all was black to me. He grabbed my shoulder, covered my mouth, and breathed, "Ssshh!" into my ear. I smiled and did the same to Romulus. We all clumped together and stood still, listening.

Something large blocked the exit. Its heavy breathing rumbled like a locomotive. Every now and then it'd snort. When it moved its bulk shook the walls of the tunnel and made dirt specks rain down on us. Visions of Venoma sprang to my mind. I gripped the Jasper cup hard, ready to swing Morphageus in a death blow before the monster could spring at us. *Why can't anythin' in my life be simple and easy anymore?*

I heard Tyrell cock his pistol. Behind me, Romulus shifted to give himself a better angle to use the saber. My Stone stayed warm, but that might be cold comfort. It looked like we had one more foe to vanquish before we'd be free of this cursed house. I heartily hoped that it wasn't that awful Venoma. Three of us might not be enough. Breathing deep to steel myself for the attack, I'd just started to rock forward when it hit me. Or rather, it didn't hit me.

The smell. Venoma's cemetery stench. The thing in front of us didn't have it. In fact, the aroma in front of me was a hundred percent different. And I recognized it.

I cackled with glee. Tyrell, alarmed, turned to shush me. Shoving his hand away, I laughed out loud, all of the tension caused by terror and death released at finding out who shared our tunnel. Tyrell and Romulus both stared at me as if I'd escaped from the loony bin. Still giggling, I pushed past the captain to confront the fell beast that blocked our path to safety. My companions both sucked in their breaths and raised their weapons to defend me from the demon.

"Hey, cutie," I said, holding out my hand. A velvety nose snuffled into my palm, looking again for an apple and finding none. Alcibiades made a disgusted sound.

"Cap'n Tyrell, it's a poor cavalryman who's afraid of his own horse," I snickered.

While the Reb officer absorbed my gentle abuse and hugged his mount, Romulus and I eased past him to the tunnel mouth. Large bushes blocked the exit from an outside view, where it came out of a low hill to the west of the house. Looking back east, we watched it burn. No renegades were in sight. But the stars were, bright and clear. We were safe...for now.

"When demons lie, their noses run."

18 / New Rules
Sunday, June 22

The tunnel turned out to be the safest place to be for a while, so we stayed put just shy of that final bend. Amongst the stores that the unfortunate owners had put up for runaway slaves were lamps, cheese, water, salt pork, hardtack, matches, and a whole host of other handy items. We filled up every pocket, haversack, and saddlebag (and stomach) with as much of it as we could. I set some cheese aside for Ernie, knowing I'd never hear the end of it if I didn't. Jasper made yummy sounds in my head the whole time.

No one came down the tunnel from either end, but we kept to a watch schedule anyhow for what was left of the night. Those lightly-padded pallets made for a better rest than the bare floor of the parlor had. Some of my aches eased up a bit. The new dream came back, but sort of fuzzy and disjointed. Maybe if someone sent it to me, the tunnel interfered with the process somehow.

Just after dawn, while we were all stretching and yawning, a troop of Union cavalry rode up to the ashes of the house. Tyrell got anxious, but they were just curious. After poking around for a bit they seemed to decide that it had just been an everyday house fire, not a military concern, and moved on to the north. If they'd fully investigated the basement, which they couldn't get to because the big house had collapsed on top of it, things might've gotten sticky for us. Finding heaps of uniformed bodies with weapons could only have made the soldiers look around with serious intent. I couldn't see any sign of the Hellfiend Legion, so they must've figured out that their big reward had escaped them, and sure wasn't worth the trouble anyway. Even if they'd thought otherwise, a hundred Yankee troopers would've persuaded them to move on to safer hunting grounds.

When everybody had left the area Tyrell moved to a nearby clump of trees that shielded him from the sight of the house. He fed and watered Alcibiades, cleaned his weapons, and washed himself. Me and Romulus kept an eye out for Roberta and Ernie. They were due back soon and would be alarmed at what they'd find. Romulus said he'd use his mirror to signal them where we were. I still didn't want to put all of my trust in the Reb, so letting him see our scouts didn't strike me as a wise move yet. There were plenty of unanswered questions that bothered me, like why the horse just happened to be in our tunnel and who Tyrell's 'people' were that he seemed so sure could outbid the Honourable Merchantry.

I'd slept through the previous morning and was glad to not miss this one. Bright and clear, the air smelled of flowers and smoke. Not unlike the scent of Jasper's magick. Life and death in one sniff. The sun smiled through puffy white clouds that reminded me of Ma's big feather pillow. Dew sparkled on the tall grass, making me imagine that fairies had sprinkled jewels there. *Heck, that's not even a crazy thought anymore, Verity.* All that natural beauty made it easy to forget that I'd just been through more violence, horror, and death since Friday night than any kid should have to see in three lifetimes.

Until I touched my Stone. Then memories of Ma and Tommy swooshed through my mind in a red swirl. So much had been happening, like trying not to be horribly dead every five minutes, that my worries for them hadn't been able to compete for attention. But now that survival was assured for a little bit at least, anxiety for my family started to choke me. What to do? I had four weeks to get to London to save Tommy. Was that even possible? With a sturdy steamship, a strong current, and no interference, sure. And if I managed to arrange all of that, what about Ma? *Is she okay? How can I help her?* All I had was 'Croatan' written in sugar. That suggested the Lost Colony in North Carolina, which sat more or less in the direction we were heading. Nothing else came to mind from the word. What to do? Assuming I made it through the battlefields around Richmond in one piece, which direction would I go? To Roberta's ship and then to Europa? Or to Roanoke to fumble around hoping Ma would turn up? The latter seemed a long shot, but darn it...it was Ma.

What to do?

"I'd say that you should go with the sure thing," said Jasper out of the blue.

I jumped a little, then looked around to see if Tyrell had seen me start. "And where've you been, mister?"

"Right here. Where else can I go? Tahiti?"

"I mean I didn't hear a peep outta you while every lunatic in Virginia tried to massacre us last night."

"You got through it all right. You made good decisions in the heat of battle. Proved you could get along without relyin' on magick...mostly. Pretty good for a new Stone Warden."

I gritted my teeth at that. "So last night was some kind of test?"

"Oh, no. The Stone doesn't make things happen, much as it seems to sometimes. It just worked out that way."

"Well, glad I impressed you. Now what's the sure thing?"

"Tommy. You know he's in London. Your Ma's an unknown."

"If Venoma told the truth."

"No reason not to. Besides, when demons lie, their noses run."

For some reason that struck me as the funniest thing I'd heard in days. Controlling my urge to laugh out loud, I moved farther back down the tunnel. "Really?"

"Really. If more humans knew about that, think of how much misery could've been avoided down through the centuries."

"So don't sign a deal with a devil if he's carryin' a hanky?"

Jasper did laugh, since nobody but me could hear him, cheering me up a lot. "Now there's a scene that Goethe fellow

Goethe seems to have left out of *Faust*."

Glancing at Romulus, I saw him peer up at the sky and squint. Maybe Roberta and Ernie were coming back. "You're awful well-read for a sword-spirit."

"Yeah, well, playin' solitaire loses its charm after the first three hundred years."

I wondered how Jasper could read anything, stuck in a wall for ages, but didn't press the point. Romulus had turned away from where Tyrell buttoned his jacket and brushed his boots. His mirror looked the size of a postage stamp in his big paw. He wagged it back and forth, shining light up into the sky. *Yep, they're here.* "So to London it is, then?"

"That'd be my suggestion. Not easy for you, I know."

I fingered the Stone, warm against my hand. "Not easy, no. Neither way."

"We can arrange to have Marshals watch the house while you're gone, see if she makes it back on her own."

That made sense. Maybe Ma would solve her own problem. *She's nobody's fool, that's for sure.* "Okay by me. First chance we get I'll see if Roberta can fly off to set that up. Unless we run into a Marshal out here who can get word to whoever is in charge of that sort of thing." I frowned. "Don't even know how you recognize a Marshal. Do they have code words and secret handshakes like the Masons?"

"You'll have to ask Ernie or Romulus about that. It's all I can do to keep the magick swords straight."

I started moving back toward the entrance. Tyrell had

finished cleaning up and headed back toward us. Romulus saw what I wanted and turned toward me before the captain got within earshot. He pocketed the mirror and smiled.

"They's all right," he said, quiet as his big voice could manage. "I messaged 'em to follow us once we sets out south. When you heads fo' the trees to take care o' business, they'll land and report."

"Sounds good," I told him. "That should be soon, I think. The cap'n looks ready to go."

Right I was. Tyrell ducked into the tunnel and motioned us out. "Looks safe enough, Miss Mary. The Bluebellies are out of sight and I think you took the fight out of the Legion. We can get on the road and see if we can find your brother."

"Fine by me, Cap'n. Your horse okay for the trip?"

"Oh, he's fine. Take more than a little dustup to fluster Al. He's done this before."

"Done what before?"

"Untied himself from the tree and took a walk. Smelled food and water in here and stayed till the trouble ended. He's trained to come to me only if I whistle, so he won't blunder into a situation and maybe make it worse."

"Sounds like a special horse."

"Oh, you have no idea, miss." He jerked his head toward the exit. "Shall we?"

We loaded Alcibiades and Romulus down with all of our supplies. It pained me to treat my friend like a slave, but he'd made it clear to me that he was willing to play the part. As his owner I wouldn't be expected to soil my hands much, and Tyrell would get suspicious if I did. So I walked beside the cavalryman's mount, a step ahead of 'Jim.' Tyrell rode, saying he wanted to get a feel for things and be up high where he could spot any trouble and react to it quick. We took the nearest road that went south. It was a narrow track but well-drained and level. Our guide seemed perfectly familiar with all of the territory we passed through. No doubt a year of war had acquainted him with every bush and path in his area of operations.

For a war zone near the northern capital city it looked awful quiet. Nothing much to hear but the Sunday church bells. We met nobody all morning as we trudged along. I didn't say much, not wanting to risk making a mistake with my cover story. Whenever Tyrell asked me a direct question I'd take as much time as I could arranging my answer in my head before speaking. He didn't seem to notice. The captain was in his element, as they say—mounted on a fine horse, armed to the teeth, escorting a young damsel in distress whose brother had given his blood for the Confederate cause. Strong foes had been vanquished the night before and he looked literally flushed with victory, face all pink with pride and glory. I wished I could have as simple a life.

After a couple of hours of traveling through the beautiful green rolling Virginia countryside, I decided that the time had come to reunite with my scouts. Telling Tyrell that I had to answer the call of nature, I skipped off of the road into a hedgerow. In less than a minute I heard the flapping of heavy wings and a flutter of red and blue dropped in on me. Roberta looked none the worse for having been out all night, perched on a rock with her spectacles a bit askew. Ernie adjusted them for her and scampered onto my outstretched palm.

"Hey!" I grinned, "how y'all doin'?"

"Better than yer, I expect," the mouse said with a yawn, knitting needle tied across his back with twine now. "No sooner do we leave you alone than yer burns the bloody house down."

"Run outta firewood, did you, matey?" asked Roberta, her head turned sideways while she dug her beak into an itchy wing.

"No, Romulus wanted some smoked ham, so I decided to oblige him," I shot back, keeping an eye on the road. I didn't want Tyrell to surprise us if he thought I was taking too long. "Find out anything about my escort?"

The parrot nodded. "Seems to be on the up-and-up, as far as me contacts know. Joined the army before Sumter's guns cooled. Has a reputation in the cavalry as a man with a future. Cool customer in a fight."

"That's for sure." I sketched out the night's events for them.

"Whooee! Wish I'd been there," Ernie declared. "Haven't had a good scrap since I gave that cat what-for."

"Be glad you weren't," I said. "Darned close call, that was. And there weren't even any monsters involved."

"Not all monsters look like Venoma, girlie. You'll find that out if you get to Merchantry headquarters."

"Speakin' of that...what else did you find out. Did you get into the Reb camp?"

Ernie put his hand on his tiny bosom like he was having apoplexy. "How can you doubt me, child? Piece o' cake, it was." He put on a thick Southern accent. "Ya jist moseys in like ya owns the place, see? Up and ask questions o' the local mice, and a coupla rats if ya don't mind slummin', and pretty soon yer in the know."

"Wow, that's scary. They teach you that in Marshal school?"

"No. But I have been livin' in a bloody theatre, you know."

"Oh, yeah."

Roberta jerked her head toward the road. "You're boyfriend's gettin' antsy, matey. Best wrap this up for now."

Ernie spoke in a rush. "Big doin's in Richmond. McClellan's great attack bogged down and turned into a siege. Gave the Rebs all the openin' they need. They're movin' everybody with a trigger finger down there. Jackson's men are hot-footin' it from the Valley. Soon as he's in place that new general, Lee, is gonna hit him. Hard."

I frowned. "When? Did they say?"

"The mice I talked to didn't have an exact date, but any day now."

"So we're probably walkin' right into the biggest battle of the whole war?"

"Sounds like it," Roberta nodded. "The birds are all avoidin' that whole area if they can."

Groaning, I started edging toward the road. "Lovely. Anything comin' up ahead we have to worry about?"

Ernie climbed aboard the parrot's back again. "Not that we saw, but we'll keep an eye out. If somethin' happens you need to be concerned about, we'll buzz yer."

"Good. Thanks. If everything stays quiet, meet us just outside of wherever we stop for the night."

"Will do," Roberta said with a wink, flapping into the sky. I watched them fly away for a moment, then broke out of the bushes. Tyrell looked anxious, but seemed reassured as he watched me fiddle with my overalls.

"I declare, women do take the longest time to do the simplest things."

I wanted to explain to him that nature's call was a lot simpler for him than for me, even if I wasn't wearing a proper dress. "You're a rugged soldier, Cap'n," I purred. "This is the first time I've lived in the out-of-doors."

"True enough, ma'am," he nodded, all chivalrous, just like I'd expected him to. "Would you care to ride up here for a while and rest your feet?"

"No, thank you, I'm good for a while yet. The more I walk the tougher my feet'll get."

"Spoken like a true soldier. On we go, then."

To tell the truth, my feet hurt something awful and I desperately wanted to sit on that horse. But it was time to talk to Jasper. Sitting with Tyrell wasn't the best place for that conversation, since I sometimes forgot to think my words and would blurt things out. While we plodded along on the dusty back road, blessedly free of anybody else (the one good thing about sneaking through a war zone is that people don't travel unless they absolutely have to), I decided that I needed to know once and for all what I was in for at midnight.

"Okay, boyo," I told him, "let's have it."

"Have what?" asked Jasper, all pretend-innocent.

"Them ground rules I never seem to get. What happens come midnight and how do I deal with you after that?"

"No free shape-shifts, for starters."

I shuddered at the thought of being turned into an animal, or worse, again. "Wow, what a burden. Anything else? Are you gonna disappear at the stroke of twelve in a puff of purple smoke?"

"Ooh, that'd be nifty! Maybe throw in a sulfurous whirlwind, too."

"Spare me. Them muck monsters smell bad enough as it is. Spill it. What exactly changes tonight?"

"Not as much as you think. I'll still be in your head as long as you hold the Stone and Morphageus. I can still defend you from imminent peril. But the magick for everything else will have to be earned."

"Earned? What you mean?"

"I mean that magick is never free. The Stone increases whatever magick you add to it, just like it increases your speed, strength, and senses."

"Will that change?" I hoped not. I was powerful happy being able to see in the dark.

"No. The Stone runs off of your own life-force. As long as

you're breathin' and in contact with it, the Stone will help you."

"But...?"

"But it can't create magick on its own beyond that. You have to make bank deposits, sort of. That's how all magick works."

Images of me handing an eye-shaded teller a bulging bag of magick flashed through my head. "Deposits?"

"The Stone can help you store magick energy inside you, once you learn how. There are a couple of ways to do that. Chauntways are the most powerful, but also the hardest. You'll need a teacher for that. We'll have to find you a mage one of these days."

Chauntways? I'm doomed. Can't sing to save my life. "Go ahead. I know you're dyin' to show that you're smarter than me."

"The world is full of places where magick energy flows, like rivers. There are also places where it pools, like lakes. Those are called Chauntswirls. In fact, they're usually near water. Enormous power there. If you know how, you can suck up that energy like a sponge. If you don't know how, one of two things happens."

"And they would be...?"

"Nothing, which'd be really embarrassin' in the middle of a Bully assault, or..."

"Yeah? What?"

"Or the magick flares up and runs around inside you like an out-of-control fire."

"Somehow I just know that can't be good.

"Well, your brain explodin' like a keg of powder usually

makes a mess, yeah."

"Great. So that's out for now. What else?"

"There's the black magick that the Bullies use. But you don't want to do that."

"I'd think not. I can just imagine what you have to do to earn that magick. Deals with demons and such?"

"Yep. Although it's easier to just cause pain or death to an innocent living thing."

"No, thank you." That got me to thinking, though. "Wait! Haven't I been doin' that with all of this fightin'? What about last night?"

"The key is 'innocent.' If someone has chosen freely to attack you, then they've abandoned innocence."

Then who have the Bullies been tormentin' to earn their power? I didn't want to know. My imagination was creative enough. An awful lot of street kids went missing in Washington City, for starters.

"So every time I step on a bug or pull a weed...?"

"Or eat chicken." Jasper had a wicked glee to his voice.

I sucked in a breath. "I'm gonna be sick."

"Don't fret. It's a part of nature. You take in a tiny bit of magick all the time with just ordinary livin'. You lose some every time you're mean to someone, lose your temper, and so on. That all balances out in the long run. It's the big stuff—murder, torture, like that—that corrupts you. The mages who do such things can become horribly powerful, but that sort of magick feeds on itself and changes the user in ways you don't want to think about."

"Oh, don't tease me."

"Let's just say that demons have to come from someplace."

"Ick! What's the other way, then? The other safe way?"

"You do me...favors."

I stopped dead in the middle of the road. Romulus almost ran me over. When he frowned at me I tapped my cup, then my head. He nodded and kept moving. "Such as?"

"I've been stuck inside this sword for ages and ages, since I was your age. No body, no feelin's, no human interaction. It's a prison. What do think has been powerin' Morphageus the last three days, workin' sundry miracles for you? **My** life-force, trapped in here by my original master. If you recharge me by makin' me feel alive, I can do things for you. Otherwise, I'll fade."

"What sort of favors?" I didn't much like the direction this was going, but it sounded better than the exploding brain or torturing kittens.

"Nothin' much. Nothin' black, anyhow. Just stuff to let me feel like a real person again."

"Like eatin' your favorite foods? Smellin' a flower you haven't seen since the old days? That type of thing?"

"Yeah. Also, lettin' me into your mind."

"Heck, you're already there, in case you haven't noticed."

"No, I'm only privy to the thoughts on the surface, the ones you use to get around with. Your heartfelt emotions and secrets are closed unless you choose to let me in, or lose so much control that they come to the surface with the rest."

Huh? "I don't know that I want you tiptoein' through my attic, rummagin' through my feelin's."

"Who am I gonna tell?"

He had me there. Unless he had more ways to make mental links than I knew about. Would he tell the other magick swords about the holes in my underwear? Were they all going to laugh about my girlie worries? Still, it sounded better than the other options. Without Morphageus I couldn't help Ma or Tommy. They'd be lost for sure.

OK," I sighed, out loud. "It's a deal."

*"I ain't gonna have to paint myself in colored rings
and crawl around naked, am I?"*

19 / A Cure for Sore Feet

Hot, tired, dirty, bored, and overall miserable. That's what
soldiers say is their usual lot. Actually, I've heard them add
lousy, cold, and wet to that, too, but we saw no rain on this
sweltering afternoon. As for the lice...well, you just had to get
used to the idea that you carried passengers. Fleas, too, most
likely courtesy of Alcibiades or the pallets we'd snoozed on in
the refugee tunnel. Those I tried to pick off when I felt them
crawling or biting. They were easier to find than the lice. Before
falling into Ford's basement I'd always smushed any fleas I'd
found on me. Now I just flicked them away, figuring the odds
were too high that the poor little guys were serving time for
some indiscretion against the Merchantry. *Indiscretion. Like
wantin' to be free, maybe, or just not dead in some
Merchantry-sponsored war or plague.* I also dwelled on Jasper
telling me about getting black magick power from killing things,
even plants. That gave me the shivers. Once I'd read about a
religion in the Golden Raj that revered life so much they wore
masks so as to not accidentally inhale a bug that might be a
reincarnated ancestor. *If I have any more revelations I may be*

headed in that direction. Nevertheless, I looked forward to stopping for the night so I could boil my clothes. I'd been living in them for three days. My underwear felt like tree bark.

It was about four in the afternoon. We'd been on the road since six in the morning, resting ten minutes out of every other hour. Tyrell set a ruthless pace, him being on a cavalry horse. He'd grown used to covering ground in a hurry. I imagined that having to stick with me at maybe three miles an hour galled him. All he talked about as we walked was how he didn't want to miss the big battle for Richmond. Just dandy. All I wanted was to find a way to avoid it altogether. Men and their glory-hunting. The world would've been a lot nicer place to live in all these past untold thousands of years if they'd settled for less glory and more bedtime stories to their kids. *I know that woulda suited this kid just fine. Never had a story from Pa, not that I remember. Ma did it, of course, but that's not quite the same somehow.* I hoped that when push came to shove Tyrell would choose me over martial fame.

Our little back road filled up with more folks as we got closer to Fredericksburg. Most headed north, away from the battle that was coming. There wasn't much more conversation other than "Good day." People wanted to put as much distance between themselves and the war as they could. Once or twice young Confederate dispatch riders raced past us in choking clouds of dust, bound for the capital. They didn't even favor us with a by-your-leave, just roared on south with their messages. The map in my head told me that Fredericksburg lay about halfway to

Richmond. We'd get to it the next day and push on through to Hanover Courthouse. Late Tuesday, if we kept up our brutal pace and I didn't drop over from sheer exhaustion, we'd make it to Richmond. We aimed to stay on the road twelve hours, making around thirty miles a day. Romulus showed no signs of tiring, limping, or even breathing hard, despite being loaded down like a pack mule. Tyrell, fat and happy on the tireless Alcibiades, had no worries, except that his rear end might get sore. Unlikely for a veteran cavalry officer. Even though I was in good shape from lots of running and sword fighting with Tommy, I would've keeled over the first day if the captain hadn't made me ride in front of him a lot of the time.

Once or twice I spied Roberta, high overhead and mimicking the hovering flight of a vulture to avoid notice. She never gave me any sign that trouble might lie ahead, which made me real happy after the past couple of days I'd had. Romulus didn't say much, just kept staring ahead with his sharp Marshal's eye, doggedly putting one big foot in front of the other. Jasper stayed just as quiet. Maybe he was taking a nap or whatever magick swords did on their own time. Tyrell stopped asking questions that seemed to be designed to catch me in a fib. He just sang patriotic songs in a quiet baritone, as if he were his sole audience. When he did "The Vacant Chair" he got a hitch in his voice that he tried to cover with a cough. *Must've lost somebody close, then. Just like everyone else since this fool war started.*

We moved off of the road around six-thirty in the evening and camped in a thicket next to a creek. After a cold supper of beans and hardtack we washed up and checked for damage. The captain tended to his horse like it was his best girl, of course. You'd expect no less. Romulus just shucked his boots, glanced at his perfectly-healthy feet, curled up like a hound, and started snoring. Boy, I wanted to whack him a good one out of pure envy. I had blisters on both feet and a bruise on my backside from where that diabolical McClellan saddle had worn a hole. To my mind, all the trouble that the Union commander had in taking Richmond could be put down as penance for having invented such a fiendish torture device.

On top of everything else, I had a surplus of livestock on my body. The lice and the fleas had to go. With Tyrell's bemused permission I got a fire going a few yards from camp, behind a wall of briars. Having established as much privacy as I looked likely to get, I set our one small pot on the fire and boiled water. Then I stripped down to my near-black bare skin and scrubbed myself while my drawers and shirt bubbled away. It had been a darned lucky thing to have found that tunnel full of supplies. I'd pocketed a tiny piece of soap and an old towel along with the other goodies (I resolved to never travel without a towel again). They now gave me blessed relief. When I'd scrubbed myself to where you could finally see the freckles again (Ma's personal indicator of my cleanliness), I skimmed the indignant insects from the top of the water. Wringing everything out, I hung the clothes on a branch, wrapped myself in the towel as best I could, and tossed my overalls into the pot. By the time they'd been de-bugged my short hair had dried and so had most of my underlayer. Pulling on the drawers and shirt, I stretched out on the towel in bliss. It seems a small thing, but being clean amidst untold grime is one of the great joys of living. That lesson would be re-taught to me quite a bit in the coming weeks.

By the time everything had dried out as much as I could expect, darkness had arrived. We were just a day past the start of summer, so daylight gave up with a grumble. I packed up my stuff, doused the fire, and returned to the main camp. Tyrell had set up a dog tent in my absence and rolled out a bedroll in it. He told me to crawl in and sleep for at least six hours straight, as I had the most aches and pains. He and Romulus would keep first watch in three-hour shifts. I didn't argue with his logic. It was sweet innocent Mary Williams he was caring for, after all. Had to keep playing my part. After whispering to Romulus that Roberta and Ernie might show up, I went out like a drenched candle.

My new dream returned as clear and sharp as it had been the first night. It being the third time through, I could start to think about what things might mean even while I floated in the dream. Romulus had to be the black dog, that seemed obvious. Tyrell might be the angel in cavalry boots, but who the other angels could be I had no idea. Marshals, maybe? If so, why no parrot feathers or mouse whiskers? And why did the Romulus-dog have a leash? I still couldn't understand what the words in the sky were. Some might have been Iberion and Gaullic, though it was hard to tell because most of the time I couldn't see the whole word. A few of them were in different alphabets. Hebraic, maybe? Arabe? Muscovite? *What's that all about?*

The people in foreign duds reminded me of the stories told about Washington's Monument. Merchantry spies? Or Merchantry refugees? Or maybe they were people I would meet in the future. No telling how this dream thing worked. My first dream had been a taste of my future, but that didn't mean that all dreams worked that way. If it warned of things to come then those Bullies were worrisome. I had a sick feeling that word would spread about how we'd treated them the other night. The next time we met they'd come loaded for bear.

That ship could be Roberta's, the *Penelope's Kiss,* my way to the Sceptr'd Isle. Tommy's ambulance. Or his hearse. Maybe mine, too. The skulls on the beach worried me. So did those three well-armed strangers. I saw now that they wore dark-green clothes that were almost black, and masks covered their faces. All of them moved like dancers. Or cobras. Who the lady fighting them might be was vague. Me, all grown up? Ma? Someone I had yet to meet? Probably not Ma, since she came in a second later to toss me onto the ship. And what did the whale mean? I knew precious little about them, but this one didn't seem like your normal harpoon-him-for-his-oil beastie. More like a god than a mere animal.

Afterwards I slept like the dead. No other dreams passed through my tired noggin. It bothered me a little that I didn't have nightmares about what Venoma might be doing to Tommy, or what peril Ma could be in. Maybe the Stone protected me from the worst of that sort of thing, just like it made me stronger in my body and let me stay calm in a fight. Too bad it couldn't prevent blisters. Now that'd be a magick rock to write home about.

It turned out I didn't need a magick stone for the overalls, just a Marshal of the Equity. A gentle touch on my shoulder woke me. For a moment I stayed fuzzy like you do when pulled from a sound sleep. Blinking, I saw Romulus, getting me ready for my sentry shift. He held out my denims, the hole repaired.

"Time to get up, Miss," he whispered. "All's been quiet so far."

"You fixed 'em? That Marshals' school's real thorough, huh?" It embarrassed me a bit that he could do that and I couldn't. In fact, I wasn't much good at anything girlie. Ma would sigh sometimes and call me her firstborn son. That usually happened when I came home with a bullfrog, covered in Potomac mud, after winning three arm-wrestling matches with the local fellows.

"'Tweren't nothin'. I always carry this with me for 'mergencies." I noticed that he held one of the tiny portable sewing kits that the soldiers called 'housewives.'

"Thanks." I pulled the overalls on and crawled out of the tent. When I stood up and put weight on my feet, everything screamed in protest, from my blistered feet and achy butt to my back and arms. The last two must've been from all of the fighting. Twelve years old and I felt like somebody's decrepit grandpa. This shaped up to be a long ugly quest. Maybe I'd save the world and then just fall apart like last year's scarecrow in the middle of my victory ceremony.

"Ouch, ouch, ouch!" I whined, trying not to wake Tyrell. The Reb snoozed on the ground next to Al, whom he'd tied to a tree. Just to make sure that the horse didn't disappear again, a slack rope had been tied around his neck and around the stirrup of the saddle. Tyrell used the saddle for a pillow, with his jacket for padding. If Alcibiades moved more than a few feet away the rope would tighten and jerk the saddle out from under his head, waking him up. I guessed old Al must've really had a talent for getting himself loose if the trooper had to take that kind of care.

"You sounds worse for wear," said Romulus. "Feet OK?"

I shook my head. "Nope. Bad blisters. I'm nearly always barefoot but I guess that didn't toughen 'em up enough for current circumstances. I may have to ride all day. That'll be bad if there's a scrap and I have trouble puttin' weight on my dogs."

"So to speak," the Marshal smiled. *Whoa! Romulus has got a sense of humor. How about that.*

"Uh...yeah." I tested my toes by trying to walk normal. Wincing, I made a disgusted sound. "Not good."

"If they as bad as all that, we has to fix 'em."

I gave him a doubtful eye. "Fix 'em? How? There some magick spell for that?"

He smiled again. "Actually, yeah."

"As long as it doesn't involve spillin' chicken blood and chantin' in Romish, I'm all for it. What do we do? Whatever it is, we have to get away from Tyrell. I don't want him knowin' about me yet."

"Come along, then." Romulus picked me up like I was the

morning newspaper. He hauled me off to where I'd washed myself earlier. Setting me down on the bank of the run, he said, "The Stone and Morphageus can do it."

"Huh? Jasper can heal wounds?" *Wow! That's more than most army doctors can do, from what I hear tell from soldiers.*

"If they's somebody willin' to accept the wounds from you."

"There's always a catch with magick, huh? Are you sayin' somebody has to want to be blistered in my place?"

"Uh-huh. If they don't make the choice then it won't work."

I looked at him for a long moment, a mosquito whining in my ear. "Nobody here but us, you know."

"Oh, I knows it."

"Awful kind of you, mister."

"Way I looks at it, we's all likely to live longer if you's in one piece."

I wasn't as sure about that as he seemed to be, but gave him the benefit of the doubt. "Then you'll have bad feet. How's that help us? It's just shiftin' the burden to somebody else in the group. As a whole, we're still crippled."

"Not if I takes the wound someplace else."

Aha. Clever. "You can do that?"

His big head nodded. "Long as the wound itself gets transferred, the place can be different."

"OK, then. How does it work?"

"You just talks to Morphageus and asks. Then we holds hands and it happens. Easy."

"Well, that sounds simple enough. Let's—" A jolt hit me.

Midnight had passed hours ago. "Oh-oh."

"What?"

"My three days are up. His magick charge is gone."

Romulus swatted a mosquito. He didn't seem to have any worries about any black magick stain from that. "Did he tell you how to accept new magick?"

"Yeah. Said I had to do him favors and such. Or pull energy from Chauntways."

He held up a hand. "No Chauntways until you knows how."

"Don't worry. He made that real clear already. We don't want to leave a smokin' crater here." I waved the tin cup. "A favor it is, then."

The instant I said it Jasper's goofy voice rang in my head. "And I know just the one I want!" The cup melted into little hands, rubbing together in annoying glee.

"Why do I have this sinkin' feelin' in my belly all of a sudden?" I sighed.

"So little faith," he pouted. "After all we've been through together."

Rolling my eyes, I said, "That's just why I'm worried. Romulus wants to accept my wounds. What'll that cost me?"

"Fifty cents."

It's that easy? "Really?"

"Oh, you wish, girlie. For a wound transfer? That's heavy magick."

I should've known. "I ain't gonna have to paint myself in colored rings and crawl around naked, am I?"

"Heck, no. This is easy. Trust me, you'll like this."

Three minutes later I felt as sick as I'd felt in a long time. Puffing away on one of Tyrell's cigars, which Romulus had to pilfer from the sleeping captain's coat, I just knew that my face looked the same color as the grass. *People choose to do this? For fun?*

"If this is what adults do," I croaked, "then I'll stay a kid, thank you very much."

Jasper laughed in my head. "Where's your spirit of adventure? What kind of Stone Warden can't handle a little tobacco smoke?"

I waved a hand to try to clear the thick fog away. "Little? It's like suckin' on a locomotive's stack."

"Sweet ambrosia, I call it!" A satisfied breathing sound filled my ears. "You humans know how to live...when you ain't bashin' each others' heads in and such."

"Yeah, yeah, yeah. Come on, fix my feet. I held up my end of things."

"Indeed you did." The cup stretched out into Morphageus, Dread Sword of Nicotine Poisoning. "I have to be in my best shape for this."

"Your Sunday-go-to-meetin' outfit?" I asked, gagging.

"Yeah, somethin' like that. Hold his hand."

I reached out and took Romulus' giant mitt with mine. He squeezed it gentle-like. It was warm and rough. My other hand gripped the sword's hilt. It felt pretty much the same way, like a person's palm. *I swear, that's the creepiest part of this whole magick business.*

"Are there magickal words I have to say?" I asked, hoping that the more I talked the less I'd have to puff on that awful instrument of doom.

"Not for this. That's Chauntway stuff. Just relax and let Uncle Jasper work his wonders."

My feet started in to itching. As much as I wanted to scratch them, something told me that it wouldn't be good for the spell. So I set my jaw and waited things out. Romulus clamped down on my hand some more. A light breeze blew away some of the foul smoke. Looking down, I saw tiny lights swirling around my feet, like blue-white fireflies.

"Where?" asked Jasper.

I sat fascinated by the lights and didn't get what he was asking. "Huh?"

"Where does he want the wounds?"

I looked over at Romulus. "He wants to know where."

"Upper arm, if you please," he answered.

The second the words left his mouth, my foot-lights whirlwinded up to his burly left bicep, which he'd already bared. I felt a sting, as if a mischievous somebody had pinched my feet. My poor hand got crunched in Romulus' fist, then released. The little lights sank into his skin like water into a washcloth. As they faded away, leaving the usual after-smell of brimstone and lily, I could see two nasty open blisters. The Marshal flexed his arm but showed no other signs of distress.

"Huh," I breathed. My feet no longer hurt. In fact, every ache

I'd had in my whole body had vanished, along with all of the exhaustion. I felt like I'd been reborn.

"No extra charge for the other stuff," Jasper told me in a perky voice as I gazed at my pristine pink feet. "Now get back to our cigar."

After dutifully sucking on the awful weed some more, and just as dutifully upchucking into the creek, I plopped down on the bank, Romulus patting my back. I guess he thought that could help, somehow. My sword looked like a cup again. I considered puking into it to teach Jasper a lesson.

Cigar stub still glowing in my hand, I heard Tyrell say from the edge of the thicket, "Ah, I remember my first stogie. How this takes me back. Since we're all up, let's breakfast and get on the road. Dawn's coming soon."

*I didn't want to think how an adolescent sword
might behave around a floozie.*

20 / Fredericksburg
Monday, June 23

Monday turned out to be a repeat of the day before, for the most part. At first light we were packed up and heading toward Fredericksburg with me giving thanks for my new feet, now free of the offending blisters. I swallowed my pride and rode on Alcibiades a lot more. Soon I'd find me some used boots. *I can't be-spell my tootsies every day. Awful hard on one's friends.*

I made sure to take care of Romulus as much as I could, bringing him water and anything else I imagined he needed. It was the least I could do for the favor he'd done me. Though he never said so, and would've rather have died first, I got the feeling that the pains of mine that he'd accepted wore on him. You'd have thought that him being so big and strong would mean that my little aches could hardly make an impression. Maybe the spell increased the misery to match the strength of the receiver, so that it'd be a meaningful sacrifice. When I asked Jasper about that he told me that he didn't arrange it that way, but that you couldn't always tell how magick would work on a particular person. After all, Romulus had already been witched into human form, so maybe the new spell ended up being that much of an extra burden because of it.

Tyrell alternated between cheerful and edgy. One minute he'd be tipping his hat to folks we passed on the road, grinning in that devilish way of his. The next he'd be quiet and alert, dark brows furrowed as he peered at each bush or tree as if an ambush lay in wait behind it. Why he got more antsy the further we traveled into Confederate territory I couldn't figure. Seemed to me that he ought to be singing his Rebel head off. After all, if we kept going the way we planned we'd pass right by his home town of Williamsburg. But then, McClellan's army had run rough-shod all over it on the advance and now troops were quartered there Maybe that knowledge had the captain concerned.

Whatever it was, Romulus bore the brunt of his bad mood. More than once Tyrell snapped at him to hurry up, grumbling about 'lazy darkies dragging their feet.' He seemed to think that Jim was sabotaging us somehow. Poor Romulus, back in slave mode, just took it quiet-like and kept on walking. Since I had to maintain my pose as his owner there wasn't much I could do to help. I had to try and tread middle ground. Whenever Tyrell launched one of his tirades at Romulus I'd bat my eyes, act all sweet, and tell the cavalryman that he imagined things. I insisted that Jim had always proved as loyal as the day is long. Making up a long tale about Jim having trekked through floodwaters once to get medicine for my late lamented daddy, I managed to distract him for a bit. Soon he'd returned to humming happy tunes and complimenting ladies on their bonnets as if there weren't a war for a thousand miles.

A little past noon we got to Fredericksburg, crossing the Rappahannock on a guarded bridge. Challenged by a sentry, Tyrell showed him some sort of paper and he waved us all through. A thriving river town of a few thousand citizens, Fredericksburg held more than its normal number at the moment. Southern soldiers and Richmond refugees, crossing paths as they moved in opposite directions, bumped shoulders with local inhabitants and slaves. Considering that a huge hostile army lay just fifty miles away, things looked more normal than I'd expected. Stores did business, checker-playing geezers sat on benches giving unwanted advice, noisy kids ran about causing trouble. The last group made me think of all the good times with Tommy. Wiping my eyes a little, I promised myself that Tommy would be able to play in the streets again, no matter what it cost me or how long it might take.

Jasper had been quiet most of the morning, but now that we were in town he started chattering away, thrilled by all of the new sights and smells. Good thing nobody could hear him but me. He hollered insults at people who got in our way, made fun of odd-looking folks, and drooled over every cigar and whiskey flask in sight. Ladies' perfume really seemed to set him off. *Please, oh please, don't let us pass any fancy girls like Silky Sadie.* I didn't want to think how an adolescent sword might behave around a floozie.

"Hoo-eee!" he whistled, almost deafening me even though no real sound hit my ears. "You mortals sure know how to live! Looky, looky! And you say this is a small backwater town?"

"Yep," I told him, eyeing the muddy river. "Literally."

"Can't imagine what Richmond's like, then. Or Washington City when we ain't bein' chased by Bullies." There was a breathless pause. "Oh, we are gonna have such a good time in London!"

Yeah, if we find a way through the big battle that's brewin'...and find Roberta's ship while being chased by the scum of the South, since there's a bounty on our heads...and get across the ocean without a Merchantry squadron sinkin' us...and make it in and out of the Proprietor's headquarters with the same skins we started with.

I stopped to scrape off a horse flop from my foot. "Don't count your debauches before they're hatched, mister. After that wretched cigar I plan to do a lot more on my own from now on."

"Hey, you never know when you're gonna need a little magickal help from your buddy Morphageus. Wouldn't hurt to bank some of that witchy energy for a rainy day."

Screwing up my face, I gave in a smidgeon. "OK, I'll sniff some perfumes while we walk."

"And maybe run your hand over some velvety fabric, like that girl's wearin' over there."

"Where?" All I saw was some tired-looking soldiers. Jasper flowed up the inside of my shirt sleeve. A steely hand popped out of my collar and nudged my head to the right.

I spotted the girl in question, who looked even younger than me, outside the druggist's. She sat on a bench, yawning, playing with a cat's-cradle. It looked like she was waiting for her ma to come out. Her velvet dress, a rich green, must've cost more than every bit of clothing I'd ever owned.

"I see her. You want me to start pettin' perfect strangers in enemy territory? What if she takes offense? Or even worse, her folks?"

Jasper snorted. "Didn't you just say you were gonna shift for yourself? Here's your first chance. Use your imagination."

"All right, but if I get my arm busted by some outraged mama I'm gonna rent you for a spittoon."

Zigzagging through the crowd, I took advantage of Tyrell's distracted maneuvering around the army wagons to skip up onto the pinewood walk. In two seconds I stood in front of the little girl. "Hey," I said with a little wave.

"H'lo," she answered with a smile. Glad to have somebody close to her age to talk to. Only child, I figured.

"I can never do that," I went on, nodding at her cat's-cradle. "Too clumsy. I got farmer fingers."

She giggled. Her voice tinkled like a tiny silver bell. *I bet you get your way a lot with all of that cutesy stuff, don't you?* "It's not so hard. Takes a lot of practice is all."

"Ain't you hot in that dress?" I asked, getting all clever. "Petticoats and velvet and all?"

"Lordy, yes," she whispered, looking around to see that she wasn't being overheard by her mama. "I declare, this is the itchiest thing anyone ever made with a needle and thread. But we're supposed to set an example for the lower orders, Aunt Polly says."

Aha...no mama. Being reared by a snooty aunt. I took on her own sneaky tone. "Well, I'm one of the lower orders and the only example you're aunt's settin' for me is that my betters is all gonna collapse of heat stroke, wearin' a dress like that in the summer. Can I feel?"

"Go ahead. I'll watch for her. Just don't wrinkle it." A real Southern rebel, this one.

I stroked the sleeve of her dress like she was my favorite hound dog. In my head Jasper made the cooing sound of a flock of satisfied pigeons. "Ooh, it is thick, ain't it?"

"Sure is. Fabric came from New Orleans. Makes you wonder who'd wear it all the way down there."

Out of the corner of my eye I caught Tyrell, hollering at Romulus. *Mad at him for losin' me, I expect.* "Sure is nice. You'll be glad to have it come winter, anyhow."

She shrugged. "I suppose. What's your name?"

"Verity," I told her without thinking, wincing inside as I did.

"Oh, real smart," Jasper snickered. "Hope the Merchantry ain't usin' ten year-old spies here."

"Boogie," my new friend said with that same 'I-just-love-everybody-even-the-poor' grin. "Brigid Louise, actually. Brigid Louise Fairfax. Boogie's what my mama calls me."

Romulus headed my way, Tyrell keeping a stern eye on him from atop Alcibiades. He kept the horse smack in the middle of the crowded street, not caring who he blocked. I eased backward off the walk. "Pleased to meetcha, um, Boogie. But Daddy's sent our hand after me, so I hafta go. See ya."

When I'd gone a full thirty feet away from her and had almost met up with Romulus, Boogie stood up, waved, and hollered in her high but surprisingly loud voice, "Bye-bye, Verity!" Half the street stopped what they were doing to look our way.

"Bye-bye, Verity," Jasper mimicked. "Have fun outrunnin' the Bullies!" He returned to his usual voice. "Gee, you think there's anybody in Fredericksburg now who doesn't know you're here...including Johnny Reb over there?"

Tyrell glared at me, frowning. I sighed in disgust. *Oh, boy. The free world might be countin' on the wrong girl.*

"Miss Mary, what was that all about?" the captain demanded, clutching the life out of his gloves.

"Nothin', sir," I said, all sweetie-pie. "Just admirin' her cat's-cradle." A thought jumped at me. "My poor brother Tommy taught me how to make them, just before he left us for the last time." I added a tiny sniffle for effect.

Softening some, Tyrell growled, "Did he also teach you to give folks a false name when holding a civilized conversation?"

"False name?" I remained the picture of innocence. "I gave her no name at all, sir."

"I clearly heard her call you Verity."

Uh...now what? Think, girlie. "Oh, that. I complimented her on her lovely dress so much that she got it into her head that I was joshing her. So I swore to her, just playing around, that

Verity was my middle name." *Weak, but better than nothin'.*

"Well, take care," Tyrell warned me. "This is no place to get separated. I'm responsible for getting you to your brother, after all."

"Yes, sir. Sorry, sir." I acted so meek and contrite that Jasper laughed his metaphysical backside off. "Where to now?"

"There's a general store yonder. We'll stock up on a few necessities and make our way out of this mess." He turned on Romulus. "And you listen to me good, boy. Lose her again and you'll feel my boot. Understand?"

Romulus seemed to shrink to half his size, and this time I didn't think it was an act. I felt for him, so lately a dog, then a slave, then free, and now being put back into bondage. Even if temporary, it had to hurt. I know it hurt me.

Hauling me up onto the horse to ride in front of him, whether I wanted to or not, Tyrell eased Al around a buggy and moved us toward the end of town. Jasper chattered about wanting to find some rabbits to pet next. I told him if we managed to save the world from all the evil sorcerers he could have a whole farm full of bunnies. An hour later, after buying some apples for his horse, sugar and flour for all, and boots (*new stiff ones. Ick!*), and stick candy for me, Tyrell had us back on the road again. Our travel day only half over, I settled in for the trip. Though I wanted to talk to Romulus about Roberta and Ernie, to see if they'd checked in the night before, the captain seemed determined to hang onto me. So I gave up and tried to relax on the hard saddle. I succeeded better than I'd have hoped, for soon

I dozed off.

I jerked awake, having been in so sound asleep that at first I thought morning had come already. Didn't know where I was, either. After thrashing around for a minute, I got my bearings. It turned out that I lay in the dog tent again, pitched next to somebody's big red barn. The comfortable smells of hay and manure pinched my nose. I made out the buzz of people talking, but they were too far away to understand actual words, even with my witched hearing. Alcibiades snorted right next to me someplace.

"It's all right, miss," said Romulus in a near-whisper. He crouched down at the tent's opening. "We's stopped fo' the night. Cap'n sweet-talked the owner o' this farm to let us stay here. A might better than roughin' it like last night."

Rubbing my eyes, I blinked and looked at him. Judging by the light it'd be dark in about two hours. "Holy cow...I've been asleep ever since Fredericksburg? That must be at least six hours."

"Yes'm. Guess you needed it."

He started to stand up, but I grabbed his shirt collar to keep him still. "Seen Roberta and Ernie? Did they show last night?"

"Just fo' a second. Said they'd be back when you was awake. 'Round about three o'clock today I mirrored 'em to meet us in the hayloft here just after sundown."

"Mirrored 'em? You know Morse code, too? Is there anything you Marshals can't do?"

A corner of his mouth went up for a second. "We's powerful

bad dancers, mostly."

I stretched and yawned. "Is that so?"

"Ernie's of the opinion that he be the exception, of course."

"Of course." I crawled out of the tent and got to my feet for a look around. The house and buildings were in good shape, fresh-painted and well-maintained, but that was as far as it went. At one time the farm might've been a prosperous one, but it looked like the Rebel army had requisitioned—the military term for 'stolen'—all of the livestock and a good part of the crops. The owner must not have been holding a grudge against the Confederate government if he'd offered hospitality to Tyrell. I noticed that his welcome didn't go so far as letting us sleep in the house, though. "So where are we?"

Romulus patted Alcibiades, who munched on one of the new apples. "Just north of Hanover Courthouse. Be in Richmond late tomorrow, I reckon."

"That'll be when things get serious." We watched a column of gray-coated infantry march past the house as fast as their feet could carry them. They must've been in a heck of a hurry to get at McClellan, for not a one of them broke ranks to forage on the farm property. In a second they'd rounded a bend in the road and were gone. "We'll need all of Roberta and Ernie's help to find a way around those armies."

"Should be easy once we gets past the Rebs," chuckled Romulus. "They say Stuart's cavalry rode all the way 'round the whole blessed Federal army only 'bout a week ago."

I'd read that, too, in an anti-McClellan paper. Maybe it was true. In a perverse way that lifted my spirits. It sounded like we could find a way past them, then. Three people would have an easier time than thousands of horsemen. Unless McClellan had learned the error of his ways and had sealed the gaps.

Tyrell barked at us from a corner of the barn. "You, Jim! I thought I told you to get some hay for my horse?"

"Right on it, sir," Romulus said, hurrying into the barn.

"Have to stay on them every second," grumbled the captain. "Go to sleep at a dead run if you aren't watchful. Anything to gum up the works of their betters."

I couldn't resist disagreeing. His attitude toward the colored folks annoyed me, though I had to be careful since Mary ought to share it. "Oh, I don't know. Jim's always been a hard worker for us. Perhaps you're letting your past experiences cloud your judgment?"

He shook his head at the poor benighted child of privilege. "It's good that you're so forgiving, but in time you'll learn that those who are too sweet get taken advantage of." With that argument-ender he turned and strode off toward the farmhouse.

Jasper piped up as Tyrell vanished into the house. "I wonder how sweet the Hellfiend Legion thinks you are?"

I laughed out loud. "The feelin's are mutual, I expect."

"Speakin' as the resident magick sword here..."

"Yeah?"

"Do you have an actual plan for gettin' to the coast, or are we just gonna read a few tea leaves?"

"I dunno. If I drink the tea first will that earn me magick

points?"

"Maybe if you pour some bourbon into it. Laudanum! Now laudanum would really charge me up."

I snorted. "But it wouldn't charge **me** up. I'm the one who'd float away on an opium cloud, mister. Don't you have any wants that are safe for your lord and mistress?"

"Lord and mistress? Sounds like a cheap stage act. Magician and a monkey."

"Yeah, but who is which? Come on, let's go make supper...and a plan."

There's an Assassins Guild?
Murderers with their own trade union?
Somehow it don't surprise me.
Probably a Loyal Order of Poisoners, too.
And a Torturers' Fraternal Association.

21 / Trouble in Richmond
Tuesday, June 24

As soon as it got dark we had a reunion in the hayloft. Sailing in through the high hatch, Roberta landed on an oak beam to let Ernie scramble from her scarlet back and down to my knee. Romulus kept watch at the top of the ladder, but we weren't much afraid that Tyrell would surprise us. After an actual hot meal, courtesy of the Grangerfords (owners of the property, whom he'd met and charmed some months earlier), the captain had declared it unnecessary to keep a watch that night. His trust in the Grangerfords meant that we were safe. Beds had been offered to us. He insisted that Romulus sleep outside, of course. I told him as Mary that I was having a fine adventure and would stay in the tent again like a real soldier. He took that as an indirect compliment, then retired to cotton sheets and a down mattress.

"Nice digs," squawked Roberta, eyeing the barn. "Better than berthin' on the ground like before."

Ernie agreed. "The barn mice like it here. Say the cat's old and slow. Prefers to snooze in the house rather than earn his keep."

"Course," our parrot ally went on, "it can't hold a candle to where we stayed last night." She paused just enough to make me fidget.

"And that was where?" I asked her.

"State capitol dome," Ernie announced with pride, running up Romulus to sit on his shoulder.

"Pigeons scooted over for us," Roberta explained. "Professional courtesy. Seems they're neutral, war-wise."

"You've really been in Richmond already?" I asked.

Ernie poked at Romulus' blistered shoulder. "Sure thing. We'd be poor scouts if we hadn't." He looked hard at Romulus, then at me. "What happened?"

I waved his question off. "He took my foot blisters. What's up in Richmond, then?"

Roberta itched her white cheek with a toe. "The Federal army's only four miles east of town. Everybody's runnin' hither and yon like their pumps have stopped workin'. Half the civilians have skedaddled already, and three-quarters of the rats, I might add."

"Typical," said Ernie, snapping his tail like a whip. "Bloody cowards. Give me a sturdy old mouse any day."

"Town's full o' soldiers headin' for the front. From what we hear this General Lee is gonna give McClellan a full broadside before the same thing happens to him. Little Mac's already shakin' in his boots thinkin' he's outnumbered. Seein' enemy sails where none exist."

I raised an eyebrow. "The pigeons told you all this?"

She peered regally at me through her spectacles. "What, you think they just sit around all day ploppin' on statues?"

"Hey, ease up. A couple days ago I didn't even know animals could talk."

"That's all right, girlie," Ernie laughed. "A couple o' days ago we didn't know humans could think." Roberta found that funny, too. Jasper guffawed so hard in my head I thought he'd wet himself. That was a prospect that didn't bear thinking about.

So there I sat, listening to a mouse and a parrot ridicule my species and give me left-handed compliments. *Won't this make for an odd memoir in my old age? Assuming I get to have an old age.* They gave us some more detailed information about Jackson's corps hustling from the Shenandoah Valley to flank McClellan, and about suspected positions of other Confederate and Union forces. Since brigades seemed to be shifting non-stop, though, that news was already out-of-date. We made plans for them to fly over us every two hours starting at noon the next day. I expected to get to the outskirts of town by late afternoon if we pushed it, which Tyrell could be counted on to do. By then I hoped we'd have enough good intelligence to decide how to get through or around the enormous masses of men in our way. If anything urgent needed to be communicated to us, Roberta said she'd send a robin friend of hers. Less likely to cause suspicion than a parrot in glasses carrying a mouse on its back, we all agreed.

I decided that walking any sort of distance in brand-new boots was a recipe for all kinds of disaster, so I used some of my velvety Boogie bank account to get Jasper to tenderize them for me. He did that by turning into an enormous toothy mouth and chomping them for half a minute. From the yummy sounds he made you'd have thought he was dining in some snooty Gaullic restaurant. When he spit them out like a tobacco chewer aiming for a spittoon, I winced at the prospect of putting icky goo on my tender toes. But they came out dry as a bone and as soft as a baby's bottom.

Other than the roads being clogged with more bodies, civilian and military, than on the first two days of our trip, nothing much changed on Tuesday. Rested from my heroic afternoon nap and an uninterrupted night's sleep, all cleaned up (an actual hot bath in the Grangerfords' house! Woo!), and full of food from a real breakfast, I felt spry and saucy. Romulus seemed to have shrugged off the wound transfer already, although shrugging off Tyrell's nasty comments looked to be more of a chore. Every step closer to Richmond worsened the Reb's tone toward the Marshal, who stayed stoic and took it all. Me, I'd have knocked him off of his horse. Then again, I wouldn't have been strung up from a tree by the locals for doing it, so maybe Romulus knew what he was about.

Jasper kept trying to get me to pilfer another cigar, but I made it very clear that I'd bathe in Washington Canal and arm-wrestle manure monsters before I ever smoked again. Nobody on the road wore their Sunday finery or their best perfume, so stranger-stroking or sniffing was out, too. I told him that if we got the chance in Richmond I'd get hold of some imported chocolate and gorge myself. Once I'd explained to him about chocolate ('God's apology for the flood') he whooped for joy. For once I agreed with him.

Just after noon Romulus caught up with me. With a worried look on his sweaty face he whispered, "Trouble, I thinks."

I gripped the cup where it hung on my belt. If he thought there was trouble I wanted to be ready for anything. "Where?"

"Not sure, but somethin' don't feel right. A darkness in the air, somehow."

"Well, we're in a war zone, you know."

He shook his head, looking all around without trying to be obvious about it. "Ain't that. More like Merchantry bizness. Your Stone's still quiet?"

Touching my chest and feeling nothing cold there, I nodded. "Warm as toast."

"Well, that's somethin'. Expect 'em to be mortals in daylight, anyways. 'Specially with all o' these witnesses."

Now I was looking around and seeing nothing, too. "Stragglers from the Legion, maybe? That boss of theirs got away. Don't how many of 'em are left. Plenty of new deserters to refill their ranks these days, I expect."

"Could be. But you oughta know, miss, that the Merchantry has its own renegades to watch out for."

*Huh? I'm only hearing about this **now**?* "Say that again?

Merchantry renegades? I thought they were this great well-oiled machine of world domination?"

"They is, but nothin' that big can hold together perfect. They's more than one opinion 'bout just how to run that machine."

"Dissension in their ranks?" *That's about the best news I've had all week.* "Good news for us, right?"

Romulus nodded, squinting into the sky at a circling buzzard. "Yes, ma'am. Unless one o' them groups has taken it into they heads to snatch you befo' you gets to London."

"Whoa! That'd explain why Venoma told me to get to London on my own but the bad guys still keep attackin' me. That bounty the Legion talked about might be from one of the dissenter groups. Makes sense, huh?"

He still watched that buzzard, which now swooped lower, right over my head. "It do, at that."

I frowned at the big ugly bird. "That buzzard one of 'em? You want me to get Tyrell to shoot it?"

Grabbing my arm hard, Romulus hissed in my ear, "No! That's Lenny."

"Lenny? He's a friend of yours?" I could believe anything, after the talking tree.

"We used t' work together...befo'." Romulus had a faraway look in his eye. *Must be rememberin' the good old days, back when he could relax by the hearth and chew a nice bone.*

"Uh...okay. Why's he here?"

"That's what I's wonderin'. Might be lookin' fo' a rabbit. He sure do love his rabbits." We followed Lenny's flight, which went lower and lower. The giant bird raced along the ground to our left, just off of the road. His talons, bigger than my own hands, snatched at something in the grass. Those huge wings beat the shimmery summer air and lifted the buzzard back up high. A large wriggling snake, a venomous copperhead, struggled to free itself from his grip.

"Good ol' Lenny," smiled Romulus. "Lookin' out fo' us, he is.

As he spoke good old Lenny tore the snake in two with one easy snap of his good old beak. After watching the pieces fall to earth he circled over us one more time. I swear it looked like he saluted us. Then he waggled his wings and disappeared to the south, where his normal prey would soon be lying in the sun, full of bullet holes.

"I suppose that wasn't just some poor innocent snake that just happened to be mindin' its own business?" I asked.

"No. You kin always tell. If he eats 'em, they's just food. If he kills 'em and leaves 'em, they's enemies."

Great. A buzzard with standards. "So now I have to worry about every livin' thing around me?"

"Not just now. You always had to worry 'bout that. And Bullies. And Venoma. And mortal bounty hunters. And maybe the Assassins Guild, too."

There's an Assassins Guild? Murderers with their own trade union? Somehow that don't surprise me. Probably a Loyal Order of Poisoners, too. And a Torturers' Fraternal Association.

"That's just wonderful. Remind me again who all is actually

on **our** side?"

Romulus gave me a grim smile. "Pretty much the whole world, miss. They's just too 'fraid to show it. That's why you's here. To give 'em courage."

Oh, so it's the blind leadin' the blind. At least I know where I stand...underneath a giant burden of 'save humanity or else,' that's where.

"Wait a minute. You say I've always had to worry about things bein' out to get me. You mean that literal-like, don't you? Like since I was born?" He didn't reply, just looked at me as if I were a drooling idiot, which I guess I was back then. "So that must also mean that I've been watched over my whole life, too? By who? I don't remember seein' any guards."

"That's the idea. We wanted you to grow up normal."

That made me see red. "Normal? Movin' from our farm in the dead o' night, with just the clothes on our backs? Growin' up with no Pa? That's normal?"

Romulus didn't look at me, but stared straight ahead as he walked. "Couldn't be helped. We tried to stop it, but..."

Stop what? Does everybody know the details of my life except me? "Then you do know what happened to Pa? Tell me! Ma won't say a word about it."

"Ain't my place to say."

"Well, whose place is it?"

I'd gotten pretty hot about the whole thing, and loud, too, I guess. Tyrell eased Alcibiades over and almost casually kicked Romulus with the side of his boot. "Say, boy, you're upsettin'

Miss Mary. Get along up front and shut your mouth."

Without another word Romulus picked up his pace and moved past the captain about thirty feet. Tyrell stared down from his giant golden horse. Al just snuffled at me, still hoping to find an apple. Both of them had a disappointed look. "What was that about?"

I reeled myself back into my role as Mary. Gritting my teeth, I said, "Just a little lesson on respect, is all. He'll be all right now." *Sorry, Romulus.*

"In my experience they remember their lessons best if you use a sharp whip. I'd be happy to—"

"No!" *Oops, that came out too strong.* I took a breath. "No. Papa always used to refuse to beat the hands. Said it just made 'em more resentful. We treat 'em like simple-minded children. Seems to work better."

"But even children, begging your pardon, miss, have to be spanked every now and then. For their own good, I mean."

I gave him a long, hard stare that must've cooled off the summer afternoon by ten degrees. "Don't even think it. You ain't my Pa...sir."

He touched the brim of his hat with a white-gloved hand. "As you say...ma'am." Spurring Alcibiades more sharp than necessary, he moved away without another word. I watched him for a moment to make sure he didn't abuse Romulus again out of spite, but they stayed well apart.

"Whoo! Remind me," said Jasper, "not to get on your bad side."

I smiled. "Too late. I can still taste that cigar."

"Someday you'll thank me for that. Besides, who's the one walkin' on two good feet?"

He had a point. It had been a fair enough bargain, considering what he might have asked for instead. I went to school with boys his age. Their minds smelled fouler than the Washington Canal. "Okay, okay. But why do I get the feelin' that when I need somethin' truly big from you that I'll be payin' some serious interest?"

"Hey, I didn't make the rules."

"Well, just remember, no pound of flesh."

"Why not? I can always heal you later. Romulus looks like he can spare it."

"What's this, pick-on-Romulus day?"

"No, it's picnic-on-the-battlefield day, remember?"

"Don't remind me. I'm not overjoyed with our plan."

"You mean you're not overjoyed with the cost."

"That, too. You're sure I can't just owe it to you? Pay later?"

"Sorry. I need the energy ahead of time to charge the magick. Couldn't give you credit even if I wanted to."

While I pondered our thin plan to get through to the other side of the feuding armies, we all kept plodding along. It seemed the only folks trying to get into Richmond from the north side were gray-uniformed soldiers and me. Story of my life, always swimming against the tide. It reminded me of the time Tommy smacked a beehive with a rock. All of the other kids had run for their lives, but I'd dashed up to see what an angry hive looked like. I sure enough found out. Ma had clucked over me all night, putting compresses on the stings, while Tommy had just made fun of me for getting what I'd deserved by being so simple.

And I get the feelin' I'm gonna get stung again pretty soon. This time there's no Ma or Tommy to make things better.

Just in time to accent my mood, clouds started to come in during the afternoon. The nearer we got to Richmond, and by three o'clock I could see the spire of its biggest church, the darker the sky became. A misty rain started to fall. The roads were hard-packed enough from travel and sun-baking that they didn't immediately turn to mud. I felt glad to be cooler, but the quick weather change, coupled with the snake incident and thinking about Ma and Tommy, glummed me something awful. To make matters even worse, distant thunder rumbled in around four o'clock, just as we hit the capital's northern outskirts. When the thunder didn't fade away, but grew in volume and duration, I knew we were in for it.

Guns. Artillery. Lots and lots of cannons firing east of town.

We're too late. The battle's already started. Now how do we get to the coast? A big detour south and then east would take forever. We might get to London too late to help Tommy. It made me want to sit in the middle of the road and cry.

Tyrell, face aglow with fighting fever, cantered up on Alcibiades, who seemed just as excited. The captain gripped his short-brimmed cap in one hand, waving it over his head in big circles. That long dark hair of his danced in the light rain.

"The show's begun, Miss Mary!" he whooped. "Now we'll

show Little Mac what a mistake he's made!" Slapping his kepi back on but askew, he held out a gauntleted hand to me. "Climb up here. My boys need me. Time to move."

Before I knew it I'd been jerked aloft into my customary place in front of him. From my high perch I saw that the crowds of civilians on the road didn't exactly share Tyrell's enthusiasm for battle. They all looked at one another in a forlorn way, like they were attending the same funeral. Alcibiades whinnied and charged down the road. People scattered as the enormous horse, resembling a glistening brass statue come to life, galloped into Richmond. His hooves made the same sound as the far-off cannon.

"What about Jim?" I asked, gripping Al's mane as tight as I could.

"Don't worry about him," Tyrell replied in a tight ominous tone. "Already arranged."

"Shape-shiftin' felt like bein' born
and givin' birth at the same time."
Jasper made a nauseated sound.
"Ooh, there's an image.
You know, livin' in your mind
makes me feel...dirty...sometimes."

22 / Lost in the Rain

Already arranged? What the heck does that mean? Can't be good. I struggled to get loose, but Tyrell had the back of my overalls in a vise-grip. We roared into Richmond like a runaway locomotive, Al's feet barely ever touching the dirt streets, almost as if he was flying. The capital city of Virginia and the southern Confederacy blurred past. I had no time for sightseeing, I just didn't want to fall from this tremendous horse. No longer the happy-go-lucky apple-muncher I'd grown used to, Alcibiades seemed transformed into some mythological beast of battle. The cannons' roar drew him like the pole draws a compass needle. If I hadn't known better I'd have sworn that fire sparked from his flared nostrils.

Tyrell matched his mount's fierce determination to reach the field of war. His eyes almost glowed from the fervor that drove him on. Every muscle taught as steel cables, the Reb captain had become a part of his steed. He leaned forward as if he could fly there like Mercury, winged sandals and all. Little did I know then how close that was to being the truth about him and Al both.

"Let me go!" I hollered, clutching the horse's neck like it was a tree trunk in a gale. "I need to get Romulus!"

"Who?" Tyrell shouted back, only half-listening. He'd been waving pedestrians and buggies aside, shouting that he was on a mission for General Lee.

"Jim," I snapped, catching myself. "We need Jim."

"Your darky has other business. It's all taken care of. Now hold on, I know a shortcut."

Alcibiades cut left quicker than my stomach or my head could keep up. Dizzy from the turn to the east, I nearly slid off. At that height and speed that would've been the end of me. Tyrell's iron hold, so annoying a moment before, had turned into a lifesaver. We dashed down a narrow side street with no traffic. That overjoyed me, because the terrifying speed at which we traveled boggled my mind. I'd been on horses before, being raised on a farm, but trotting a fat old plow horse and galloping a mighty cavalry charger were night and day. My pulse and my mind raced like lightning. No wonder men rushed out to join Stuart's horsemen.

"Yee-hah!" Jasper screamed. "This is the best thing ever! You're earnin' bucketloads of magick, girl!"

I struggled to focus my thoughts on him and still concentrate on staying astride Al. "Yeah, well, I'm about to lose bucketloads of my lunch if we don't slow down!"

"Go ahead! Less weight'll only make us go faster. Woo-eee!"

We were coming to an intersection with a major street. While I tried to think of a snappy retort to Jasper, not easy when your bones are shaking apart, a refugee wagon pulled right out in front of us, piled high with a family's worldly belongings.

That's it. We're all dead. Here endeth the Quest.

"Hang on!" Tyrell hollered, letting go of me to get both hands on the reins.

Hey! If I hang on any tighter I'll strangle your horse!

My Confederate captain urged his horse up. Our one chance was to jump the wagon. The awful shaking stopped as all of Al's feet left the ground. As we sprang up into the misty air time seemed to slow down to nothing. No sound reached my ears except the pounding of my own horrified heart. Amidst it all I had several clear thoughts.

We ain't gonna clear the wagon. It's too high. Even Al ain't strong enough. It's up to me. And this is a life-or-death situation, Jasper.

Whipping the tin cup from my belt, I aimed it down at the street. My will charged down my arm. Just as our momentum began to slow, Morphageus sent a pair of steely hooves down beneath Al's rear legs. For an instant we were astride a six-legged horse. The extra boost proved just enough. We clipped the leg from a chair atop the wagon, and almost the driver's head, too, but we made it up and across in one piece. Tyrell and I both 'oofed' from the impact of the hard landing. Alcibiades skidded to a stop, shaking his head as if he couldn't believe he'd made the jump. Tyrell panted from the exertion and the terror. At least my secret was still safe. Both he and the wagon driver had had their eyes closed.

There was a long pause while we all caught our breath. Beyond belief we were alive and well. The wagon pulled away, driver muttering curses at us. Then I got loud proof, in my ears and in my head, that men and boys are all the same.

Tyrell and Jasper, as if they'd planned it, let out a tremendous Rebel yell together. I swooned from the aural assault.

"Aaiee-yahh!" the Confederate screamed. Alcibiades reared up in agreement. The captain waved his cap to a couple of admiring boys who had seen the jump but not my magickal assist. They took off their own hats and tossed them into the gray sky, cheering us and beaming.

Then we were racing off east again as if nothing had happened.

Alcibiades showed no signs of tiring. In fact, the magnificent beast gained speed as we careened through the city. Mothers yanked their kids onto sidewalks, carriage drivers shook their fists at us, wounded veterans shouted encouragement to their fellow soldier, and Jasper kept hooting about how much fun it all was. I could only think of one thing.

Need to get off of this fool horse. Now.

There were too many people around to use Morphageus, so landing with a magick spring wasn't any good. I had to do it on my own, or as on my own as practicable. All of my senses stayed heightened by the Stone, I'd noticed, which also sped up and deepened my decision-making. None of that had to be recharged the way Jasper claimed the sword did. Must've just fed off of my soul or life-force or natural freckled cuteness. If I concentrated, most of the fear of being on a half-controlled horse faded away, as did the confused blurring of my vision while I searched for a way off. I even managed to dim Jasper's non-stop cackling.

Tyrell no longer held onto my overalls. *Guess the wagon episode taught him to use both hands.* That made my jump easier. Before he knew that I planned to leave I'd let go of Al's neck and slid to the right. Up ahead I spotted the one chance of a landing that might not involve breaking any of my treasured bones. I sure hoped that the Stone-enhanced senses also improved my aim and coordination.

Springing out from the speeding horse with all my might, I stretched out my arms in front of me. Zipping through the rainy air like a red-haired arrow, I darted straight at my target, a big round communal horse trough, eight feet across. No animals drank from it, though a couple of geezers stood next to it gabbing. Discussing the weather, maybe. They were about to get something better to talk about.

'Did I ever tell you about the time a girl flew into a horse trough? Soaked my best suit, she did.'

I feel for you, fellers. My best suit was about to get drenched, too. Heck, my only suit at the time. *Oh, well, it's rainin'. I'm already wet.*

Sure enough, the Stone guided me straight into the slimy

tank. A split-second before I hit I twisted around to land in a ball, back-first, hands covering my head. The water didn't turn out to be much softer than the ground. At least, that's how it seemed at the time. The wind got knocked out of me and I swallowed a mess of water before I managed to scramble up to clutch the side of the trough, gasping. Let me share some wisdom with you: water tainted with mule spit is not the nectar of Olympus.

A pair of ancient but strong hands lugged me out of the trough and onto my feet. Getting my overalls grabbed all the time began to annoy me. Twisting away, I freed myself and shook all over like a soaked dog. People stared at me as if I'd cheated death, a pretty accurate summation of events. I gave the onlookers, including the pair of elderly gents who looked close to heart failure, my most winning smile and a big shrug.

"That's why I prefer to ride in a buggy!" Folks laughed as I snatched up my cap and sprinted off the way I came, leaving a wet trail behind me on the street. My drawers squished like sponges and my overalls weighed a ton. I felt like I ran in a dream, where everything's in slow-motion and you don't manage to get anywhere. But I had to return to where I'd lost Romulus. Richmond was too big and chaotic to find somebody if you let it go for too long. Getting turned around a couple of times, eventually I had to slow down and ask somebody to show me the road from Hanover Courthouse. They pointed me in the right direction and after about half an hour I got to the place where Tyrell had kidnapped me.

No Romulus. Nowhere, no how.

Controlling my panicky breathing, I dashed into every store on the block, asking if they'd seen a giant shaved-head Negro anyplace. Nope. I had no luck asking people on the street, neither. But since they all clearly thought I'd lost my mind—soaked to the skin, hair matted, eyes wild, raving—maybe all they wanted was to get away from me. It seemed as if he'd been swallowed up into the earth. Later on I found out that this was just what had happened, more or less.

After fifteen minutes of useless searching I plopped down on a bench outside a cobbler's shop, the pounding in my head echoing the thump of the guns. I sat alone in a strange town in wartime, a great battle had begun, my only family in mortal danger, and now my trusted guide had vanished. *Verity, you're in a world of trouble.* But darn it, I was still the Stone Warden, born to save humanity and restore the world to its natural order. *Time to do what great heroes do.*

I cried. A lot.

I bawled like every baby ever born. I wailed until my throat rebelled. I blubbered until snot ran down my shirt. Oh, I did it right. And at the end of it, of course, I had improved my lot not one tiny bit.

Not true, to be honest. After making such a fuss someone was bound to ask me why I bawled. That someone turned out to be a soldier working for the Provost Marshal. A military policeman. His worried round doughy face, rain running down it, appeared in front of mine like a big wet pie.

"Honey," he asked in a slow drawl that told me he came from way south of Richmond, "maybe you'd best tell me what the trouble is."

Sniffing, I gulped air, collected my thoughts, and reassumed my Mary Williams role. I spun him much the same tale I'd told Tyrell about my lost brother, but added a bit about losing good and faithful Jim, Pa's best hand, who'd raised me from a pup. If I didn't find Jim my Daddy'd whup me, not to mention that I'd be all sorrowful about losing my best friend. That last part didn't require much in the way of a performance.

"Loose slaves have all been rounded up and put to work diggin' fortifications, darlin'," the plump soldier told me. "North and east o' town. That's what I've been doin' all day. If we see 'em we line 'em up and march 'em off. Sometimes folks point 'em out to us, then we grab 'em and add 'em to the bunch. Don't recall seein' that buck o' yours, though. But there's other details besides mine."

"Where do you send 'em?" I asked, calming down like oiled waters as I grasped at this straw. "Is there a central place they go before bein' sent to the works?"

He wiped his face with a bandana no drier than the rest of him, his musket slung over his shoulder, muzzle-down to keep the water out. Another red handkerchief had been wrapped around the lock for the same reason. "Naw, we just git 'em all out to either the Williamsburg Road to the east or the Mechanicsville Turnpike farther north. Whichever's closest. Somebody there decides where to send each bunch."

For the first time I looked past him to see his detail. Five other soldiers, as bedraggled as hobos, stood guard on maybe a dozen forlorn black men of all shapes and sizes. None of them was my Romulus. "Where are y'all goin'?"

"North side. The fightin's all out the Williamsburg way. Federals sent out a forced reconnaissance, ran into Huger's brigade. Sharp work over there. But General Lee's afeard that McClellan will take the chance to move around us to the north, so we're to extend the trench line."

This was the best-informed sergeant I'd ever run into. Most soldiers seldom knew anything more about the tactical situation than, "Well, the colonel says fer us to go get 'em yonder."

"Could I tag along with you? See if he's there?" I begged, putting on my best and cutest face. It wasn't much, after the rain and crying and whatnot, but I tried. "I'd be ever so grateful."

"Land sakes, no, child!" His horrified expression told me that he'd prefer charging Yankee double-canister. "It'd be as much as my backside's worth to take a little girl out there. For all we know the entire Yankee army's about to charge into Richmond with all they got. Your pa wouldn't thank me if I got his baby captured or worse."

I stuck out my lower lip in a great big pout and let it quiver a bit. My tear-stained eyes started to well up some. A catch came into my breath as if an enormous sob was on the way. Tommy would've been proud. I hadn't been spending all that time at Ford's Theatre for nothing.

My performance worked...sort of. The sergeant must've had

at least one daughter, because he had the look of a man who'd do almost anything to avoid the waterworks. "All right, all right. Tell you what. I cain't take you with us, but I can look 'round when we get there and see if your Jim's in sight. Where'll you be so I can send a message?"

Good question. Sticking where I was wouldn't do. Tyrell might retrace his steps as I'd done and come looking for me. I couldn't afford to waste time running from him or figuring out another escape. "Where's General Lee's headquarters?"

"Out along Nine Mile Road, just past Battery Five. Widow Dabbs' house. A little more than a mile east of town. 'Bout two miles from where we sit." My benefactor cocked his head at me and squinted. "Why? You surely ain't thinkin' o' goin' out there?"

"Why not? I imagine that General Lee's sittin' in the best-protected spot we have."

"I allow that may be true, but that don't make it safe for a girl, 'specially when there's a big push on. Patrols ain't permittin' any civilians up that way without they got themselves a pass." He stood up and backed away from me, moving toward his detail. They looked like they were getting fidgety and wanted to get going. "I can tell you, honey, no man worth his salt's gonna give you one. Heartless, that'd be." He tipped his hat and waved at his men to move out, nudging the captive men ahead of them. "If I find your man, I'll send word to this here cobbler. It'll be from Sergeant Wilkes, that's me. Now that's there's all I can do. You take care now."

The soggy detail marched away, taking my best chance at finding Romulus with them. Watching them trudge east, toward the mounting gunfire, I felt empty. A long sigh left me and I sagged against the pole holding up the shop's sign. What now? Sit and pray that a busy soldier in the heat of battle remembered a promise to a stranger? And even if I did, what if Tyrell came back? Or worse, Bullies? I recalled the snake that the kindly buzzard had dispatched. It had been following me, spying on me. For who? For how long? What information had it passed along? For all I knew, battalions of Merchantry agents, eager for bounty, were in Richmond already. I needed to get to Lee's headquarters, spin a sob story, free Romulus, and get to the coast. Sitting in one place was probable suicide.

I need a disguise. Too many enemies are nearby and know me on sight.

"I agree," said Jasper. "Lovely cannonball into that trough, by the way."

"Thanks," I thought to him with an imagined scowl. "Do you have anything helpful to say or are you just lookin' to gloat at my predicament?"

"Hey! Your predicament is my predicament."

"Then maybe you'd like to suggest a way outta this mess."

"You already have."

"Huh? What?"

"Thought of a way out. You need a disguise, you said. I agree."

The rain had tapered off to nearly nothing. It hadn't been much to start with. I shook my short hair and slicked it back out of my eyes. "And I suppose you're offerin' to help with that?"

"How could I not? You're my favorite Stone Warden."

I started walking down the street, planning to turn at the first intersection and get onto a side street or alley, where I was less likely to get spotted. "No, thanks. Shape-shiftin' ain't my cup o' tea. Felt like bein' born and givin' birth at the same time."

Jasper made a nauseated sound. "Ooh, there's an image. You know, livin' in your mind makes me feel...dirty...sometimes."

"Hey, who forced this little kid to smoke a cigar the size of her arm? Don't talk to me about foul."

"Be that as it may, I can help you with your disguise. You'll hardly notice it this time. Cross my heart."

I slunk into a tiny trash-filled alleyway, getting a snotty look from a mutt there. The dog had been sniffing a filthy drunk lying asleep next to a doorway. "No shape-shiftin', I said."

"Okay, okay, I heard you the first time. This won't be a shape-change. At least, not a real one. It'll be a glamour."

"And that'd be different...how?" I moved past the snoring man, my wonder-nose rebelling at his stench. The rain had done little to wash him off.

"Instead of witchin' your body into a new form, which is a powerful spell and makes you feel like a sheet of paper somebody's wadded up—"

"Exactly right."

"A glamour puts the image of what you want to be into the minds of observers. Everybody sees you as President Lincoln or whoever, but you haven't made a physical change at all. If you look in a mirror you see your actual face and body, unless you will yourself to see the false image."

That sounds too good to be true. I told him as much.

"It's perfect for what you want, to fool people. Shape-shiftin' is for when you need the actual attributes of a thing as well. Glamourin' you into a beaver wouldn't have helped you swim the river, for instance. You still would've been Verity, blubblin' your way to the bottom of the Potomac."

"So I just wish to look like somebody else and other folks see me that way? All other folks? Everybody I meet?"

"Yep. Looks and voice. Unless they're a mage huntin' specifically for a glamour. Not likely any of 'em around here at the moment."

"Anything else I should know about it before I say yes?"

Jasper sniffed. "Your suspicious nature makes me cry, my girl."

"Yeah, well, I figure developin' a suspicious nature is gonna to keep me alive in the future."

Laughing, he said, "Now you're learnin', dearie. There are two kinds of glamours, the one you want and the type that reaches into the mind of the observer for the best image."

I stared at the drunk clutching his half-full whiskey bottle and shivered at the thought of what he might like to see if he happened to wake up right then. "Why would I want that?"

"To create an emotion that you can manipulate. Fear or joy or love. You can make somebody see you as the thing they're most afraid of, for instance. Harder to control, harder to maintain. Unpredictable, since you won't necessarily know what they're seein' in you."

"But I don't want that one anyhow, right?"

"Nope. The simple kind will do for gettin' through town unnoticed. Plus, a passion glamour needs more energy than a vizard glamour."

I frowned. "Vizard?"

"Mask. It's in Shakespeare. I thought we met in a theatre?"

"Pardon me for not knowin' every antique word in the world. I take it that when you say 'needs more energy' that also means 'costs the girl more to use'?"

"Well, now that you come to it..."

I sighed. *Why do I suspect this'll be worse than the sorry cigar episode?* "Let's have it."

My tin cup popped into the shape of a hand, index finger aiming back at the wretched fellow on the ground. Following the pointing digit, I saw that it led to the bottle.

I felt my stomach heave at the thought. "Oh, no," I moaned aloud.

The hand became a toothy smiling mouth. "Oh, yes," it said with honeyed glee.

> *I stepped around the corner of the shop*
> *and upchucked whiskey into the alley.*
> *"Hey!" Jasper whined, "I wasn't done with that."*

23 / How to Glamour a General

"I look prettier than a leading lady at Ford's," I said to myself, gazing in the window of a dry goods store. At least, I hoped it was to myself. That vile whiskey I'd stolen from the poor man in the alley might've been fooling with my senses.

The lovely young thing who stared back at me from the shop window looked to be in her mid-twenties. Like mine her hair shone coppery-red. But where mine sat straight and boy-short, hers flowed past shoulder length and was gathered in a jeweled white snood. Her shoulders were broad without being mannish and her waist, cinched in by a torture-chamber corset from the look of it, was narrow as a pencil. *And I have a bosom! Oboy!* Perfectly-proportioned, too. Not too large so as to look silly or cheap. Arms and hands long, slender, and smooth, the vision's neck matched the rest and led up to a chin with just the slightest point. Miss Cutey-Pie's face could only be what Ma called a 'man-melter.' Baby-soft skin, white as a dove's belly, a delicate nose you just wanted to reach out and tweak a little, and dark blue lamb's eyes underneath saucy eyebrows. Lord only knew what part of my mind had been hoarding this image. The wishful-thinking part, no doubt.

"Please," I muttered, looking up, "let this be me in ten or twelve years. Is that too much to ask?"

Jasper spoke up, speech slurred just a little. "Now I know you're drunk," he teased. "Who'd want to look like this all her life? What a burden."

I tried to touch the plush green velvet dress worn by the stranger. No mystery where it came from. It looked a lot like Boogie's. My tiny friend's skirt hadn't gone all the way to the ground and her hoop hadn't been as pronounced, but other than that it was mostly the same dress. Mine had fine gold thread trimmed along the cuffs, in imitation of the 'scrambled eggs' that Confederate officers wore on their uniform sleeves. Where Boogie's hat had been a giant-brimmed girlie affair, I wore a feminine version of a soldier's kepi, also with gold accents. An open-weave suggestion of a veil curtained my features but didn't really hide a thing. *Yep, this is surely a husband-catchin' outfit.* When my fingers stroked the top of the skirt I gasped. All I felt was rough dirty denim. Gazing down, I saw that I still wore my soiled wet overalls and flannel shirt. I raised my head and looked at the shop window once more. Yep, the stunning vision again. *That's scary.*

"My voice'll be different, too?" I asked Jasper out loud, hoping to hear for myself. Sounded the same to me. Two ladies who walked by at that moment looked over at me, but their expressions only said that they wondered why I yakked to nobody, not that I sounded odd.

"You'll have to will your ears to hear it the way you want, just like you did with your appearance," Jasper told me, giggling. He sounded like the raw whiskey had affected him more than me. Maybe he was just trying on 'drunk' for size. I doubted that he could really feel alcohol like a living human.

I sent my voice low into my throat, raised my chin, and said into the window, "Could you get me a nice cold lemonade, sir?" The tones I heard now were rich, warm, sultry. They licked my ear like a cozy fire in mid-winter. *Whoa!*

"Absolutely, ma'am," purred a new voice behind me. The glass reflected a handsome short-bearded man of middle years, dressed like a banker or lawyer in a fine black suit. "And any other service I could perform would be a distinct pleasure." He tipped his hat and smiled.

Well, time for a test run, Verity. Now or never.

The three healthy swigs of rotgut I'd had ten minutes before gave me the courage to turn to him. Twice I almost lost my balance, but he didn't seem to notice. I could feel the flush of the firewater in my cheeks. Hopefully, he'd put it down to coquettishness.

"Why, aren't you just the sweetest thing!" I cooed, putting on all of the southern charm I could muster. "You know, I was standing here, all a-twitter over this battle I keep hearing about, flustered over what indignities our brave boys must be suffering, and foolish phrases must have positively leaped out of my mouth. Now what might I have said to deserve the attentions of such a charming gentleman as yourself?"

That's layin' it on with a trowel. But my admirer ate it all up, so I guess my acting still measured up to Tommy's standards. In fact, Prince Charming here looked like he wanted to eat **me** up. I half-expected to hear myself say, 'Why, Grandma, what big teeth you have!' *Careful, kiddo. Your head's swimmin' as it is.*

"You expressed a desire for a lemonade, ma'am. Do you still wish it? I'd be more than happy to—"

I waved him off. "A lemonade! Oh, flighty old me! I couldn't bear to indulge in something so selfish with those guns roaring at our men. Dear me, no!" I touched his sleeve with two delicate fingers and looked at him sideways. "However, if you would be so kind as to direct me toward Nine Mile Road, I will gladly sing the praises of your gallantry till they echo from the clouds above." I'd heard that line in some dreadful touring production only a month ago. It'd made me roll my eyes and gag then, but it seemed appropriate now. My tummy lurched. *And if you don't get away from this fellow in a heartbeat you're gonna roll your eyes and gag all over his expensive imported boots.*

"Anything for you, ma'am." In three brief efficient sentences he lay out my route. *Ah, a lawyer, then.* I gushed as my new character required, thanking him as if he'd just given me a new house, and bid him a fond good-day. No sooner had he lifted his hat and headed off down the street than I stepped around the corner of the shop and upchucked whiskey into the alley.

"Hey!" Jasper whined, "I wasn't done with that."

"Yes, you were, bucko," I whispered, wiping my mouth on my sleeve. *Adults drink this stuff? On purpose? They actually pay good money for it?* With that kind of judgment small wonder they'd all blundered into this horrible war. "And for the record, that tasted worse than the tobacco."

"Been on this earth twelve years and you don't know how to live," he clucked.

"I want to keep livin', that's the thing. Maybe even see age thirteen or fourteen. And where did you ever get the idea that children should drink whiskey, anyhow?"

"Well, if they'd have given me a grown-up I'd have taken her. Rearin' you is no picnic, believe me."

"Rearin' me? We're the same age, ain't we? Technically."

He tried to speak in a ghostly old-man-in-the-mountain voice. "I'll have you know that I am as ancient as the Seven Seas and as venerable as the—"

"Oh, shush! You may have been stuck in that sword forever, but you don't know beans about real life. If you did you wouldn't be puttin' me through these foul experiences so you can see and feel. Don't come at me with that high-and-mighty tone."

"Hoo! Ain't we full of ourselves now that we look all mature."

I groaned, dizzy and sick. "All I'm full of is alcohol." Looking around, I could see that no one took much notice of me. Good so far, as long as I didn't attract attention by any drunken foolishness. "We need to get goin'. Find Romulus. A brisk long walk should help clear this poison out of my system."

"Poison!" Jasper sounded like he thought I'd gone loco. "How can anything that creates such exquisite sensations be called poison? Ah, the aroma!"

"Smells like turpentine."

"The delicate flavor!"

"Tastes like cough medicine."

"The silky mouth feel!"

"Burns like Prussic acid."

"The dreamy impression of floatin' on air!"

"The miserable impression of my snoot in the mud if you don't quit goin' on about it. Help me concentrate until the wooziness passes. You're sure this glamour will last till we get out to the lines and talk to General Lee? It won't fade because of the whiskey?"

"No, you should be fine. It's not time-limited like the shape-shift. It depends on your energy reserves, which you have plenty of at the moment. Whee!"

At least somebody's happy about my first and last drink. Twelve years old and a tragic victim of demon rum already. Ick.

"You're welcome," I thought to him in a surly manner. I crept along the crowded street with mincing steps. People stood in clumps, trying to analyze rumors about the battle and make those agree with the sounds of firing that we could all hear from the east. The artillery booming had been joined by massed musketry, which at this distance resembled someone tearing a giant canvas sheet. I hoped with all my heart that Romulus hadn't been trapped in the middle of it all.

Following my admirer's careful instructions, and stopping once more to fertilize an alley, I made it across Richmond without getting too lost. Everybody I met beamed and said hello. The disguise worked like a charm (an appropriate figure of speech, considering). I suspected Jasper of having added some passion glamour to it, making folks see me as their best friend or favorite relative, but he said no. I'd just overdone the attractiveness of my false image when I'd engaged the spell. A common problem with beginners.

"Truth to tell, this glamour may be worse than stayin' as yourself," he nagged. "Nobody pays any never-mind to kids, especially grimy ones on side streets. But now you're strollin' down a main avenue of the capital of the Confederate States of America, lookin' like every man's notion of a plantation princess and givin' out signals like a queen bee in heat. Stop grinnin' at everybody!"

Sure enough, I held a perpetual smile that I'd been sharing with all and sundry. My face ached from flashing my gorgeous new teeth, like I led a grand illumination on a national holiday. I forced my face into a more neutral pose. "I can't help it. Must be the novelty of the whole thing. Most of the time nobody pays me the slightest attention."

"That's 'cause you dress like a plow hand."

"Hey!"

"Uncle Jasper calls 'em as he sees 'em."

"This is practical. I work backstage a lot.'

"Whatever you say. All I know is that your boyfriend wears a dress more than you do."

"Boyfriend? Tommy is not my—!" That brought me up short. *This'll bear thinkin' about, I suppose. But not now.* "Dresses are uncomfortable, itchy things. They trip you up with all of their petticoats and skirts. Hoops are ridiculous and corsets are a crime. Only men could've invented it all."

"That's just the liquor talkin'. I think, deep-down, you love to get all frilly."

"This from a dumb old boy. What do you know, Mr. 'ancient as the Seven Seas'?"

He sighed. "Maybe nothin'...yet. But one of these days you'll need a magick favor and then I'll get to romp through your brain's attic. I can hardly wait."

That made whiskey and cigars sound like a church picnic. Time to change the subject. "Um...This glamour will hold no matter what, right? Even if somebody touches me? Shakes my hand, or kisses it? They like to do that down here."

"The vizard is solid, don't you worry. I'm a trained professional. Can't you still feel it on you?"

I focused my foggy senses on my outsides. Sure enough, the tightness on my skin, like what you'd get from a real long scrub with too-strong soap, still pinched me. A sort of buzz, different than the whiskey thrill, hummed through my bones. It felt like the aftershock of a close lightning strike. Beneath it all lay the faint tang of brimstone and lilies that always hit my nose when Jasper did something special.

"Yep, I feel it, all right. I just hope it works on General Lee."

"It should, unless he's even more of a paragon of virtue than they say he is. Why do you need to see him, anyway? The passes are probably bein' handled by some major workin' for the Provost-Marshal."

Keeping my face frozen into a widow's mask, I worked on ignoring all the people I passed. We'd been walking for nigh on an hour and not much of Richmond proper was left. Soon we'd be out of town and into the danger zone. "Because I don't want to waste time arguin' with a lackey if it turns out he wants to be troublesome. Better to go straight to the top and get a signed order nobody can challenge. We can't afford to risk lettin' Romulus get caught in army red tape. The longer he lingers in some trench the more danger he's in." I touched my imaginary dress where the Stone lay hidden. "And while I'm there, I want to see if my Stone goes cold. Find out just how high up the Merchantry mages go in this war."

"Makes sense, exceptin' that your general's up in the thick of the action right now, judgin' by the noise."

He had a point. Now we stood twice as close to the point of contact as before. The din of cannon and muskets hit me like an angry slap in the face. Granted, my hearing made it much louder than it was, but still I felt it rather than heard it. It no longer sounded so much like thunder as it did standing inside of a giant steamship engine going over a waterfall.

"Not much we can do about that now," I told him. "Just keep goin' and try to make somethin' happen. If we throw up our hands and sit, hopin' for a miracle..."

"Disappointment is likely to ensue," Jasper muttered, finishing my thought. We were starting to sound like an old married couple.

Richmond lay behind us. Ahead Nine Mile Road, a narrow dirt path starting to go a little bit muddy with the light rain, ran over rolling fields into a line of trees. Somewhere beyond them and to our right raged the fighting, near the Williamsburg Road. A few houses, some shacks and a handful of nicer, more substantial dwellings, sat scattered along our way. None looked to be occupied by their owners. Lots of the front yards were full of officers on horseback, consulting maps or peering through spyglasses. One property had been turned into a hasty storage depot for ammunition boxes and such. I saw no civilians at all. Everybody'd skedaddled when the guns had started, if not before.

We kept on going. After a few more minutes we came upon Battery Number Five that the plump soldier had mentioned. It looked out to the east on a vast field of stumps, where a small forest had been cleared to make a good field of fire, as well as to build the bastion itself. The Rebs had made it of earth reinforced with logs. Gabions, giant wicker baskets filled with dirt, lined the outside wall to absorb Minie balls and shrapnel. Shaped like a star, the fort squatted low, over fifty yards across. Each point of the star could reinforce another, so that an enemy reaching, or even breaching, a wall would take crossfire from other areas of the bastion. Lee's troops had porcupined it with cannon, threatening the north, east, and south. A couple hundred men manned the guns, ready to deal death to any attacker. They were supported by a regiment of infantry, standing alert with gleaming bayonets fixed on their muskets. I'd read about this type of defense in *Harper's Weekly* not too long before. Trying to force your way into Richmond along this stretch of road would make for a bad and bloody day.

I resisted the temptation to drive their commander crazy by waving and giggling at them all with my saucy glamour. *Best to keep your head down, kiddo, and not draw attention till you have to.* Maintaining my pace, I plodded down the road, expecting at any moment to be challenged by somebody from the fort or a cavalry patrol. Nobody did so. I guessed that the bastion's defenders had their own worries and left that sort of thing up to the scouts. Passing the fort with a sigh of relief, I checked on how my real self was doing. Most of the wooziness from Jasper's vile whiskey had gone. My feet didn't stumble or slide, nor did my stomach heave. *That's good. Need a clear head here directly, I expect.* But now I felt so thirsty that my tongue seemed to swell up. Guzzling the last of the water from my canteen, which I'd poured into the tin cup so that it would look less suspicious, I felt a lot better. Except for the fierce headache that had just started, I gave myself reason to hope that I might survive my youthful brush with intemperance.

"So far, so good," I said to Jasper, eyeing the road in front of me. Stumbling into a hole in my weakened condition wouldn't be good. The fort lay a few hundred yards behind us. Somewhere near ought to be the Dabbs house, if that Provost sergeant's information was to be trusted. He'd been accurate enough about the battery.

"Good for you, maybe," Jasper moped. "The whiskey's all gone and I have a headache."

"What do you mean **you** have a headache? I'm the one with the hangover. You're a disembodied spirit moochin' off my intake."

"Oh, don't I wish that was true." He sounded genuinely miserable. "Seems when the rules changed my energy got even more mingled with yours than before. Believe me, right now I feel your pain."

I tried to conceal my delight from him, not sure if that was even possible now. "Honest? You ain't just joshin'?"

"Do I sound like I'm joshin'?" What he sounded like was a kid with the influenza.

"Hard to tell with you, boyo." I made a nasty spike out of the cup, grit my teeth, and jabbed a little finger onto it.

"Ow!" he yowled. "What're you doin'?"

Sucking on my finger, I let out a muffled laugh. "Just checkin' on your veracity."

"Well, check it some other way. Don't have to poke me full o' holes. Darn!"

"You know, to be strictly accurate, you just stabbed yourself."

He let out a growl. "Go ahead. Have your fun. Your next favor's gonna be a doozy."

"Good luck comin' up with somethin' worse than the first two. If I understand you right, you'll feel every bit of it right along with me."

"That may be, but my evil creative imagination can dream up things that'll gratify me but horrify you."

His tone of voice made him sound like one of those stage villains out to have his way with the ingénue. I didn't much care for it, but right then I had bigger worries, like the butternut-clad soldier standing in front of me with his hand raised. Stopping as ordered, I stood as sweet and pretty as I could manage.

"Afternoon, ma'am," he drawled. "I'm 'fraid you can't go any further."

Pouting, I stuck my hip out and put a hand on it. "Can't I?"

"General Lee's strict orders. No civilians in the battle zone."

I gave him a soft little laugh. "And good for you, followin' your orders so well. But what makes you so sure I'm a civilian, Captain...um—?"

The soldier, who couldn't have been more than five years older than the real me, flushed red as I ran my poked finger across my bottom lip. Boys are all the same. Sweet silly old hound dogs. "Uh, Private, ma'am. Private Sawyer."

"My mistake, Private. I am positively blinded by your command presence."

"Not at all, Miss—?"

"Mahoney. Alaena Mahoney." I'd been thinking for a while about what name to use. My Grandma had been a Mahoney, from Belfast. Easy to remember in a pinch. And I used her pet name for my ma for the same reason.

"You ain't a civilian, Miss Mahoney? Pardon me for sayin' it, but I sure don't recall seein' anybody in the army as purty as you and no mistake."

Yep, a girl can sure get used to this. Might have to think about changin' outta these overalls some day, when all this quest business is done with.

I let him wriggle for a second while I gave him a brilliant smile, then I really turned on the charm. "Why, aren't you just the most splendid thing on two legs! A lady could get positively spoiled hearing such a handsome man talk like that. Turn my head, you will. But to be serious for just a moment, Mr. Sawyer. I have an important message to deliver to our great and good General Robert E. Lee." I touched his sleeve just like I'd done to the lawyer in town. "Personally." He whimpered like a famished dog staring at a bone.

And that was how I found myself being escorted into Confederate headquarters like the Queen of Sheba.

Tyrell grinned at me and touched his hat brim with a finger.
The instant I saw him the Stone froze solid.
Then the shooting began.

24 / Witching Robert E. Lee

The Widow Dabbs lived in a fine white two-story house with green shutters. I saw no sign of her, so I guessed she'd been moved into Richmond like the other civilians. As with some of the earlier dwellings we'd passed, the front lawn served as observation post, map reading center, and officers' lounge. Not a lot of that happened in the rain. Most everybody stayed inside, except for a pair of glum sentries and a lieutenant in a gum overcoat sitting on top of the roof, eye jammed into a huge telescope. Every now and then he'd holler some military gibberish like 'enfilade' or 'flying battery' down to a sergeant in a second-floor bedroom. That man would scribble hasty notes and slap them into the hand of a private, who'd dash down the stairs and deliver them to a clump of officers crowded around a map. Then they'd make noises like a bunch of high-ranking chickens, clucking and babbling. Every few minutes a messenger would blast up on a sweaty snorting horse to gasp out something that would set them a-fussing all over again. No sooner would they send him back with a written or oral command then another would arrive to make them all flutter some more. *If that makes for efficient military maneuverin' then my name's Horace Greeley. But heck, they're all generals and colonels, so what do I know?*

Private Sawyer, duly chastised for disobeying his orders and bringing me into Lee's headquarters, stood back at his post near the road, getting rained on again. Perhaps as a reward, the drizzle showed signs of ending soon. So did the battle. Most of the heavy artillery fire had already tapered off, leaving just the occasional rattle of muskets. From what I could overhear, which with my ears was pretty near all of what they said, the Yankees had pulled back after finding out that the Williamsburg Road hadn't been abandoned after all. They'd heard rumors of a Rebel flanking movement and hoped that the defenses had been stripped to send men around to the north. When that proved untrue McClellan moved his reconnaissance brigade back to where it'd started. General Lee had been up at the battle line since the guns had first started dueling. One of the couriers brought word that he was on his way back, now that things were quieting.

They'd not known how to react to me, women at headquarters being as rare as oars on a duck. Their first reaction had been to send me packing, rain or no rain, but Southern chivalry won out over military logic. Instead they plopped me on a comfy wing chair in a corner of the drawing room and tried to question me as to just what I thought I was doing. That didn't last long. By now I'd learned how powerful this glamour could be. Turning the tables on them, I complimented every man in range on his hospitality, good looks, military genius, and general Confederate adorability. In three minutes my feet were up on a footstool, I'd been given a towel for my wet face, and hot coffee filled my cup. I felt like a prize racehorse being readied for the big event.

One colonel managed to recall that there was still a war on. "Miss Mahoney, you say you have a private message for General Lee when he returns?"

I nodded, sipping my coffee and nibbling on a sweet roll somebody'd found for me. *Great! I'm starvin'. Tyrell has all of our supplies on his horse.* "I do, indeed."

"And you can't tell any of us because...?"

"Because she hasn't bothered to invent it yet," said Jasper to me, snickering.

I tried to ignore him and focus on my new character. Out with Mary Williams, in with Alaena Mahoney. "Ooh, aren't you just bursting with inquisitiveness! Believe me, I would dearly love to share my news with all of you and get out of harm's way. Really, I would. Not to disparage the fine company in which I find myself, of course. But the party who entrusted the information to me insisted that he was on a mission of extreme delicacy for the good general. His instructions were quite clear: from my lips to General Lee's ears only. The information is that sensitive." To help my cause I lingered on 'lips.' The poor man's brain visibly shut down for a second. *Is it really that easy to turn men into marionettes? Have to keep that in mind.*

"Uh...well, then...," he stammered. "Perhaps we'll just let you sit there a spell. The general's on his way, according to his aide."

"You are the soul of kindness, sir," I purred with a warm smile and a wink. He shuffled off to look at the map, eyes a bit crossed.

I must use this power only for good.

"You must use this power to get us the heck outta here," Jasper insisted.

"Don't fret," I thought to him, keeping an eye on the room. "Things're goin' perfect so far."

"So far. Let's not push it. Get hold of Romulus and let's go."

"You know that's not all we're here for. Relax. Have some more coffee." I sipped out of the cup, feeling the brew warm my insides. Real coffee, too, not one of those awful chicory substitutes forced on the South by the Union blockade.

"Mmm," he sighed. I could almost feel his toes wiggle, if he'd had any. "I like this stuff. You're rechargin' your magick again. That sweet roll ain't hurtin', neither."

Most of the whiskey had cleared from my head. The coffee and food dimmed the headache, too, and quieted my upset stomach. *I could almost take a nap. That'd be real nice.* I caught myself before I let that happen. Falling asleep and then being awakened by General Lee could easily lead me to say the wrong thing. And I'd only get this one brief chance to speak to him, I felt sure of that.

"Nothin' outta the Stone, I see," Jasper observed.

"Nope. Not cold, not glowin', not dancin' a jig. All's quiet on the evil front."

"Fine by me. Wouldn't do much for your stealthiness to have to use Morphageus in here."

I smiled to myself. "Can you imagine the letters home if we had a fight right now?"

Jasper imitated some hapless Alabama major writing home. "'Dearest Beatrice. You'll never believe the amazin' occurrence I had the misfortune to witness yesterday. A veritable paragon of Irlannish femininity whupped up on the flower of Confederate manhood with a glowin' sword. I swear it's true, as I live and breathe.'"

"Let's just keep our wits about us so I can live and breathe. We may have to change things in a hurry if our plans go wrong. Listen."

I told him what I wanted to do and asked if it'd be possible."

"Oh, sure," he told me. "It's possible. Cost you a little extra, though."

I'd been afraid of that. "What?"

He paused for dramatic effect. "Is that a bottle of sherry on the sideboard?"

"No! Are you crazy? I am **not** drinkin' again, even to save my own skin."

"Or Romulus?"

That brought me up short. *Darn you, Jasper.* "OK, but just one—"

He giggled. "Just joshin'. I don't need the headache any more than you do. Bring on the sweet rolls!"

And that's why crumbs covered my lap when the head of the Army of Northern Virginia stomped in, mud on his boots and his fine gray coat.

You've seen photographs of Robert E. Lee and maybe you think you have some idea about him. Trust me, you don't. I controlled a room full of men with a magickal spell. He did it with...well, I can't rightly say what he did it with. Class, maybe? Presence? Bearing? Whatever he had, I knew Verity didn't have it, not without the Legacy Stone, Morphageus, and every Marshal of the Equity to be found in Northern America. As soon as he entered the room I sat up straighter, just like when my school's headmaster had burst in last year looking for the student who'd locked him in the outhouse (it'd seemed like a good idea at the time).

Taller than most, but not President Lincoln's height, General Lee looked to be about fifty years old, maybe a bit more. Though he didn't go past Abe in altitude he sure had him beat in looks. The room was jammed with strapping young lieutenants and captains in their twenties but you only looked at the general. His hair and beard had turned gray, to be sure, but that only made him seem more like King Arthur searching for a Round Table to sit at. A lifetime of soldiering, from the Mexican War to commanding at West Point, had made him into a weathered oak, all the weaknesses worn away. His eyes sparkled with a fire that I'd see in many people after that day. It came from seeing men fight one another, from smelling powder burn, and from hearing steel smash against steel.

I'm sure I stopped breathing for a second. Later on it came to me just why. Here stood the sort of man I'd always thought Pa would be, if we hadn't lost him.

I touched my chest, in that awe-struck way you do when something just amazes you, but also because I wanted to check the Stone's reaction to him. Now that I'd felt such a strong pull toward him, I really wanted to know if Lee used dark magick to control the Confederate army, if the Honourable Merchantry had a mage in at the top.

Nothing. Not a peep from the red rock around my neck. General Lee did it the old-fashioned way. That didn't mean he wasn't a Merchantry man, but at least he was no black sorcerer.

Stuck in my corner, I made no immediate impression on him. Okay with me. I needed to get my thoughts—and my lies—together. He put on spectacles and bent over the map, which must've been hard to see in the fading light. Although the rain had pretty much all stopped, the dark clouds that had brought it remained, making it darker in the sitting room than usual for just past six o'clock. An aide lit a lantern and hung it up to help his general read. The room got real crowded. More aides and brigade commanders, men who'd accompanied Lee when he'd ridden out to the sound of the guns, pushed their way inside. My sensitive nose began to get overwhelmed with the smell of unwashed bodies, sweat, gun smoke, mud, manure, and everything else that went with a hard day's soldiering.

"A sharp fight, but those people are right back where they started," Lee said, almost to himself. His voice had a soft quality with a strong core, like a saber resting in its velvet scabbard. It sure did suit him.

"Yes, sir," agreed the colonel who'd questioned me earlier. "Heintzelman's Corps, probing for a weakness. Guess he found out that there isn't one in this army."

Everyone laughed but Lee, who still managed a small smile. I felt like a guest at somebody else's family reunion, watching all of the young men cluster around the revered patriarch in search of praise, wisdom, or both. We didn't have reunions at our house, there being just Ma and me. *Now there's just me. Hope that ain't permanent.*

Lee stood up from the map table and tucked his spectacles in a pocket. Taking a sandwich somebody offered him, he said, "I wish I shared your optimism. That would leave me less anxious about tomorrow's attack. Have we heard from General Jackson today?"

A baby-faced major stepped forward, not much past twenty. "Yes, sir. He expects to have his corps ready in the morning. They're moving now."

"I dearly hope they aren't too worn out from all that fast marching from the Valley. I fear he pushes them too hard sometimes."

"General, he hasn't let us down yet. His Foot Cavalry will give Little Mac a bloody nose, you wait and see."

"Well, waiting is all I can do now. I just—"

Lee paused. A heavy silence fell over the room, as if everyone held their breath to hear what he'd say next. I was curious, too, seeing as how he stared straight at me with a surly frown.

My colonel broke the tension. His face said that he hoped Lee didn't bust him to private for admitting me. "Ah, sir, this is Miss Mahoney. She claims to have a message for you and you alone."

The Rebel leader handed the sandwich over to whoever had given it to him. "Does she?"

"She does." Lee looked decidedly unhappy and the colonel felt that displeasure radiating his way. "We...agreed that she should stay till you returned. The information is highly sensitive."

"So she says." I got a hard glare from the general. I tried my winning smile on him, but that just made him scowl some more. *Okay, so much for my magical man-control. Now what?*

When in doubt, brazen it out. I stood up, brushed the crumbs from my overalls, and stared right back at him. Instead of my delicate charm, I switched to hard-edged spymistress. "I do say, sir. Your men were right to admit me, civilian or no. I did not ask for this assignment, but here I am, ready to do you and yours a great service, I think. Shall we go somewhere and talk or shall I walk back to Richmond and catch my train to New Orleans?"

For a long moment I thought I'd overdone it. Then Lee took a long deep breath and said, "Major Taylor."

The youngster perked up. "Sir?"

"I'll be in the kitchen with Miss Mahoney for no more than five minutes. Make sure my horse is seen to. When we are done you will detail two men to make sure that the lady gets safely back to town."

"Understood, sir." Taylor moved off to do his duty. Lee waved his hand to show me the route to the Widow Dabbs' kitchen, which lay at the rear of the house. With a polite nod I swept through the soldiers, who parted for me like the Red Sea for Moses. Well, maybe it was for their general, but it felt good anyhow.

When the kitchen door had closed behind us, Lee crossed his arms and said, "So you're a spy?"

One part of me tried to maintain the character and the conversation while the other part of me spun wheels and gears to stay ahead of events. It was hard work. "You make it sound so...low."

"It's just that you don't look like most of the spies we employ. Don't misunderstand me," he smiled, raising a palm. "Intelligence either saves an army or breaks its back. I can't afford to look down my nose at spies. Nor at crystal ball-gazers or tarot card readers, if they help me to win battles. We're outnumbered here, as everyone knows except George McClellan. Is your information a help or a hindrance?"

"Good question," Jasper laughed in my thoughts. "Do you have any idea?"

Thanks. Just what I need right now. Focusing on Lee, who eyed me like Zeus considering who would get the next thunderbolt, I said, "That depends on whether your army is a help or a hindrance...to me."

Lee burst out laughing. He even slapped his thigh. "You! And just who are you? Someone's bedmate who overheard something she thinks she can profit from?"

Whoa! So that explained his hostility. He thought I was a floozie, a soiled dove, even, trying to sell second-hand information. I had to rid him of that notion in a hurry, and just then a brilliant idea came to me.

"No, sir," I hissed, cold and sharp, "I am not here for money, not even the worthless bills of your runt government. I am here at the express direction of the Honorable Merchantry of Esteemed Gentlemen. My message comes directly from the Proprietor."

I knew I'd guessed right when the fear flashed in Robert E. Lee's eyes. It only showed for a split-second, but I caught it. This veteran soldier, master of all men and every situation, had learned to be afraid of the Merchantry. Directly afraid. He knew it for true, not for what some folks believed by rumor. Either he'd fallen foul of it himself or...

Or I wasn't the first Merchantry representative to visit the Confederate government.

That made awful sense. How else to explain this horrible useless war? The Merchantry was in it up to their eyeballs, of course. If they hadn't manipulated things to get it started then they sure as heck were pulling strings to keep it going. Their shadow businesses no doubt traded with both sides in weapons, ships, food, and anything else profitable, while the misery charged up their black magick. No wonder Ernie and Romulus hated them so much.

Give him credit. Lee tried to bluff his way through me, just like he did against the Union army. "The Proprietor? Oh, really? And who might that be?"

"Like you know, either," snickered Jasper.

"Will you just hush and get ready to pull that ace we talked about?" I snapped with a thought.

"Okay, Okay, don't get huffy. Jeez."

"That won't wash, General," I said, wagging a finger at him. "You've already been spoken to by some of my friends, haven't you?"

Even now Lee played tough. I could see why McClellan feared him so much. He was nothing if not bold. "A pretty woman waltzes into my headquarters with no Merchantry password or sign and you expect me to just—"

This was what I'd been waiting for, a reason to show my Merchantry bona fides and end the argument. I sent a thought to Jasper. *Here's hopin' it works.*

The Stone flushed hot against my skin for an instant. The vizard glamour gave way to a passion glamour. Ripples of buzzing energy crawled across my face as the image changed. Instead of Alaena Mahoney, saucy Irlannish temptress from New Orleans, Lee saw the thing he feared most, a terror pulled straight from his own mind by Jasper's magick. I saw it flash in my own thoughts and shuddered.

His daughter, her face cold and pale in fevered death.

I found no mirror in the kitchen for me to check myself with, but Lee's eyes were looking-glass enough. The general, who'd seen countless men killed in battle—arms blown off by shells, brains splattered by musket balls—most feared his grown child's end from simple sickness. His strong knees buckled. It wrenched my heart out to watch, but I had to press my advantage before I lost it.

"You doubt me?" My voice now sounded gloppy, as if filled with new-turned grave dirt and maggots. "You think me a fraud?"

"No!" he cried in a hoarse whisper, not wanting to alarm any of his men and let them see him in such a state. "I believe. Only a Merchantry mage could do such a thing."

I let the glamour fade back to Alaena. "Then listen well and you may never have to see me again. You begin an offensive against the Federal army tomorrow, yes?"

"We do. We hope to destroy them utterly and end this war."

"You will not! You will only push them back. The Army of the Potomac shall live to fight another day. Do we understand one another?"

After a long, sad pause Lee choked out, "Yes. I see. The war must go on."

I nodded. "It must. This is the will of the Proprietor."

To my amazement, Lee mastered himself in moments. Glaring at me, he snapped, "And that is all that matters, these days. I'll give you your blood, much good may it do you."

Despite having been a soldier all of his life, Lee wanted a quick end to the war to minimize the carnage. *Good for you, General. Please disobey this order, if you can. Even if it means my side loses. Enough is enough.*

"Then my mission is completed," I drawled, all honey as if nothing awful had just happened. I turned to leave the kitchen, then whirled back. "Oh, one more thing, if you please. One of my men is undercover as a slave. He got careless and your pioneers have him working on entrenchments north of here. I need him back as soon as possible."

Lee pulled his order book from a pocket and scrawled out a very general message for the recipient to give me whatever I required. I tucked it into the top of my overalls, which must've looked like an impressive adult bosom to him. It got no reaction from the already-stunned Lee, though. We put on our best happy faces and returned to the sitting room. Everyone there did their best to act busy, as if they weren't dying to know what had gone on in the kitchen. Too bad for them. Lee kept mum about the specifics.

"No changes, gentlemen. We attack as planned tomorrow. Is the escort ready for Miss Mahoney?"

Major Taylor said yes and motioned for me to follow him outside. I curtsied to General Lee, who nodded once at me and turned back to the map. *OK, I've been dismissed. Now where's that escort?*

Two cavalrymen sat on their horses, holding a mount for me. I froze. One was Tyrell, who grinned and touched his hat brim with a finger.

The instant I saw him the Stone froze solid. Then the shooting began.

This is the end of *Brimstone and Lily, Part One.*
The next volume will continue directly from this point
(an excerpt appears below).

If you enjoyed this book (or even if you didn't), please
leave a brief review on Amazon, Goodreads, etc.

Thank you for reading.

www.terrykroenungink.com

From *Brimstone and Lily*, Part 2:
Beware the Sword of Mirth

But my fight looked to just be starting. Since no more bullets came my way, I made Morphageus into a tin cup again and stuffed it into the bottom of my haversack. As I moved my gaze down to see what Stonewall Jackson thought of his men's performance, I saw that the famous commander had already ridden out toward the action. My head pounded from the sickening thrill of the thing. I panted like an overheated mutt. Every muscle shook from the strain of being under fire and clinging to my tree branch. That explained why, even with most of the battle noise gone, I didn't notice the ravens swooping in to scratch my eyes out.

The spyglass saved me. I still had it out at its full length and swung with both hands. Two feet of brass caught my first screeching attacker dead in his beak. He made an *urk* sound and fell away. His friend following close behind took advantage of my follow-through to try to slash open the top of my scalp. Lucky for me I'd found that old hat on the road. It jumped off my head, still in the raven's claws. Wrapping my legs around a branch, I whipped my still-intact face around to try to spot the rest of the flock.

I counted at least eight of them, and these were no ordinary ravens. They were the size of eagles, with sickly green glowing eyes. Their taloned feet were as large as an adult man's hand. Sharp as bayonets, their black beaks seemed to my frightened eyes to be longer than railroad spikes. *Great. Evil demon birds from the bowels of hell are tryin' to rip me to shreds and I'm stuck alone in a tree.* And they laughed! They all hooted and cackled as they tried to do me in. I wasn't seeing the humor in the situation, but then the mouse seldom enjoys the hunt as much as the cat does. My Stone-enhanced reflexes kept me safe for a while, since I could see them clear, even though it was full dark. Time after time I clubbed a heavy feathered body, sending it away with a yelp. But two more would be on me in a flash, pouncing from another direction. They never gave me time to reach for Morphageus, which must've been their object. Word had gotten around the Merchantry that Verity the Valiant was no slouch in a fair fight, even if only twelve. I started to take damage. My overalls, tough as they were, opened up shredded gashes. An ear bled buckets from a beak nip. The back of my left hand had a nasty talon slice. A pair of the birds teamed up to wrench the spyglass out of my grip. Then the rest took turns smashing into my body. I was about to be overwhelmed and knocked fifty feet down out of the tree.

Covering my face to protect it, I waited for my legs to give out and let go of the branch that held me up. One more good body blow would do it. But it didn't happen. Instead, the ravens stopped laughing and started snarling. Their sounds changed to pained grunts. I took the chance to see what went on. Right then I learned what good friends I had.

Pirate queen Roberta, as furious as Blackbeard, had shot up from the ground to light into the raven flock. Her white beak, made for crushing iron-hard nuts, snapped the leg from one of the enemy birds before he even knew she attacked. Trailing blood, he shrieked and dove away. The crimson parrot roared her rage and dug her terrible claws into the body of the next raven. With a whiplike change of direction she smashed him head-first into the trunk of the tree. His limp carcass fell to the ground like a rock.

Two more ravens resumed their attack on me, ignoring Roberta's wrath. A mistake they didn't live to regret. The angry parrot beheaded another with one chomp of her terrible beak while a shrieking gray-brown ball of fury dove from her back onto the other. In mid-air Ernie threw Romulus' dreadful Bowie knife. It thunked into the tree next to my ear. "There you go, missy! Give 'em what for!" he cried, landing on the neck of his enemy. Before the growling raven knew what had hit it the stout mouse plunged his sharpened knitting needle lance into its vitals several times. "From hell's heart I stab at thee!" he snarled.

Somebody besides me has read that odd book? No more time to think, for our foes weren't giving up. Wrenching the big blade free, I cut at another black-feathered attacker. My stroke missed, but it flapped away. I didn't want to risk trying to dig the cup out of my haversack and fight with it. It'd take too long and I might drop the thing. Four more of the fearsome ravens remained and they redoubled their efforts to do me in. But now I had a free hand to hold onto the branch with. Clutching the limb with my bleeding left hand, I took vicious swipes at the huge birds to keep them at bay. Roberta had picked up Ernie again and my allies glided in to help me. I hoped they'd arrive in time. Now the ravens were gouging at my neck with their straight razor-claws. I could feel sticky warmth running down inside my shirt. *Hope that ain't as serious as it feels.* One foul bird kept pecking at my eyes, forcing me to let go of the branch to cover my face while I slashed desperately at the ones on my neck. That gave them their chance. That horrid evil cackling stabbed my ears again as the lot of them leaped onto my back and pushed me out of the tree.

Thanks to the Stone boosting my reflexes, I didn't break my back on the first thick limb I hit on the way down. Twisting like a cat, I dropped the knife before I could land on it and struck the heavy branch with both hands in front of me. If I hadn't been able to see in the dark it would've clobbered me with no warning. As it was it drove the breath out of my lungs with a loud *oof* and flipped me backwards head over heels. Wildly snatching at anything and everything, I managed to get hold of enough vegetation to slow my fall just enough so that when the next large hunk of wood came my way I just did hang on. Though bruised all over, lip bleeding and chin scraped raw, I hadn't crashed into the earth like a speeding comet.

I also hadn't gotten free of those pesky ravens. The deadly quartet had followed me down, slowed by the thick foliage and Roberta's feisty pursuit. Ernie had leaped from her back to give her more freedom of action. Shouting something that sounded like "Long live the queen!", the plump mouse skittered along the oak's trunk just like squirrels did, his lance in his jaws. A look down told me that I had a ten-foot drop to the ground. That same look also told me that the odds were about to shift in my favor.

With giddy giggles of imminent victory, my dark enemies plummeted down at me, beaks and talons ready for the kill. Just then my dark friend stepped out onto my limb and swung a branch thicker than my leg. Romulus had climbed the tree to come to my rescue. Like a cheap ball smacked by the star batter in a game of rounders, the lead raven disappeared in a puff of feathered goo. Shrieking at this sudden vicious counterattack, the rest of the birds slowed their dive and scattered. Now Roberta raged amongst them like a red tornado, cursing in her salty piratical way. Ernie added as many needle jabs as he could get in. In short order the ravens decided that they'd had enough punishment and flew off into the night.

My arms and legs gave out together. Like an empty potato sack I went all slack. Romulus caught me in his great arms before I could finish the ravens' work for them by falling out of the tree and breaking my neck. The Marshal draped me over a shoulder as gentle as he could and climbed down. Setting me on the grass, he knelt down on both knees and asked, "Miss Verity?" I must've looked awful, judging by his worried look. Bleeding from every bit of exposed skin, clothes torn to ribbons by beaks and claws, lip swelling up to the size of an apricot. The blood inside my shirt felt like dried paste. I reached up to my head with a trembling hand and tried to talk.

"It's okay miss. Ol' Romulus is here. Is you bad hurt?"

"I...I..." The words didn't want to come out of my bruised chest. It hurt to talk.

"Yeah? What you say?" He looked like a father on his child's death watch.

"I...really liked that hat."

Two mice, round as apples, stomped up to my face. Standing on my aching chin, so close it made my eyes cross, Ernie sniffed, "Yep. She's fine," and scampered off out of sight.

Making all sorts of pained ah's and ooh's, I sat up with some help from Romulus. Ernie had climbed onto the giant's shoulder. Flapping in from someplace behind me, the dread pirate Roberta landed on his other arm, which he held out for her. My new straw hat, now with fashionable raven-claw accents, dangled from her pale curved beak. I wanted to kiss her.

"Here, matey," she said, dropping the hat into my outstretched fingers. "A girl just ain't dressed without a fine chapeau."

ABOUT THE AUTHOR

Terry Kroenung taught literature for 30 years, mostly at Niwot High School in Colorado, where he inflicted his Shakespeare impersonations and love of Eeyore collectibles on tomorrow's leaders. An Advanced Actor/Combatant with the Society of American Fight Directors, he owns more swords than any sane human has any need of and spent countless hours choreographing fights with his students (thus, the gray hairs and nervous twitchings of his poor principal). As unplanned preparation for writing *Brimstone and Lily* he served as an U.S. Army infantry officer on the East German border, a Confederate Civil War re-enactor in Virginia, and a pirate at street festivals. His youthful cigar smoking and whiskey drinking resulted in just as much misery as Verity feels when indulging.

The smart-aleck dialogue and puns come naturally, alas...more's the pity.

www.ingramcontent.com/pod-product-compliance
Lightning Source LLC
Chambersburg PA
CBHW030641260626
47157CB00007B/2429